I0680585

ChangelingPress.com

Krampus Bah Humbug

Crymsyn Hart

Krampus Bah Humbug

Crymsyn Hart

ISBN: 978-1-60521-803-8

Publisher:
Changeling Press LLC
315 N. Centre St.
Martinsburg, WV 25404
ChangelingPress.com

Printed in the U.S.A.

Editors: Pat Sager, Treva Harte
Cover Artist: Angela Knight

The individual stories in this anthology have been previously released in E-Book format.

Table of Contents

Claiming Cupid 4
    Chapter One...5
    Chapter Two 14
    Chapter Three...21
    Chapter Four...29
Krampus Does Dallas 38
    Chapter One...39
    Chapter Two 47
    Chapter Three...56
    Chapter Four...64
    Chapter Five 71
Forging Krampus 82
    Chapter One...83
    Chapter Two 95
    Chapter Three...108
    Chapter Four...119
    Chapter Five 132
Krampus to the Rescue 141
    Chapter One...142
    Chapter Two 155
    Chapter Three...163
    Chapter Four...176
Krampus, Bah Humbug 186
    Chapter One...187
    Chapter Two 195
    Chapter Three...202
    Chapter Four...210
    Chapter Five 216
    Chapter Six...222
    Chapter Seven 227
Y'all Tied Up 235
    Chapter One...236
    Chapter Two 247
    Chapter Three...260
Crymsyn Hart 273
Changeling Press E-Books 274

Claiming Cupid

Crymsyn Hart

When Krampus' gingerbread men bring him a find caught in one of his nets, all thoughts of eating the handsome winged man fly from his mind. Krampus learns his guest is Cupid, the Incarnation of Love. With Cupid missing from the real world all love is at risk of evaporating. But Krampus intends to claim Cupid for his own -- even if it kills him.

Chapter One

"Master."

Krampus looked down at the one who had disturbed him. A two-foot-tall, battle hardened gingerbread general with a missing gumdrop button and a bite taken out of his head. A frosted eye patch had been filled in where his raisin left eye had once been. His edges had started to crumble the way cookies did. They could fix that by charring the cookie edge, but Krampus wasn't sure how long this cookie had left to serve him.

"What do you want? Has some of the livestock escaped again? Did you catch one of your men snacking on my humans again? I've given them enough warnings not to be lenient. I do get a hankering for gingerbread once in a while."

"No, Master. Nothing like that. We found something in the nets. It didn't look like a sugar plum fairy, so I wanted to bring it to you."

"Let me see it." Krampus was intrigued. His gingerbread hardly ever brought him something interesting. Sugarplum fairies were a delicacy and went well with human meat pie, but they were difficult to snare even with the finely woven nets he had cast in the garden. At the thought of their sticky sweetness, Krampus' mouth watered.

His gingerbread men, along with a couple of toy tin soldiers, dragged in something caught in a golden net. The creature was unlike anything he had ever seen. It looked human. Was the same size as one of them, but it had large white fluffy wings. One of the tin soldiers took something slung over his shoulder and presented it to Krampus. "We found these on him."

Krampus bent down and took a golden quiver of

arrows with feathered hearts on the end and a large bow from the soldier. It was tiny in his large fingers. This being was not from his world. If he was then they would have been the same height, but Krampus could fix that.

"Release him and leave us."

The tin soldiers left the room, but the general remained. "Uh, Master?"

"What is it?"

"When you're done with him, me and the boys were hoping we could have the leftovers. He looks tasty." The gingerbread general licked his lips, revealing needle teeth.

"If there is anything left, then yes. If I keep him, you're welcome to three of the human stock. But wait for my orders on that."

The corner of his mouth twitched trying to hide his excitement. "Yes, Master. Thank you." The general left the room and closed the door.

Krampus slowly unwound the fine golden net from the strange creature. He took care when removing the weave from the large fluffy wings. When he untwined the strange being, he turned him over to find the most perfect specimen of humankind he had ever seen. Shiny bronze skin with light blond hair that curled around a heart-shaped face. Perfectly pouty lips were relaxed in unconsciousness.

A nasty gash across his forehead marred the beauty of this captured angel. Dread rolled through Krampus as the recognition set in. *If this being is a real angel, I'm in for some shitty luck.* He had to make sure this creature recovered. First thing to do was to make him the same size as Krampus.

The realm he lived in made him a giant. When he interacted in the human world, he was a looming figure of seven feet. To mortals he brought here, Krampus towered twenty feet tall. This creature was no ordinary human. He lifted him in both hands and laid him on the sofa. The angel appeared to be a small child as he lay on the couch. Krampus waved his hand over the being

The cold grip of the spell sapped his energy. His powers had waned because Christmas had passed and spring would soon be upon him. They would return in full force as the summer turned to fall. The room frosted over in a white film to include the angel. Once the film cleared, the angel had grown to match Krampus. He found a rag, got a bowl of water, and pressed it to the cut. The blood came away easily.

Once he was done, Krampus took in the rest of the angel's physique. His abs were toned and expertly cut. Gold lamé shorts clung to his hips and left nothing to the imagination. His desire stirred as he studied the bulge hidden by the golden cloth. He tore his gaze from it and admired the shapely thighs and calves. Brown leather sandals encased his feet and twined around over his ankles and were tied with a neat heart-shaped bow.

Nothing else about him seemed to be hurt. Krampus hoped his wings were intact. The golden net was meant to snare the sugar plum fairies and break their wings.

"What are you and why did you wander into my realm? Unless you wanted to become a real live tree topper for me next year."

"It wasn't my choice. I was blown off course by the West Wind. He thought it'd be amusing to play a little joke on me. I ended up tangled in your nets and clubbed by those… things. I guess they dragged me to you. Who are you? You don't look like any of the other

Incarnations I've met."

The clearest green eyes like the holy bush held Krampus mesmerized. The angel's voice was low and yet lyrical. It took him a second to process what he'd said. *Incarnations.* "You mean like Claus and Nyx?"

"Saint Nicklaus yes. And Nyx. She's the embodiment of night. Why would you mention her? Only those who linger in the dark associate with her."

Krampus chuckled. This angel had knowledge about those beings who held specific offices like Claus, Mother Nature, Jack Frost, all the holidays the humans celebrated and a few more who were older than all of them like Death. "Claus is my nemesis. We rarely see eye to eye. Nyx keeps to herself, but she does come down from her temple from time to time."

The angel cringed. The terrified gleam in his eye didn't make Krampus feel delighted as fear normally did when he saw it in a human's gaze. He put up his hands hoping the angel would see he wasn't about to hurt him.

"Who are you?"

"I'm Krampus. Who are you?" He licked his lips at the angel's rocking body. He didn't remember when a male had tempted him so, but this angel was immaculate perfection.

"Cupid."

He grabbed a blanket. Krampus tried to wrap it around Cupid's trembling shoulders but he flinched. Krampus placed it over his wings and his fingers brushed the other male's flesh. A hot flash of desire gripped him. He bit his tongue to hold in the moan. Cupid grasped his hand and stared at him. Once those green eyes had him, his will drained away, Krampus found himself sitting next to the other man. His hand rested on Krampus' thigh.

"Tell me who and what you are?" Cupid's voice remained stern but soothing.

"I'm Krampus. Some call me the anti-Claus. I take naughty humans and bring them to my domain. Some of them are delicious. I'm the dark Incarnation of Christmas. The opposite of Nicklaus. Winter and Christmas I am in my prime."

"What do you intend to do with me?"

Krampus tried to think of a lie to ease Cupid's mind, but instead he found himself telling him the truth because this being had him under his power. "At first I thought I might eat you. My gingerbread men sure wanted to. Upon further inspection, I thought you were an angel and even I wouldn't want to mess with one of them. I have my limits."

"You're not planning on making me dinner?"

Krampus slipped his clawed hand over Cupid's and met his gaze. The words flowed freely from his lips. "Not unless you want me on my knees sucking your prick. I want to fuck you more than anything else. You rouse feelings in me, more so than most."

"You're a most peculiar creature." Cupid wound his free hand through Krampus' goatee. "What do you know about Valentine's Day?"

Krampus' eyes rolled back when Cupid ran his fingers along one of his horns. He traced his fingertips along the hard ridges until Krampus' hoof thumped against the wooden floor. No one else knew touching his horns inflamed his passion until he was so hot he could have melted snow. Cupid leaned in close, teasing him with those perfect lips.

"Tell me what you know."

"Humans created it to sell cards and flowers. They venerate cherubic children who are supposed to flit around, shooting arrows at mortals, to make them fall in love."

Cupid smirked. "You don't know anything about it. But I guess that makes two of us. I know nothing about you. Who would think a talking goat would be St. Nicklaus' nemesis? There's something about you." He moved his hand up Krampus' thigh and squeezed his cock through the thin material of the pants he wore. He sucked in a breath and yearned for more from Cupid. "At least it seems we have compatible anatomy."

"Yes."

Cupid rubbed him until his dick firmed. "You are a big boy. Do you want me to release you from my hold so I can show you my gratitude for freeing me from that net?"

A shock of longing electrified Krampus' nerves. He stiffened and cried out. He thrust his hips against Cupid's hand as he manipulated him. Never had any being had such control over him. As much as he hated to admit it, he enjoyed this man having power over him. It was so easy to give over his will. He knew part of it was because Cupid used his influence on Krampus. He stared into those deep green eyes and felt the hold over him wobble.

Krampus took Cupid's face between his hands and kissed him. Cupid stiffened, but met his tongue. Cupid slipped his hands over Krampus'. They were warm and inviting. The kiss softened as he dropped his hands and trailed them down Krampus' body, mingling with the dark hair on his chest. Krampus sucked in a breath when he found his nipple and pinched it. He broke the kiss.

"Tell me about what you do for your Incarnation?" He sat back against the sofa.

Cupid's smile turned devilish. "Why not get me

something to drink first?"

"You're a cocky prick."

"I'm used to getting what I want." Cupid walked his finger along Krampus' arm. A tingle shot along his nerves, but it didn't overwhelm him.

"You don't need to use your power on me. I'll get you a drink and then you can thank me for saving your sweet feathered ass." He left the room and went into the kitchen where he had some mulled wine heating in a cauldron over the fire. The gingerbread woman ladled the wine into cups. She went back to prepping dinner. When he entered the room, Cupid stood before the fire examining his wings.

"Are they broken?" He handed a cup to Cupid.

He sniffed the drink before sipping it. His expression lightened when he tasted it. "I can taste the cherries and cinnamon. Nicklaus has something similar. Although he doesn't break it out often. Yours is better."

"We do have some things in common. Your wings?" Krampus set his mug down and touched the curve of a wing.

Cupid stretched them out and grimaced. "They're sprained. It'll be a couple of days before I can fly. I'm fine to do other things. Where are my bow and quiver of arrows?"

"Planning on shooting me with them?" Krampus retrieved the items and held them out to Cupid.

Once he touched them, they enlarged to their normal size. What had once been a tiny bow became a long bow with arrows that were over two feet long with sharp metal tips. Cupid picked one of the arrows with a black feather at the end of it. "If I shot you with this one, you'd become obsessed with someone. Obsession can turn deadly. The pink ones are for puppy love, a simple crush. The red ones are for true love. They can be the most dangerous."

"That's what you rule over, love?"

Cupid set the bow and quiver next to the fireplace and then sipped his wine. Krampus admired how the flames flashed off his chiseled flesh. He was a statue brought to life created by an artist who had the skills of the gods. His eyes sparkled in the firelight. The power that radiated off Cupid warmed him even more than the flames. He was the moth being drawn to the light of the man before him.

"Love is the main facet of who I am, but there are so many layers to love. It's tough to categorize them all. I'm sure you have many different things that embody what you rule over too."

"I've never thought about it. I enjoy terrorizing humans. Especially the naughty ones. They taste the best. Sometimes, those who have my bells aren't really wicked. If they're good enough, I let them go."

"Is that how you determine who you use your power on? Bells?"

Krampus grabbed a beat-up stocking that hung on the mantle. Stuck in the toe was one of his bells. He drew it out and showed the other Incarnation. The old bronze bell had darkened with age. It was the size of a small orange with a red ribbon looped through the top of it so it could be hung on a tree or a doorknob. Etched into the bell was his name and his image. "Once it rings, I hear it no matter where they are. It summons me and I take whoever is supposed to be taken. Sometimes the humans are marked. Other times it's harder to see."

"Marked how?" Cupid's fingertips brushed the bell, but he pulled them back with a hiss. He stuck his fingers in his mouth.

"Something about their aura or in their soul. I don't know which, I can just see it." He dropped the bell into the sock and hung it back on the hook. When he had a moment, he would fix it and make sure his gingerbread sent it back out into the world to where it was supposed to go.

He circled Cupid's wrist and drew those fingers away from his mouth. Krampus kissed the ends seeing they had been singed. He drew his tongue over the wound and met those intense eyes. "The bell wasn't for you to touch. You're not naughty enough."

"Sure about that? How naughty do I have to be?"

Krampus drew the fingers fully into his mouth and wrapped his tongue around them. He sucked on them slowly and pulled them out. His cock firmed at the thought of what they could do. Of seeing the other male bent over and those glorious white wings spread out while he claimed Cupid. He enjoyed the taste of the other man which reminded him of something sweet. He tried to pinpoint what it was and then realized it was strawberries. Something he only had when they came into season. *What will his prick taste like*?

"It all depends. But I think we've beaten around the bush enough, don't you?" Krampus twined his fingers through Cupid's. "Do you want to come up to bed with me?"

"I'd love to. I can't wait to take your hairy ass."

Chapter Two

Krampus led him through the house. As they passed the kitchen the gingerbread woman cook whistled at Cupid. He chuckled as they went up the stairs. They made it into the bedroom where Krampus shut the door. Cupid jumped when the lock clicked,

"Planning to keep me here locked up forever? If you do, love will wither and die around the world. Would you want to be responsible for that?"

"I could tie you up with tinsel to the bedposts, shove a candy cane up your ass, and watch as the gingerbread men suck your dick. It might be a fun show, but I'd rather not let any of my minions have at you."

Cupid sauntered over and tugged on the waistband of Krampus' pants. He worked the buttons loose and slipped his hand over his cock. He hissed in a breath and kept his gaze focused on Cupid. His dick firmed even more, but he held in a show of his passion. Cupid's perfect mouth turned up into a sneer. "You're a big boy. Bigger than I thought. I like that."

Krampus walked his fingers down Cupid's torso and over the shorts. His guest was already hard and ready. He wanted to take the man and make Cupid cry his name. "You're not half bad yourself. You sure you know how to use that?"

The other Incarnation cupped Krampus' balls and squeezed them. A zing raced from the base of his shaft and through him until his heart slammed into his chest. His legs wobbled. He could barely hold in the moan from needing to give into the craving to be claimed by the other male. He understood it was part of Cupid's power overwhelming him so he could make Krampus do what he wanted.

The first instinct he had was to fight him off, but Krampus let that power wash over him until the yearning encompassed his entire being. The pressure built in him as Cupid moved up his shaft. The silky flesh of his hands worked over him until he couldn't hold it back any longer. He grabbed Cupid's arm and cried out. His guest snickered.

"It looks like you know how to use yours, too. Although, you're almost there." He grabbed his shaft and squeezed.

The pain brought him even closer to orgasm. "What are you doing?"

"Just making sure you're focused on me. You're not going to come yet." Cupid released him and left him panting. "Take your pants off and get on the bed."

"You're not the master of this domain," Krampus said through clenched teeth.

"Haven't you figured out that I am? Right now, you will do as I say or you won't have the pleasure of coming until I leave."

"You don't rule that aspect."

"It's associated with love. I have a little influence over it. You've already let me in so I could taste your desire for me. Therefore, I already have power over you. Now get on the bed and show me your cock." His tone darkened.

Krampus felt the tug on his mind from the order. He shimmied out of his pants and laid on the bed, propped up against the pillows. Cupid's smile lightened his expression and the hunger in his eyes made the anticipation of his touch all the more agonizing.

Cupid slid his shorts off.

Krampus let his gaze slide over the rocking body and the size of his prick as it stood at attention. He licked his lips at the thought of what they were going to be doing with it. Cupid crawled over the bed to Krampus. He trailed his fingers along Krampus' inner thigh until he let the bliss capture him. He lifted his hips and brought his cock closer to Cupid, waiting for him to take it into his mouth.

All the other Incarnation did was flick his tongue over his lips, giving him a taste of the pleasure he could bring him. Krampus tried to remain calm and wait, but the anticipation was killing him as he hungered for the other man's touch.

"Are you going to leave me hanging with blue balls?"

"I thought about it, to see what you'd do. I rather enjoy seeing the dark spirit of Christmas being at my beck and call. One would say I could use you for anything I wanted. I do have some dark appetites."

He growled and lunged forward. As he came up, Cupid snapped his fingers. Something caught his wrists and pulled him backward. Krampus looked down and saw red ribbons had bound him. He struggled against them, but he couldn't get free. "Keeping me prisoner in my own home? I can make sure my gingers eat you up."

Cupid slid his body over Krampus' and snuggled up to him. The fragrance of strawberries filled his nose. "You're used to ruling and not giving up that control. People fear you and you like it. I know longing. It's part of what I am. You saved me from your nets and your oversized cookies. Let me give you what I know you crave."

The words worked into his mind. They made sense. He loved fear and how it always flavored the meat of the humans he ate. "What do you propose?"

Cupid pressed his lips against Krampus' and

plunged his tongue into his mouth, tugging on his bottom before releasing him. He moved lower over Krampus body and bit his nipple. Krampus jumped in pain and excitement. Cupid raked his fingers through the thick fur of Krampus' coat, kissing down his stomach until he came to his cock.

"This is what I propose." Cupid spread his wings and cast him in shadow. He laved his tongue along the length of his shaft.

Krampus moaned from the light pressure of Cupid's tongue on his sensitive skin. Cupid wrapped his lips around the tip of his prick and sucked it in. Krampus strained against his bonds, trying to get Cupid to take in more so he could give in to the passion washing over him. Cupid inched down on him. A small whimper escaped his lips as Cupid's tongue circled around. But then the Incarnation of lust stopped and looked up at him.

"You taste like smoke and cloves." His fingers slipped along the base of Krampus' shaft and he rubbed the skin.

"Please," Krampus whimpered.

"That's more like it. First, a little something you might enjoy." He snapped his fingers and a short riding crop appeared in his hand. He raked the stiff bristles along his dick.

The rough ends made him thrust his hips up. Krampus was at Cupid's mercy. Not knowing what he would do made it all the more maddening. Cupid took the crop and hit his prick. The sudden slap of the bristles sent pain and joy burning through him. Cupid beat him repeatedly until his dick pulsated with need. He writhed in the bed. His entire body had become an extension of his cock.

He lost all sense of himself except the bruised

flesh and how much yearning he had for Cupid to grant him a release. He had thought the other Incarnation was an angel, but he knew now Cupid was a devil.

After one last hard slap, Cupid threw the crop away. Krampus had lost all of his vaunted control. The only thing remaining was his throbbing dick. He struggled against the ribbons and growled. Cupid chuckled and flicked his tongue over the soft head.

"Now you're ready. I could keep this up for hours until you truly learned to appreciate me, but we've done enough. You've been a very good boy." Cupid took all of Krampus' length into his mouth and sucked on him like a candy cane. He raised his hips as Cupid increased the rhythm. His wings flapped in tempo to his head bobbing. Krampus clenched his claws into the meat of his palms.

Cupid dragged his teeth along the length of his cock. Krampus groaned. He couldn't hold back anymore. Cupid went down on him one last time and he came. His lover didn't stop sucking until Krampus was completely spent. Once he was done, he collapsed back onto the bed. Cupid released him. He climbed along the bed and snuggled against Krampus.

"Are you going to free me?"

Cupid twisted his finger in his pelt and squeezed his nipple. Krampus grunted and felt himself stir once more. He wasn't going to admit how the winged Incarnation turned him on by dominating him or using pain.

"You would do well with a pair of nipple clamps and a cock ring. I'd attach them together with a long chain and tighten them ever so much. I'd love to see you on all fours with your furry ass up in the air paddled until you don't know your own name." Cupid ran his finger over Krampus' lips.

He darted his tongue out to catch a taste of his lover. He wasn't about to agree that what Cupid suggested sounded wonderful. He would beg him to do all of it and more. Krampus took in a breath and tried to regain his emotions. It was difficult with the ardor of passion clinging to his brain. Cupid's wings flared out and the tip of his feathers brushed along Krampus' inner thigh until he cringed. He needed more of the man.

"What about you?" Krampus forced out.

"Me?"

"Yes."

"You mean my pleasure?"

Krampus writhed in the bed. "Yes."

Cupid kissed him once more and moved his lips over to Krampus' ear. "I want your tight hairy ass. Will you give it to me?"

To have him in any way would be heaven. He never would have realized what it would have meant to give up his control and let someone have it over him. If the other hadn't been caught in his nets. Or how much he would have enjoyed it. "Why don't you undo these straps so you can claim it?"

"Now we're getting somewhere."

With a snap of his fingers the restraints disappeared. Krampus turned over. He got up on all fours and presented his ass to Cupid. He glanced back at him as the Incarnation settled behind him. He scraped his fingers down Krampus' back. "Oh, I like this; thick and dark. And your hooves are wonderful. But it's your ass and your cock I really enjoy. Spread your legs for me, big boy."

Krampus did as he was told. He hung his head and Cupid spread his ass cheeks. It took him a moment as he fumbled around. Krampus couldn't see him, but he felt it when the man settled on top of him. The other man pushed upward. Krampus didn't experience the pain he thought he would from Cupid entering him from behind. Instead, the other man's hand slipped around his waist and grasped his prick. He firmed once again as he moved upward. Cupid moved between his ass cheeks, groaning as he slid between the firm mounds.

The Incarnation pumped his cock against Krampus' backside while stroking his dick. Krampus sucked in a breath. Cupid thrust upward at a faster pace. The breeze from his wings cooled Krampus' back.

"Gods, you feel so good, Krampus."

He moaned again, trying to keep pace with his lover as his hips rocketed forward. Cupid didn't give up his hold on his shaft. He moved just as fast as he did before. Cupid grunted and pumped him until he cried out. A couple more strokes and Krampus felt himself release as well. The ecstasy soared through him until they both collapsed on the bed.

Chapter Three

Krampus opened his eyes and found Cupid snuggled up next to him. His golden-haired angel had rocked his world. He'd never imagined anything like they had shared the night before. The craving for more inundated him. He trailed his fingers along the curve of his lover's spine and watched him stir. Cupid turned over, but he opened his eyes for a second. Those green eyes met his. The gaze reminded him of the evergreen of the trees he had in his living room every year and the mistletoe that grew wild in the garden. He loved to eat the berries when it came into season and enjoyed it when the cook made them into a pie. Cupid rolled back over and fell back asleep.

Krampus' stomach growled. When his lover didn't stir, but remained sleeping, Krampus eased himself away. Grabbing his robe, slipped it on and headed down to the kitchen. The aroma of breakfast and sizzling meat made his mouth water.

"Pork?"

"Yes, Master. The human stock has gotten a bit low. We decided to take a few of the swine. I hope that's satisfactory," the gingerbread cook said to him. She stirred the fire. Black scorch marks adorned her arms. This chef had been with him the longest. Although, looking at the deterioration of her crumbling edges it didn't seem like she had very long.

"That's fine. I'll inspect the herds later along with the rest of the livestock. Pepper, isn't it?"

The cook stopped and stared at him before bowing her head. "Yes, Master."

"Have you been training an assistant?"

Her frosting mouth turned into an "o" before she dropped to her knees and wrung her hands. "Please,

Master. Don't eat me. Don't feed me to the humans. I have many years left of service to you."

He sighed and took her arm. "Get up. I'm not going to feed you to the livestock and I don't have a taste for gingerbread. I was only asking because your cookie is starting to crumble around the edges. You can't keep adding new bits of cookie to yourself with frosting. Soon you won't have anything to add it to."

"No, Master. I haven't started training an assistant, but I will do so right away."

"Good. Make me two cups of hot chocolate, and some eggs to go with the pork."

"Will you need enough for your guest as well?"

Krampus smiled. "Yes. Leave them on the table and I'll bring them up to my guest."

"As you wish."

He looked at her and shook his head. He glanced at the clock and saw it was still early. He had time before they needed to get back to work. Krampus walked into his workshop. During the night, the tin soldiers had gone out and gathered up the bells he had outstanding that hadn't rung in the past year. So far they had brought back several dozen. He hadn't had a chance to look at all of them, yet. Cupid was an interruption he hadn't planned on the night before.

He sat at his workbench and took up the tweezers. Krampus took one of the bells and used the tweezers to see if the ringer was still in place. It wasn't. *Damn it*. Some of the old ones stopped working from time to time. What he really wanted was to put the bells down and go back up to Cupid.

With the thought of Cupid, his dick hardened again. He wanted to go up there right now and fuck the sleeping man. But he wasn't about to wake him. Instead he forced himself to focus on his work. The tweezers slipped in his grip, but he picked them up again.

A dark shadow grew over the room that blotted out any light from the fire or the candles. They were eclipsed by the shadow and the darkness that came with it. A cold settled over him. It was more than just the cold he could bring with the frost or the snow he had at his disposal. This was a soul crushing, inkiness that could devour any light in its path. Only one being had that kind of power. He got up slowly and turned around.

The inky blackness pulled in on itself and shaped into the form of a woman. Sparkling dots swirled across her dark skin. She moved, a walking shadow, with her dress woven of the fabric of the night itself. Stars twinkled across the cloth and comets grazed her arms. Their trails followed across her body. Dark hair sprinkled with different colored orbs flowed down her back. Her silver eyes stared at him from her darkened skin. A small amount of fear flowed over his spine. If there was any person he would be terrified of, it would be this creature.

Krampus set the bell down and bowed his head. "Nyx, you honor me with your presence. What brings you down from your temple?"

"Krampus, it's been a long time. How are you?" Her delicate lips turned up into a smile. As she moved, the orbs in her hair moved up and down the strands. He looked at them closer and realized they were planets. Her very make up seemed to be stitched of the universe itself. She took his hand so he looked up into her eyes. Being so close to her he could make out her human features better.

The curve of her cheek and the roundness of her face. Her eyes were large and yet when she turned her head they could have been smaller. All different cultures of humanity appeared to be represented in her face. Then again, all mortals looked out at the dark and dreamed. All lived under the same night sky. Even those who thought of her as evil, as Cupid had brought to his attention earlier, knew nothing of what she truly was.

Hell, even he didn't know to what extent she was truly human or something else. Her power came off her in cold waves. Shadows danced around her trying to cover up all the light in the room. Something had brought her down from her temple and he didn't want to experience her wraith.

"Several decades at least. You haven't changed a bit. Still as beautiful as ever." He kissed her hand.

"You always were the flatterer. I think the only one better at it than you is Tempest. And he hardly ever has the time."

He chuckled. "I see you haven't lost your sense of humor."

"Of course not. Many of the things seen requires one to keep it." She walked over to his workstation and picked up a bell. It floated above her palm and rang. The sound pierced his ear being so close to him. The sound died down as the bell spun until it glowed. It grew so bright he shielded his eyes. When the radiance subsided, the bell had vanished. Hovering above her palm was a fiery ball shooting off little flares. It gave off enough heat he could feel it where he stood. Nyx took the orb and placed it against her shoulder. Her skin absorbed it and the new sphere floated out of sight.

"I was going to need that bell."

"Nonsense. It wasn't working and there was no hope of you repairing it. Why do you think so many of them have gone out of order? St. Nicklaus has a way of making sure they won't ring. I suggest making new ones. Although it would require you to fire up your furnace and go out into the smith shop. I don't think I've ever seen you do that."

He ground his teeth. It would figure his nemesis had put some kind of a spell on the bells so they wouldn't ring. *I'll get him back one way or another. He thinks children love him. Wait until this year. I'll make sure my gingerbread wreak havoc and eat a few of his elves. That will show him.* "I can fire up the furnace and forge some more. The supplies were getting low anyway. I was going to fix these and cast them back out into the world. It feels like so many more are naughtier every year. I guess it's time for new ones. You telling me about the bells wasn't why you came here? Did you want something to drink or eat?"

The door opened. His gingerbread cook opened it and was about to say something when she noticed Nyx. Her frosting mouth let out a scream as she backpedaled and left the room. From the look on her face it almost seemed she was going to toss her cookies. Krampus smirked and focused his attention back on his guest.

"I'm fine. It seems your staff don't like me."

"They are more frightened of you than anything else. As much as this visit and catching up is wonderful, you haven't told me why you've come. Nyx, you don't make social calls. Unless you're a bit lonely and decided to take me up on my offer I made all those years ago? I could rock your world."

Nyx laid a hand on his cheek. A cold spark passed through him. "While the invitation is very tempting, I'm not here for any physical activities. Although it's been a while since I've had a go-around with anyone. Last time I knocked the moon out of orbit for a few minutes and a couple of planets were destroyed."

He slid his hand over hers. "Sometimes you have to give in to pleasure to see what will happen. Not everything we do is scripted. I'm sure you know that." He brought her hand to his lips and sucked on one of her fingers. A splash of red appeared across her dark cheeks like a star going supernova. He darted his tongue across her fingertips. She sucked in a breath. Nyx's silver gaze darkened.

When she didn't pull away, he drew his tongue along her finger. She moved closer. Her delicate silver eyelashes fluttered closed. She tasted like ash mixed with honeysuckle. Nyx groaned when he pulled away and claimed her lips. He kissed her gently until she returned the kiss with a hunger and longing. How lonely was this true goddess among the Incarnations?

Surely someone had given her the attention she deserved. She dwelled alone in her temple far above everyone looking down on all the worlds. It made him realize how lonely she truly was as her fingers wound through his hair and ringed his horns. He intensified the kiss and raked his fingers down her back. Cold energy pulsated into his palms and up his arms until his head spun. Their tongues met and twisted together until she pulled away, breathless.

Krampus took a step toward her to reclaim the dark beauty. She put her hand up to stop him. "This wasn't why I came here. I'll have to extend an invitation for you to come to the temple and see the view from the top of the world."

"I already like what I see before me. You are the true temple."

"That forked tongue of yours is going to get you

into trouble one of these days."

"My forked tongue can do wonders if you would just let me."

Shadows swirled between them until they obscured the room. The darkness grew until it blanketed everything, blotting out the light even from the fire. Krampus sighed, but he still sensed Nyx's presence all around him. "And they say I am the evilest of the dark Incarnations. Surely, they haven't met you."

"Not many have. Enough banter. The other Incarnations are in a tizzy because Cupid has gone missing. The West Wind revealed he was getting even with the little brat for something he did and blew him off course. West said Cupid might have ended up heading in this direction. Have you seen him?"

"Cupid? Small cherubic fellow with white fluffy wings?"

"That's what he wants the humans to believe. Don't let him fool you. He's more Adonis than cherubic. Under those innocent green eyes of his is a devil some say is even worse than you. However, if he's gone missing, or even worse, been killed, then chaos will break out first among the humans. Then it will come down to us."

"I didn't realize he was so important."

"Mortals associate him with Valentine's Day, but he controls more than just mortal love and romance. He and his cherubs make sure certain species mate. He doesn't affect just this world, but others as well who know him by other names. If there is no love, then creativity will die off. The muses will wilt and blow away. It may not seem like it, but we're all important entities in the grand design of things. Even you who terrorize human children in the winter seasons. You keep the balance with St. Nicklaus."

"Shit." Krampus hadn't realized how important Cupid was. *Good thing I didn't let the gingerbread men eat him or there'd be hell to pay.* "My cookies found Cupid caught in one of my nets. They brought him here for me to examine."

"You didn't let those cannibals eat him, did you?" Nyx growled.

"No. They didn't. Although they wanted to."

"Thank the Incarnations."

"No thanking god?"

"Which one?"

"True. There are so many," Krampus replied.

"Where is Cupid now?"

"He's upstairs asleep in my bed."

"What did you do to him?"

"Why would it be me to have done something bad to him? I might have the horns, but he is the devilish one."

Nyx smirked. "I see you discovered that for yourself. Yeah, he knows how to play people. Don't let him fool you into thinking he is in love with you."

"I didn't think that at all."

"Good. So you'll be able to give him up?"

"He can leave whenever he wants. I didn't tie him to the bedposts. He's sleeping. I'll let him know the other Incarnations are worried. Or would you like to go up there and tell him yourself?"

The darkness swirled around him and cool hands slid along his arms. "No. I'll take your word for it. I should go. I'll let the other Incarnations know Cupid should be coming back soon." Nyx pressed her lips to his in a quick kiss. "I suspect I'll see you soon." The darkness floated away and the light and warmth returned to the room.

Chapter Four

Once he was by himself again, Krampus glanced at his table but didn't feel like working on the bells any longer. His stomach grumbled. He left the room and went back into the kitchen, where his cook had set out the plates he had asked for and left them covered on a tray on the counter. He grabbed the tray which also had hot chocolate on it and brought it up to his bedroom.

Cupid sat cross-legged in the middle of his bed with an arrow up against his eye as he gauged its shaft.

"Did you find any flaw?"

Cupid flashed him a smile before he placed it in his quiver. "No flaw. Although I have to make more. I lost a few when I was blown here."

"Are you hungry?"

"I could eat."

Krampus set the tray down on the bedside table. He uncovered the plates and held one out to Cupid. He picked at his food and ignored the silverware. They ate in silence for a few minutes until Cupid licked his fingers and handed him back the plate. Krampus examined the man as the sheets were tangled around his legs. His blond hair remained tussled. Nyx's words rang in his mind about Cupid not letting him trick him into thinking what they had was love. He could understand that because what he felt was a strong attraction, but the other Incarnation didn't have a hold on his heart.

"Thank you."

"You're welcome. So…"

Cupid touched his hand. "You were wondering what's happening next."

"It had crossed my mind. You can't stay here

forever."

"No. I can't. Was that why Nyx showed up?"

"You were aware of her coming?"

"I'm not as innocent as I made out when you first released me. I know about Nyx and the other darker Incarnations, including you. It's just that one likes to seek you out. And one can't not know when Nyx is around. Everything goes dark. She's very powerful. Some would argue she might be the most powerful of all of us. There are others though, Death, for example. Azrael has the power to touch souls and bring them to wherever they go. I'm sure there are others."

"You rule over all facets of love. That's pretty powerful as well."

"Yes, it is. What did Nyx want?"

"She came here to tell me the other Incarnations had reported you missing. They were concerned you might have been hurt. She wanted to know if I had seen you and to make sure you were all right."

"And you told her I ended up caught in your net."

"I told her."

Cupid trailed his fingers over his robe and tugged at the tie. "You desired her, too."

"I did." There was no use in denying it. Krampus found the female Incarnation attractive, and he had made an offer to her before about them hooking up. But she had never taken him up on the offer. Today was the first time she had actually extended an invitation for him to visit her in her temple.

"I'm not jealous. I've had many lovers. You're just another one to add to my list. It was fun. Don't you agree?" Cupid slipped underneath his robe and cupped his half-hard cock.

Krampus gritted his teeth and grabbed Cupid's

wrist. Cupid chuckled at the gesture, but he didn't stop touching Krampus. "Last night was fun. But you forget this is my realm. Even though I gave myself to you and let you dominate, you never gave me the chance to repay the favor." When he released Cupid, a piece of silver tinsel wrapped around Cupid's wrist. The other end attached to the bedpost. Another strand shot out and took his other hand and dragged Cupid across the bed until his head was against the headboard.

"Touché, but like Nyx said, you can't keep me tied up here forever."

Krampus dropped his robe. "I don't intend to keep you here at all. After this you can go when you want. But I wanted to return the favor. Can't I do that?" He crawled onto the bed pulled the sheet off the rest of the way revealing Cupid's firm cock.

"What are you going to do with me afterward?"

"You're due for some pleasure and I want to taste you before I let you go. Because I don't know when I'll have the opportunity to do this to you again."

Cupid shrugged. "Then come here and do it to me, furry man. Wrap those lips around my cock and use that forked tongue of yours. I want to feel it. Make me come."

The thrill of what his willing captive said jolted him. He crawled over the bed and kissed the inside of Cupid's thigh. He tasted sweeter than strawberries. Krampus nipped along the sensitive skin and couldn't resist nipping a little harder until he tasted blood. Cupid groaned. He looked up and the man's head was thrown back as he drew in short breaths.

"More?"

"Yes," Cupid moaned.

Krampus licked a spot on Cupid's other thigh. This time he bit him harder, making sure his pointed teeth made an impression in his skin. Cupid jumped this time, but he thrust his hips up. Krampus cleaned the blood with his forked tongue. The wounds healed almost immediately, but the impression of his teeth were left on his flesh. It had made a permanent impression on the other Incarnation, claiming him for his own if anyone else tried to do so later on. Cupid bucked his hips forward. Krampus flicked his tongue over the other Incarnation's dick. He could already taste the salt of pre-cum on the tip.

He savored the salty sweetness before wrapping his lips around the shaft and sucking all of him down. Cupid thrust his hips upward, making him scrape his teeth along the sensitive skin. Krampus slid his fingers along the man's thighs learning the muscles underneath the hairless flesh. Even that small touch made him hard. But this time he wasn't going to give in to his desire. He wanted to make Cupid his. Biting him was one thing, but bringing him pleasure was another. Krampus trailed his claws over the male's flesh until he came to his navel. He summoned a bit of his magic. He released Cupid's cock and blew across his body. A pale white frost laced across the man's body.

"Fuck, what did you do?" Cupid cried out.

Krampus smiled and blew across the top of his lover's cock. It turned pale blue, slightly frozen from the inside out. "Just using a bit of magic. Then I can suck you like a Popsicle. Do you like it?"

"It's like I can feel you everywhere. Don't stop now."

Krampus slid his lips over Cupid's frozen prick. The Incarnation bucked under him, shoving his shaft further into his mouth until he almost gagged. The flesh might have been frozen, but his length remained warm. He moved his lips along the skin slowly before wrapping his tongue around the shaft. Cupid bucked against him. He wanted to maintain the bliss of the encounter, but by the sound of the man he pleasured he wasn't going to last very long. Krampus looked up to see Cupid struggling with his hands wrapped around the tinsel. The tendons strained on the man's beautiful face. A jolt of pleasure speared him seeing the other man in agony because of his nearing release.

He quickened his pace and sent a bit more magic zooming along Cupid's veins. Another anguished cry came from his lover. Krampus could keep this up for a while, but the longer he had the feathered Incarnation in his grasp the more likely others might come looking for him. And he couldn't keep the male to himself even if he wanted to. They all had parts to play in the scheme of things. He went down on his lover again, increasing his rhythm until Cupid's cries had regressed into animal noises and panting.

The magic hold he exerted over the manifestation of love faded as Krampus focused on wrapping his tongue around Cupid's shaft. He scraped his nails across Cupid's torso and twisted his nipples. The other man grunted and arched his back off the bed. At that moment, Cupid came and Krampus drank down his strawberry flavored seed.

Cupid pressed himself against Krampus and kissed him. Krampus cupped the perfect ass housed in the gold lamé shorts and poked his nails into the mounds. Their tongues darted and touched, twining together, until Krampus pulled away. Cupid stroked Krampus' prick one last time sending a zing of longing through him. He didn't want to leave, but had to.

"It's been a wonderful experience," Cupid murmured.

"It has. It's a good thing the West Wind blew you into my net," Krampus replied. He adjusted his robe and tried to ignore his hardened member.

"I could stay and take care of that for you." He walked his fingers down Krampus' stomach.

He caught Cupid's hand before he slipped it underneath the belt of the robe. "And if you do that, then you are never going to leave here. The other Incarnations wouldn't be too happy if I kept you all to myself and love started to break down in the human world."

"Humans are so overrated. Don't you agree?"

He stepped away. "I enjoy humans. The ones here are nothing more than animals and make good eating. The ones from the human realm are clever. And they are so naughty. It's amazing to see some of the things they do. One of them actually lived in the mouse hole in my living room for a while. He didn't think I knew he was in there. It amused me to see him antagonize the gingerbread men who kept trying to eat him. In the end, he got tiresome and I returned him back to his world."

"Was he as good as me?"

"When I bring them here I am a giant to them. The tin soldiers and cookies are about their size. You were so small when the cookies brought you to me that you fit in the palm of my hand. I had to use my magic on you so you and I could be equal."

Cupid took his quiver of arrows and settled it around his neck. "I'm glad you did. It was fun. I'll have the bite marks to prove it too. No one is going to believe this story. My cherubs would never think the great Krampus had conquered me."

"I'm not sure who conquered who, but it was amazing." Krampus slipped his hand into the pocket of his robe and pulled out one of his working bells. He slipped his hand down into Cupid's shorts and nestled it next to the Incarnation's dick. "If you ever want to meet up again, just give this a ring. I'll hear it no matter where I am. Either I can come to you or you can come here." He sent a blast of cold through the other man.

His lover's eyes fluttered shut. When he breathed out a fog of white came out. "Fuck. I could go for that."

"Just a lasting taste so you don't forget me."

"I won't forget you, Krampus. I'm glad West blew me this way." Cupid stretched his wings to their full extent until he resembled the angel Krampus had thought the Incarnation was.

"Me too. I guess your wings weren't as badly sprained as you thought they were."

"Guess not."

"Were they sprained at all?"

Cupid winked. "Guess you'll never know." He grabbed Krampus' face between his hands and kissed him quickly, tugging on his lip before pulling away. "Gotta go. Places to be and people to shoot."

A gust of wind swept through the room and forced the shutters open. Cupid ran to the window and dived out. Krampus raced to the window in time to see Cupid spread his wings and soar high into the sky. He lingered there until he was out of sight. As he closed the shutters, an arrow whizzed by his head and landed with a *thunk* into the wood. He gripped the shaft and freed it from the wood. Wrapped around the wooden shaft was a message. He unrolled it and a bunch of red glitter hearts fell out. As the hearts fluttered to the ground, they turned into various pastel heart-shaped medallions that clattered onto the stone floor. They spelled out a message.

"Be My Valentine."

Krampus chuckled at the sentiment and went to retrieve the hearts. They rearranged into one big heart shape and fused together into one silver medallion. He picked it up and found the silver coating it was actually some kind of covering. He ripped it off and saw the chocolate underneath it. He broke off a piece and wasn't surprised it tasted like strawberries. He rewrapped the chocolate heart to save it for later.

Krampus thought about his encounter and wondered if he would ever see the feathered Incarnation again. If he did, would it be the same? Yet, even as he thought about the night they'd spent together, his thoughts turned to Nyx. She had invited him to her temple. He had never been there. She wasn't attached to anyone and she was lonely. Although, how could the night be desolate when there was so much underneath and in it, he wasn't sure. Then again he wasn't in her shoes.

Krampus set the heart on his workbench and looked at the rows of bells the tin soldiers had gathered. Many of them were old. He passed his hand over them and felt a bit of magic other than his. Krampus refocused on the colder sensation and caught the happy energy he associated with Claus. He gritted his teeth and gathered up the bells. They were useless. Nyx was right. He had to recast them and make new ones. Only melting them down would make sure the spell was broken. He slipped them into the pocket of his robe.

"Master, your guest left you something." The gingerbread cook came into the room holding something on the tray. He took the dome off and found a white feather inside of it with a written note.

For another time. Sometimes feathers are better than crops. See you later, my fine hairy ass beast.

Krampus shook his head and thought about what would come between them in the future. He knew there would be another encounter. Just when it would be was something he had to look forward to. Right now he had to think about getting his bells done. The anticipation of what was to come made him hard again. He set the feather on top of his mantle where he wouldn't lose it. Each time he looked at it, the memories of what they had shared would go through his mind.

The general gingerbread came into the room. "Master, are you going to inspect the livestock?"

Normal life called. "Yes. I'm coming. Lead the way. You know maybe we should plan something to have for Valentine's day. Maybe make you some companion cookies. Would you like that?"

The one eyed general grinned. "Sounds tasty. It would make the men happy."

"Good. Good. I'll talk to the chef first thing. Let's go look at the humans and see if they are ready to eat."

Krampus Does Dallas

Crymsyn Hart

Krampus never thought he would find someone to care for again. Then he met Dallas when the rodeo came to town. Surprises continue with the new man in Krampus' life when Stephen shows up looking for Dallas. Krampus won't let Dallas out of his sight, but when Dallas is called back to the rodeo, Krampus is in for the ride of his life.

Chapter One

"Master? Master!"

Krampus's grip on the hammer faltered. His strike on the metal he used to make the bells was off its mark. "I told you not to interrupt me!" He flung the hammer at the nearest gingerbread soldier. The hammer hit the cookie hard enough it shattered. His companion fell to his knees and bowed his head. Krampus wiped the sweat from his brow and reached down to eat a piece of the gingerbread he'd crumbled. The heavy taste of molasses sat on his tongue. *Next time I need to use less molasses and put in a bit more cinnamon.*

"Forgive me. Please don't eat me."

"Shut up and tell me why you came in here, before I do decide to eat you." He'd been in the zone and told his tin soldiers and his gingerbread guards not to disturb him for anything unless the house was burning down or someone decided to drop in.

The gingerbread soldier held up a piece of yellow paper. Krampus snatched it out of his grip. He took another glance at the cookie. His edges hadn't been burnt yet to preserve him. No frosting had been applied to fix cracks in his cookie body. Krampus took another bite of the crushed cookie and focused back on the flyer.

"Where did you get this?"

"We went to the market. They were handing them out and putting them up in the shops in town. We thought you might be interested since you've been…"

"I've been what?"

The soldier shrunk back. "Nothing. Nothing. Forget it."

Krampus knelt down next to the gingerbread cookie and touched his shoulder. The fire crackled in the hearth. He needed to get back to working on the bells, but he didn't want all his soldiers to be talking behind his back. "What are they saying? I promise I won't eat you. You caught me off guard when you came in. I'm sorry about your companion."

The younger gingerbread man looked up. His raisin eyes widened and one of his gumdrop buttons was about to come off. "There is talk among the others that you've gone a little crazy spending all this time out here. You don't interact with us anymore. You don't want to talk to anyone about anything. Ever since…"

"Ever since my winged friend left."

"Yes. We thought this might be a good distraction."

Krampus studied the advertisement once more. A rodeo was coming to town. "I could use the distraction. You're right. I've been holed up in here. I've made more bells in the last month than I have in the last few years. I think I can stop. This last batch isn't something I need. Go tell the others it's okay if you attend the rodeo, but in shifts. I don't want to leave the house unguarded. No need to let the human stock escape. Tell the cook I want a meat pie. Find the plumpest human and get it to the chef. And pick a couple for yourselves too."

"Master? Are you sure?"

"Why not? Go and have some fun. I'm sure we all need it." Krampus got up and stretched. The warmth of the forge combined with the heat of the day had gotten to him. He laid his leather apron on the workbench and set the yellow sheet aside as he dunked his whole head into the barrel of water he used to cool the metal he worked with.

When he came back up he shook his head to dry his hair and horns off. Feeling a bit more relaxed, he looked at the large bull printed on the sheet of paper. It intrigued him. He had never been to a rodeo before. Not many things came to the town sitting below his vast estate. When he went into town, the townsfolk were afraid he would come for them one night during the Christmas season. However, he didn't let his bells get passed around in his realm. They were all cast into the human world, so whenever one rang there a corresponding bell rang on his tree in the living room. It stayed there all year round, but most of the time he ignored it.

Krampus went back into the house. A scream came from the back and then a loud thud. He passed the kitchen. A cauldron bubbled over the hearth. The scent made his mouth water, but it sounded as though dinner was going to be a while. He went up to his bedroom and grabbed a cloak and threw the hood over his head.

Outside, the sun began to set as he headed down to the village. As he walked, he passed a wagon train parked on the outskirts of the village. The heady scent of animals caught his nose. A large bull pulled a cart and snorted as the cold air descended with the night. Spring had come, but it remained chilly. His fur kept him warm. He pulled his cloak lower over his face and stopped to watch as a group of men and horses set up a fence. He realized the men and horses were actually one and the same. *Centaurs. Strange for a rodeo. I don't think this is going to be the ordinary rodeo I was expecting.*

A whip snapped across the bull's back. It bellowed as the tip of it hit its flesh. Whoever sat on the wagon snapped it again. The large creature reared and jerked the wagon up off its front wheels. The enormous animal shook in its harness and it broke free of its yoke. *Poor creature. Must be what they use to pull the wagons and then use in the rodeo.* He didn't see any other animals around, but that didn't mean they weren't there.

"Somethin' you lookin' for?"

Krampus glanced over to the gruff voice next to him and saw a short, round dwarf with a crooked smile and a few missing teeth. Several of the other workers gathered behind her. One of them had a club in his hand he kept slamming on his palm. He almost threw his cloak off to tell the dwarf off. Krampus didn't want to spook them. It was good to have the distraction of the rodeo. He already felt some of his malaise and mourning over his winged friend lifting. Krampus had tried everything to distract himself and he hadn't realized how much of his frustration he had been taking out on his gingerbread.

Something poked his right leg. He glanced over to his other side and saw an even smaller woman dressed up as a clown in a pink tutu, with a pitchfork in her hand. "Hey, she asked you a question. You got a problem? If not, move it along. Don't need no dirty town rats hanging around here looking for trouble or begging for food."

He held up his hands. "My apologies. I was taking in the sights. It's not often we get a rodeo in these parts. Especially such an exotic one."

"Heh, there's more to it here than what you see. We'll be opening up tomorrow. Then you can come and see everything. Maybe get a taste of what we got to offer. I'm sure a big boy like yourself can use some distraction."

Krampus chuckled. The little woman had no

idea. "You could say that. How much for your bull?"

"He's not for sale. Without him there wouldn't be a rodeo."

"Really? Then why do I see four other bulls already grazing in the pen you've set up. Is he special or something?"

"He's not for sale."

Krampus pulled a coin from his purse. He leaned over careful to keep his face hidden. He slipped the coin into the woman's hand and trailed his talons over her wrist. She didn't flinch, but gave him a curious look. "Anything's for sale. I want him. Or maybe you might find you won't have a rodeo any longer."

"Ha! Empty threats."

"Really?" He waved his hand and expended a bit of power. Frost shot over the ground. White lacey lines crept up onto several of the wagons. They buckled under the weight of the frost. He curled his fingers and a wagon wheel splintered. Another branch of frost circled around the other bulls he saw and crept closer. The cattle stamped in distress. One of them snorted fire and pawed the ground. The frost thread wound around the bull and turned the whole thing to ice.

"Enough!" the smaller woman entreated him.

Krampus released his power and the cow returned to normal. "How much for the bull?"

"Five gold pieces. He's skin and bones."

He took out five gold coins and slipped them into her palm. "Another piece of advice. Make sure you check with the land owner next time you decide to set up on his property."

"This is no man's land. We already checked."

He lifted his cloak so the woman could see his face. "You sure about that? I'll pick up the bull on my way back."

Her face paled and she backed up a few steps. She opened her mouth to say something, but he put a finger to her lips. The dwarf woman nodded. "Anything you want, sir."

"Good. Isn't it nice that we got this all worked out?"

"Yes, sir."

"Have a good evening." Krampus moved through the crowd that had gathered around them. He entered the town. The shops had closed up for the day. The road was dry and in need of rain. The only rowdy place was the tavern. He slid inside. Few people noticed as he walked in, but they didn't say anything when he sat down in a corner booth. He sat back and watched the place fill with the laborers of the town. A waitress came by and set a mug down on his table.

"You sit at a table, you gotta order food."

"Fine. Bring me whatever's on the menu."

The waitress came back with some kind of stew and bread. He dipped the bread into the broth and took a taste of it. He coughed at the seasoning. Besides having an overabundance of pepper, it was edible. His stomach growled. He thought about his interaction with the owner of the rodeo. He'd bought a bull. *Why the hell did I buy the bull? I don't need it. Now I'm stuck with the beast. I'm sure it's had a taxing life.*

He glanced up from his meal when the noise level dropped. A group from the rodeo entered the tavern. One of the thugs who had stopped him approached the bartender. The group followed behind him.

"A round of ale for the lot."

The bartender crossed his arms over his chest. The corner of his mouth twitched. "Your kind ain't wanted here. Best if you get out before I have someone throw you out."

"We have a right to be here just as anyone else." The thug sat at the bar. The rest moved into a table that emptied out since they had come in. The rodeo participants all looked as though they had a difficult life. All were tanned and wrinkled from years in the sun and hard work. Krampus didn't envy them. The tension in the bar grew. He sat back. The bartender and the other patrons surrounded them.

A cloaked figure slipped past them and hovered by Krampus's table.

"Why don't you sit here? It looks like everywhere else is taken." Krampus found himself saying.

The man looked at him. "Why do you care?"

"I don't. Sit or don't sit."

Krampus pushed the plate aside and laid a couple of silver coins on the table. They would more than cover the cost of his meal and the ale. He didn't want the waitress to hassle him any longer. The man glanced at the coins and the unfinished bowl of stew. He sat down and reached for the stew. Then the stranger pulled his hand back.

"You going to eat that?"

"Have at it."

The stranger's hands were dark, almost like polished black marble. His arms were decorated with long-healed-over scars. The man took the bowl and brought it in close to him, protecting it. When he ate, the hood of his cloak fell away, revealing a bald head, a strong jaw and a flat nose. His eyes were gold when he looked up at Krampus. Something in that gaze stirred Krampus's desire.

"What?" the man asked around a mouthful of bread.

"Nothing. I just noticed you were hungry. I could make it worth your while if you wanted to come back to the house with me."

"So you can fuck me? I'm not a whore. I see how you're looking at me."

Krampus held back a smile. "No. I wasn't considering sex. I just meant I have better food than what you have there. Plus, you can sleep in a bed. It looks like you might need it. No strings attached."

The other man eyed him. "I thought you said you didn't care."

"It's obvious your companions don't care about you or you would've come in with them. And you wouldn't have been hiding your appearance. I'm surprised you're still with them. Of course, I could be way off on my observations. Come or not, but I'm leaving." Krampus got up from the booth and left the tavern. After he rejoined the darkness, the tavern door slammed shut.

"Where are we going?"

"Follow me."

Chapter Two

Krampus and his companion walked in silence. They stopped at the rodeo. He didn't see the bull he'd bought.

"Where's my bull?"

The little woman he'd found there put her hands on her hips. "He wandered off. I can't keep an eye on him if he ain't mine, now can I?"

"You don't want to piss me off, dwarf."

"I don't give a hoot who you are. Threaten me again and you'll get a taste of my own power. Go find the bull yourself."

Krampus pulled in a breath. The coolness of frost wrapped around his fingers, but the stranger from the tavern touched his arm. He looked over at the other man.

"It's not worth it. I'm sure you'll find your animal. It can't have wandered too far."

He saw the sincerity in the other man's eyes. "Fine. Follow me."

They walked past the rodeo up to Krampus's manor. As they walked, they didn't see a bull. It was dark, but he wasn't about to go looking for the animal. When they entered the castle, the other man gasped as the door shut on its own. Krampus chuckled. A gingerbread cookie scurried down the hall, but otherwise he didn't see any of his servants.

"Who are you?" the other man asked.

"I'm the master of this land. Who are you?"

"They call me Dallas."

"Dallas. Is that what you call yourself?"

His guest seemed taken aback by the question because it took him a few minutes to answer him. "I -- I don't know. I don't have a name. That's what they call me."

Krampus touched his arm. Dallas jerked away. He pulled his hand back and put it up, showing he meant no harm. "That's a shame. Come into the study. I have some brandy that will warm you." He led him into his study and poured the drinks. He handed one to Dallas and set his own on the desk.

"You got that food coming?"

"I will." Krampus pulled a cord by the fireplace. A few moments later one of the gingerbread soldiers opened the door.

"You rang, Master?"

"Holy shit! It's a talking cookie!"

"Get my guest some food. Tell Cook some venison and pork meat pies. Would you like anything else?"

"Do you have apples?"

"We do."

"Can I have some of those too?"

"Of course. And a plate of apples."

"Yes, Master." The cookie left the room, leaving behind a small pile of crumbs.

"Who are you really?" Dallas asked.

Krampus removed his hood and lay the cloak over the back of the couch.

Dallas gasped. "My Lord Pan. Forgive me. I didn't realize it was you." His visitor knelt before him. Dallas's cloak fell around his shoulders and revealed more lash marks.

His whole back must be striped with them. What have these people been doing to him? "You have me confused with someone else. People don't bow before me. Who is this Pan you're referring to?"

Dallas clasped his hands together and pressed them to his forehead. "I've prayed for this moment that you would finally appear and liberate me from my bondage. As promised, I'm yours to do with as you please. I will be your slave and serve you for all time for freeing me from the hell I've lived in."

Krampus knelt and gently took his guest's hands and lowered them. He lifted Dallas' chin. Tears streamed down his face. The relief in his eyes moved Krampus's heart. *I'm not going to play the ruse either.* He wiped Dallas's cheek. "I swear to you I'm not this Pan you think I am. My name is Krampus."

"If you are not my god, then why have you offered me this kindness and released me from the rodeo I have served? You bought me from them. I am yours."

He expected Dallas to be afraid of him, but he looked at him with awe. "*Bought*? I bought a bull. I bought no man."

"I am the bull you purchased."

"How can this be?"

"I'm both man and beast. I was bound to them until someone released me from their service." Dallas got up slowly and looked at Krampus with his golden gaze. Something deepened within Krampus and moved between them. "No one has ever cared before. I've been bound by a spell. Someone had to want me -- I don't mean in a sexual way -- because no one has ever wanted me. Something in you wanted me. That's why I thought you were my god. Are you sure you aren't?"

"No. I'm not this deity you prayed to."

The door opened again and the gingerbread brought in a tray with the food. He set it on the table and then backed out of the room. Krampus took a plate and handed it to Dallas. The other man dug into the food and all was silent. Krampus took a slice of apple and ate it. The sweetness surprised him. He thought about what Dallas had told him. The idea that he had broken Dallas free of some kind of spell made him wonder exactly who or what this man was to the rodeo.

"There's more where that came from. You don't have to eat it all in one sitting."

Dallas slowly put down the pie. "Sorry. I just haven't been fed in a couple of days."

"Haven't been fed? What did they do to you?"

Dallas gazed at him for a long time. He shrugged off his cloak and turned to show Krampus his back. Fresh stripes lined his flesh along with a map of old scars that showed how he had been mistreated. "If I don't pull the wagons hard enough or if I don't buck high enough when I have a rider on my back, I get these. This was from this evening. I saw you looking at me while I pulled the wagon. You released me, so I wanted to find you. I followed your scent. I thought you might be the mighty Pan. I'm not sure what to make of you. Walking and talking cookies? A large tree with bells on it?"

"You're a shape shifter. I never would've thought. I saw them beat you. Even before that, I thought you were a magnificent animal."

Dallas's whole demeanor changed when he smiled. "You thought I was magnificent?"

"I did." Krampus took one of the napkins, dipped it into the liquor, and touched the cloth to the stripes on Dallas' back.

The other man winced and hissed in a breath of pain. "What are you doing?"

"Tending to your wounds. They need to be looked after before they get infected."

"The others have healed fine."

"The others have healed horribly. You never

should've been whipped. No one deserves to be treated this way. I can stitch these up if you like."

"No need. I heal pretty quickly. One part of my fucked-up life."

"Now you're free. What are you going to do?" Krampus felt a tug on his heart at the thought of Dallas leaving.

"I don't know. You freed me. I am yours to command." Dallas stood up and placed a hand on Krampus's chest.

A jolt of warmth ran through Krampus. He felt himself stir from the sudden contact. "But you got angry when you thought I was soliciting you for sex."

"I wasn't in the mood then. And I had to be sure you wanted me for me. Not just my body. I saw it in your eyes." Dallas slid his hands down along Krampus's chest and twined his fingers through his brown fur until he cupped his cock.

Krampus groaned at the pleasure of it. "There *is* something about you."

"You saved me. Now I will do anything for you." Dallas pushed his lips against Krampus's lips and kissed him hard.

Krampus let himself ride the desire. The strong animal smell titillated his senses. It hadn't been so strong before, the scent of the bull that lived underneath Dallas's skin. The other man rubbed his hard shaft, but Krampus couldn't let himself get caught up in the moment. This man didn't have any right to be used by him or by anyone else. He deserved to be free. "Dallas, wait."

"Don't you want me?" The hurt in his voice made Krampus's heart ache.

"Yes. I want you. You're beautiful. Magnificent. I need to know you want to be with me not because I freed you from some spell or because you're trying to repay me for the food I've given you. You thought I was your god. I'm no god. I'm just the opposite. I eat humans. I steal naughty children at Christmas, and some adults from the human world. I'm not the nicest creature to be around."

"I know what I know. It doesn't matter if I just met you. I want this. This isn't me trying to pay you back for anything or show you gratitude. I know you want me. Is that good enough for you?"

"Yes."

"Good. Now shut up, get naked, and bend over. I'm taking you by the horns."

* * *

Krampus was surprised at how forceful Dallas became. The other man's eyes glowed in the firelight. Dallas snorted. His cheekbones shifted and his nose elongated.

"Is everything okay? Your face has changed."

"It happens when I get aroused. Don't worry about it. Sometimes I can't keep all of the beast contained."

"I understand. But don't you want me to pleasure you? I'm sure you --"

"Shut up so I can take your furry ass. That's what I want."

Krampus wasn't about to argue with the man. He liked knowing Dallas knew what he wanted. Before he could comply, Dallas turned him around forcefully and tugged lightly on his hard prick. Dallas bent Krampus over the arm of the couch. He kicked Krampus's feet apart and pushed him down until the material of the cushions rubbed against his face. Krampus groaned when his lover grabbed his ass cheeks and squeezed them. The pain felt good, but he wanted more of it. The weight of his lover pushed him lower. Dallas ran his fingers over his ass and rimmed his asshole until he inserted a finger and then two, stretching him.

He groaned.

"You like that?"

"Yes," Krampus whispered.

The bliss in him rose, leaving him barely able to hold on. It had been so long since he had felt it. He wasn't sure he if could perform. Krampus hadn't been with anyone since his former lover had winged off and left him.

Dallas cupped Krampus's balls and squeezed them. He jumped from the sudden pain. It soon became over shadowed by the pressure he felt from Dallas as he slipped his cock inside of him.

He expected the other man to be slow about it. However, he plunged inside of Krampus, claiming his ass quickly. Krampus bucked against him. Dallas held his balls while he drove into him again. The musky scent of Dallas's sweat filled his nose. His weight against Krampus's back seemed to have doubled, as did his body mass.

Sharp nails scraped the tender skin of his scrotum. Heavy breathing filled his ear. Krampus pushed back against his lover until they found a rhythm. Dallas released his sack and moved to his dick. Talons dragged over the tender flesh of his shaft. He sucked in a breath. His cock tightened even as Dallas pumped into him and manipulated his length.

Krampus bit his lip and tried to remain in control, to make the pleasure coursing through him last longer. His nerves burned with building pleasure. Krampus gripped the sofa as heat rose within him. He tried to keep the tempo between them going.

Dallas's grip on his cock quickened. Short bursts of warmth tickled the sensitive hair around his ears. Each puff of air made them flick back and forth. It was both maddening and enticing all at the same time.

"Harder," Krampus cried.

The words slipped out before he realized he uttered them. He couldn't hold it in any longer. He was going to come. He needed to feel all of his lover inside of him. There was no more pain, just the craving to be filled and the desperate desire for release. Dallas's claws stung as he pumped Krampus's prick, sending another jolt of agony rode up his groin to become mixed with the pleasure of their joining.

His lover thrust into him. His breathing quickened. Krampus sensed Dallas was hovering on the precipice. One last tug on his prick and he came with a wail that filled the room. The release brought him to an ecstasy he hadn't known he could find again. His body burned with it. His mind exploded with points of light as the orgasm took him. Dallas moved into him one last time, then slumped over. The added weight brought Krampus back to himself. Out of breath, he turned his head and looked at his lover.

Gone was the man. Instead a man with a bull's head remained. His erect cock glistened from their union. Dallas tried to turn away, but Krampus put a hand on his shoulder and shook his head. He kissed Dallas's chest, tasting the flesh and salt along with the musk of the animal. Short bursts of air came from Dallas as he sipped in the air. Krampus took his perky, dark nipple into his mouth and sucked on it. He nibbled as it hardened even more. He trailed his fingers down Dallas's chest, feeling the slick skin, and grabbed his cock. He fondled it slowly as it remained firm.

He looked up once more. Dallas's face returned to a mixture of the bull and the human, with short black horn buds growing from his temples. Krampus released him and pressed his lips to his lover's. Dallas returned the kiss lightly until Krampus flicked his tongue over the other man's. Dallas met his tongue and they deepened the kiss. Their tongues danced and Dallas's hands roved over Krampus's body becoming tangled in his fur. His hands trailed lower until Dallas patted Krampus's prick once more. He stirred, but pulled away.

"What did I do?" Dallas asked.

"Nothing, dear one. I don't want to take advantage of you. This was lovely. But you need to rest after all you've been through today."

Dallas began to protest, but Krampus put a finger to his lips. "We have tomorrow and tomorrow. Endless tomorrows. You need to sleep and recoup. I only want what is best for you. Understand?"

His lover nodded.

"Good. One of the gingerbread soldiers will show you to your room. Rest. I'll be here if you need me."

"Okay." Dallas gave him a quick kiss.

The door opened. A cookie waited there for orders. "Show my guest to a room. Make sure the fire is stoked and get him whatever he wants. Understand?"

"Yes, Master." The gingerbread servant bowed. A few crumbs fell to the floor from around his jagged edges.

"Good. Come back here when you're done." Krampus's stomach growled.

Chapter Three

Dallas followed after the cookie as Krampus put his pants back on. He sipped his drink and sat on the couch thinking about their coupling. A smile played on his lips. The warmth of the fire and the liquor improved his mood. Feeling bloomed inside of him when he thought about the bull shifter. He watched the coals in the fire as they glowed orange and the door opened. The cookie servant stood before him, waiting for orders.

"You got him settled in?"

"Yes, Master."

"Good. Come here."

The cookie didn't hesitate. Krampus grabbed the gingerbread and bit into its shoulder. The gingerbread man screamed, but Krampus took another bite. *The gingerbread's gone stale. Yuck.* He threw the half-eaten cookie into the fire. It writhed as the flames came to life and licked at its limbs. It cried out again, but Krampus paid it no mind. *There's more where he came from. All I need is a baking sheet.* The room smelled of molasses and lifted Krampus's spirits even more.

Krampus woke the next morning to the sound of a bell ringing. He jumped up and followed the sound in to the hall. Dallas stood by the decorated fir tree fingering one of the brass bells. The other man trailed his fingers over the sharp needles of the tree. They were a contrast of emerald against his nearly onyx skin. Beams of sunlight illuminated the man's shiny skin. The toned muscles of his back and his ass, even those ragged pants he wore, made Krampus realize how much of Dallas was a bull and not a man. The lash marks marred his perfection. How could they have mistreated him so? They only saw him as a beast of burden. Something to be used and abused in their rodeo. Nothing to be cherished the way he should be.

Dallas unwound one of the bells from the branch. Krampus placed a hand on top of his. "Best not for you to remove them."

Dallas jumped back as though he had been lashed. He looked down and stepped further away from Krampus. The other man hung his head. "Forgive me, Master. I meant no harm. The only bells I've seen are the ones they put around my neck or around the necks of other livestock."

A small sigh drifted from Krampus's lips. He lifted Dallas's chin to stare into the dazzling gems of his eyes. "First off, call me master only if you wish. I won't make you. I may have bought you, but you're not my servant. Second, I wasn't scolding you about the bell. I have newer ones in my workshop and in my study that haven't been spelled yet. Once the bells are removed from the tree, they lose their magic. I have to replace them or respell them. It's easier to replace them because they are from my predecessor. Don't think I am angry with you because I'm not. If you stay here, you might find I have particular appetites that you don't approve of."

"You want me to leave?" Dallas's eyes widened.

"No. You're not my slave. Come and go as you please. I'm not going to force you to stay here. But if you do, there are some rules to the house you have to abide by. And if you call me anything, call me by my name."

Dallas's shoulders slumped in relief. "You're Krampus."

He shook his head. "To the whole world and others, I am. Krampus is the incarnation I hold. Like Cupid or Nyx. I occupy an office until it's my time to move on. That time varies. I've been doing this now for hundreds of years. I enjoy it, but I do have a name."

"What is it?"

"Clover." He hadn't revealed it to anyone in so long it felt foreign on his tongue.

"Like the flower?"

Before he stepped into the role of Krampus, he had been something else. Although he had forgotten most of his past over the years. "It's not a flower, but a plant. And yes." He ran the back of his hand down Dallas's cheek, careful not to catch his talons on the supple flesh.

"How about I call you Clo?"

"Maybe. I'll have to see how it works out, Dallas."

"What are the other rules I have to abide by?" Dallas slipped his hand down Krampus's chest and stopped at his waistband.

Krampus stirred at the touch. He caught his lover's chin to get his attention. "I eat humans when I have the hankering, and keep them with the livestock out back. They aren't the humans you are used to. Mostly a step above stupid animals. When one of these bells rings during the holiday season, I bring the naughty humans back here. Sometimes I eat them too, but mostly they get what they deserve. The gingers and the tin soldiers are protective of me unless I tell them otherwise. You may not agree with some of my ways, and voice your opinion if you like, but don't come between me and my work. I don't expect you to eat long pig with me, but know that I do."

"Will you eat me?"

He chuckled. "I'll lick you and suck you until you cry my name."

"Sounds wonderful." Dallas rubbed Krampus's

prick until it hardened in his hand. "*Master*."

Krampus hung his head. "What do you want?" he barked at the gingerbread servant's interuption.

"There's a man outside claiming he has business with you and your guest." The gingerbread man met his eye and then looked away. His edges were crisp. Plump raisins made up his eyes. The gumdrop buttons down his chest were bright orange and green. White frosting for a mouth turned down in a frown. He rubbed his hands together. Krampus caught the sour scent of fear coming from the servant. Terror tainted the taste of the cookie. He wasn't about to eat him, even though he was hungry.

"I'll be right there," Krampus said. The servant left. He glanced back at Dallas. "Any idea who might be at the door? Last night you led me to believe you had no other ties to the rodeo."

"I don't know what they want. I wasn't allowed to keep any personal things save a few scraps of clothing for when I was human."

"Okay. Let's go see."

Dallas grabbed his arm. "You're not going to give me back to them, are you?"

The terror-stricken look in his eyes melted Krampus's heart. It was obvious his lover didn't want to go back to the life of traveling on the road and being used as a beast of burden. Krampus had no desire to give him up. "You're a free man. Come and go here as you please. I wouldn't give or sell you back. There's nothing for you to worry about. If you have no ties left there, then whoever this is shouldn't be a problem."

They went to the front entryway. A man lingered in the hallway. The two-foot-tall tin soldiers held him at bay with their bayonets. The terrified expression on the visitor's face brought a small smile to Krampus's lips. He didn't recognize the wary-looking man from the ones he'd seen the other day at the rodeo.

"What do you want?" Krampus tried to keep his voice even and not spook him more than he already was.

He took his hat off and held it against his chest. "S-sir. Forgive me for interrupting you. I've come after the rodeo. I…" His eyes widened when Dallas stepped out from behind Krampus. "It's you. They said you were gone."

"You know him?" Krampus asked.

"He's… how did you find me?" Dallas asked the newcomer?

"I've been following behind you for over a year. I lost my way a few times because I never knew where you'd be. I've had to take odd jobs. I was saving up money to buy you from them. I finally saved up enough and found you again. I went there this morning and they said you were already sold. I --" He stepped toward Dallas, but the tin soldiers pushed him back. The other man wrung his hat in his hands.

Krampus could see now he was younger than he appeared. Years of hard work had worn on the man. His blue eyes were intelligent. But his body was shaped and sculpted by the years of hard work the man had done.

"Give us a moment." Krampus pulled Dallas away. "Tell me the truth. I deserve that much. Who is he?"

"No one I thought I'd ever see again. I swear it, Master."

Krampus gritted his teeth at the fear he heard in Dallas's voice. "Is he your lover? Is that why you're afraid to tell me about him?"

"Sometimes the owner of the rodeo would pimp

me out to the highest bidder. One night I was supposed to pleasure a wealthy nobleman, but he couldn't perform. He blamed his limp member on me, saying I had spelled him. He made his servants bring me out into the courtyard and flogged me. The damage was bad. I passed out from the pain. When I came to, I was on my stomach lying on a straw pallet. Stephen was tending to my wounds. He told me his master left me to die. Stephen didn't realize I would heal from the wounds. Mostly they don't leave marks, but this time they did. The scars you see on my back are the result of the last beating. They used a silver tipped whip, which made it slower to heal. The wounds will eventually fade."

"What happened after you were well enough to leave?"

"It took five days to heal me. The rodeo came back for me, but the nobleman lied to them. Stephen was so gentle. He hid me from the nobleman. When I was well enough, he helped me escape the nobleman's castle. I made it back to the rodeo, and I didn't think much of Stephen."

"Really? Because he cared for you and you didn't show your gratitude to him at all?"

Dallas shuffled his feet. "I never thought he'd find me. Stephen didn't want to let me go. But the longer I was away from the rodeo, the stronger the feeling I had to go back to them built. It was part of the spell holding me. It ensured I would return. But you're right. Stephen was the first person, besides you, to show me any sort of kindness. But he never said he loved me. I never thought he'd find me again."

"Do you love this man?"

"I -- I hadn't thought about it. I assumed him lost. And you, I have feelings for you as well."

Krampus wasn't going to deny the love he felt for his new companion. "Come. We'll sort this out." He went back to the new visitor. "Dallas says you saved his life and in that time you fell in love with one another. He wasn't sure he'd ever see you again. Is this true?"

"Can I come in, sir?" Stephen's eyes showed his fear of Krampus.

Krampus found it stimulating, and wondered what it would mean to have this man share his bed. He wasn't about to let Dallas go. "Come in and sit. Do not touch anything. What you see does not leave this house. Understand?"

"Y -- yes, sir." Stephen entered.

A tin soldier closed the door. Krampus ushered the two men into his living room so they could sit on the long sofa in front of the fireplace. The flames burst to life as they entered. Stephen jumped and perched on the edge of the sofa. Dallas stood between the sofa and Krampus. He could feel his lover being torn in both directions. He sensed the fear from Stephen and the yearning from Dallas to spend the night in the other man's arms.

Krampus pulled a bell in the corner, signaling one of his gingers. A few moments later a ragged cookie entered. Frosting bandages wrapped across his left arm. The tear in the gingerbread had been patched over roughly with new batter. His raisin eyes were dried out and the cookie edges crumbled more than Krampus liked in a servant.

"Yes, Master."

"Make up another room for our guest. Give him whatever he wants. Make sure to set out towels and other implements in the grotto."

"As you wish. Master, there's another visitor for

you."

He rolled his eyes. "Who is it now?"

"I don't know. They would not give any name."

"Great. Dallas. Follow him out to the grotto. I'll be back in a few minutes."

"Are you sure?"

Krampus kissed Dallas quickly, savoring his silky lips and the wonderful taste of him. Like cloves. "Yes, dear one. We all have things and people in our past."

Dallas deepened the kiss quickly and broke away. "Thank you."

Stephen and Dallas left the room.

Chapter Four

Krampus went to the door ready to disembowel the person who'd intruded upon his day. It was bad enough Stephen had come, but he didn't hold it against the man. Dallas seemed pleased to see him. Krampus knew his lover wasn't revealing everything on his mind. They were getting used to one another. Although in a short time he had grown in his heart. Maybe it was from Cupid's influence many months ago. He appreciated his last lover's affection because otherwise he wouldn't have been ready for Dallas. He would have gone past and let them keep on beating him. Cupid made him remember he had once been human. Once upon a time, he'd had a past.

He shooed his toy soldiers away. Krampus longed to be in the grotto with the other two men. He didn't think Stephen would mind having a tryst with him. He looked sturdy enough even though he was fearful of him. Most people feared him. The feeling made him smile. But he lost that smile when he saw the rodeo's owner.

"What do you want, dwarf?"

"I need Dallas back." She held out the five gold coins he'd given her.

"I don't think so. He's worth more than that."

The woman dived into the bag at her waist and withdrew five more gold coins. "This enough?"

"You could give me a fortune and it wouldn't be enough. The way you treated him is deplorable. You used him as a beast of burden and sold him to the highest bidder."

"I have a business to run and I do as I see fit. You going to sell him back to me or not?"

"I'm not. Find someone else to fill his spot."

"Bastard. I can't. Do you know how special Dallas is?"

"I do actually. He's sweet and you didn't see that."

"He's more than just a shape shifter. He's a minotaur."

"I know what a minotaur is. Why did you sell him to me in the first place?"

"Because you startled me. I wasn't expecting to meet the Lord of the Manor and have it be the Dark Lord of Christmas. I've heard rumors you eat flesh."

"I do when I have a hankering for it. I'm still not selling Dallas back to you."

She threw up her arms. "Fine. Can we come to a deal, then?"

"Depends on what it is."

"I need him as the main attraction for the bull ride. He knows how to buck the riders off at the right time so I make a good bank. I'll cut you in for half the profits."

Krampus stroked his goatee. "Come with me."

He motioned for her to follow him. They walked through his house until they went outside and down the stairs into the natural grotto on the property with a pool large enough for several people. As he walked down the steps to it, he heard Dallas and Stephen murmuring to one another. He cleared his throat loudly to get their attention. Dallas glared at the owner of the rodeo as he sat in the water with Stephen next to him.

Dallas rose from the frothing water. He strolled toward them with fury in his eyes. "What is this bitch doing here?"

"She has a proposition for you."

The dwarf didn't blush though she came up only

to Dallas's groin and was eye to eye with his cock. "I need you for one last night for the main event. I'll give you half the profits if you can buck 'em like you have in the past."

"Why the hell should I help you?" he roared.

Krampus placed a hand on his lover's shoulder. "It could be a lucrative deal for you."

"You want me to go back to work for them? After what I told you?"

"I'd come with you. No one would think of doing you any harm and you'd come back home with me. Your purse could be lined with coin." Krampus whispered in his ear. "Think of it as getting back at them. She's at your mercy. You control the negotiation. It'd give me pleasure to see you bucking, and then I could get to ride you."

"I'll do it for you, but not for her." Dallas pushed his lips into Krampus's and gave him a hard kiss. "I expect a reward after I'm done." He squeezed Krampus's cock.

"I can promise you that."

Dallas released him and glared at the dwarf. "Fine. Seventy-thirty split. Krampus is the last one to ride me. That's my final offer. Take it or leave it."

"Son-of-a whore-flying-fuck," the woman muttered. "Fine. Be there at sundown." She walked off.

"Well, that was fun. Are we done with that bitch?" Dallas asked.

"For now. Are you getting along with Stephen?"

"It was wonderful until she showed up. We were waiting for you. I was telling him how you saved me and brought me back here yesterday. How well you treated me. He wanted to show his thanks to you as well. But I think the mood might be broken."

Krampus cupped Dallas's balls and rolled them

around in his hand. His lover's eyes fluttered shut. "Are you sure about that?" He summoned a bit of his power and rolled the cold through Dallas just a little bit to make him shake. The bull shifter groaned as his prick hardened. Krampus sent a little more into him until his hips bucked forward.

"Clo, I need you. I need Stephen. God that's cold. I want more."

"Then you can have it."

Krampus released his hold on his lover, entwined his fingers through Dallas's, and led him toward the grotto. The warm water bubbled. Stephen's eyes widened as he approached. Krampus saw the fear of being there in his eyes. Dallas went back into the water. He kissed Stephen and whispered something in his ear. He relaxed. Dallas gestured for him to join them. Krampus undressed and stepped into the water with them. He sat on the other side of Stephen.

"Are you okay with this?" Krampus leaned in close to Stephen and ran his nose down his cheek, taking in the manly smell of him.

"I-I don't know. Dallas says you won't hurt me."

Krampus slid his fingers along Stephen's inner thigh. "I know what they say about me. I'm evil and I dine on human flesh. I don't deny I have particular tastes, but you don't have to worry about that with me. Dallas says he cares for you, and I care for him. He's different. I can bring you pleasure, if you let me. We both can." He let a bit of his power ride along Stephen's flesh. The man's breathing intensified until he squirmed around and bit his lip. "Does this hurt?"

"No," Stephen murmured.

"Do you want more of it?"

"Yes."

"Then kiss me," Krampus purred.

Stephen met his lips. They were fuller than Dallas's. Stephen kissed him with a bit of trepidation, unsure of what was going to happen. Krampus was good to his word and cupped Stephen's cock and eased a bit of his cold through the man's rigid member. Once it hit the human male, he broke the kiss and moaned.

"Are you going to spoil him and not me?" Dallas squeezed Krampus's ass.

Krampus pushed his tongue against Stephen's. The other man accepted the kiss and pressed up against him from the seat of the grotto. Krampus tried to ignore the other man as Dallas cupped Krampus's cock and rubbed it slowly. He lost his grip on his cold power and gave into the ecstasy building within him. He closed his eyes and let his head fall back against the bull shifter. Stephen kissed down his chest until he came to Krampus's nipple. Stephen swirled his tongue around the pert nub until Krampus squirmed, both of them playing with him.

"This was not how I assumed this would go," he murmured.

"How did you see it, Clo?" Dallas asked.

"I thought you'd be in the middle," he answered.

The human male bit his other nipple. Krampus screamed in pain and pleasure. He slid his hands over Dallas's and pressed his claws into his flesh, because he didn't want to hurt Stephen. He wouldn't heal without a mark the way Dallas did. The bull shifter grunted, and he loved hearing it.

"We can do that." Dallas nipped at Krampus's throat and bit him deeper so Krampus could experience the same kind of pain and bliss.

His hips bucked forward and bumped into Stephen's. Krampus broke away from between the two and moved so Dallas was in the middle. He ran his fingers over Dallas's strong back, and the muscles bunched as he stepped forward and caressed Stephen. Krampus sucked on Dallas's skin, tasting the salt and the sweat. Dallas moaned, but Krampus only paid attention to his throbbing prick.

Stephen wrapped his hands around Dallas's neck and pulled him closer. Krampus trailed his nails around Dallas's side and twisted his nipple. The bull shifter leaned his head back. Krampus met those tasty lips in a quick kiss. He reached around Dallas and grabbed hold of Dallas's dick. It bobbed away from him in the warm water. The water swirled around them, getting no higher than a couple inches above their waists. It warmed him and made him aware all his movements were sluggish as they cut through the water. The temperature relaxed him.

"God, that feels good," Stephen moaned.

Krampus realized he was stroking the man's cock and not Dallas's.

"I think he likes you," Dallas whispered.

"I guess so." Hearing the soft groans from Stephen made his pulse race. His balls ached for release. Dallas ground his ass along Krampus's cock. He thrust his hips in the same rhythm. They were all going to come fast. He slowed his strokes on Stephen's shaft. Krampus positioned his cock between Dallas's ass cheeks. The friction as they moved together was nearly unbearable. Dallas kissed Stephen. Krampus watched the exchange and nearly lost it.

He gritted his teeth while focusing on thrusting between Dallas's tight ass cheeks. He closed his eyes and leaned into the bull shifter as Krampus worked Stephen's cock. Dallas wound his hand over Krampus's to work Stephen's cock as well. The thrill of all three of them touching in some way stirred Krampus to gain a bit of his control again. He stiffened as a blast of cold touched the other two. He drove upward as Dallas tried to find a rhythm with the human.

They were coming and there was no stopping them. Stephen couldn't hold it any longer. He reared against them and knocked Dallas back a bit. Krampus almost lost his footing. Dallas grunted. When he did, Krampus saw horns protruding from the sides of the shifter's head. He released Stephen's cock and grabbed hold of Dallas's horns. The bull shifter snorted and roared as he came.

Krampus held onto them as the ecstasy built within him. He couldn't hold back any longer. His cock was ready to burst. He shut his eyes and gripped Dallas's horns as he rocked back and forth. He heard the water splashing and his heavy breathing, but he couldn't stop. The cold power within him burned along his nerves until he lost control and it passed through his other two lovers. He cried out once more, and then he came at last.

Chapter Five

Krampus pulled his hood lower over his face. He didn't want to scare the townspeople. Stephen had gone ahead with Dallas to the rodeo. The sun had set a couple of hours ago. From the roar of the crowd and the blazing torches, he knew the makeshift rodeo was in full swing. All the townspeople were gathered around the fences to watch the festivities. Scents of fried food and sticky sweet treats filled the air. Children ran around shouting at one another. Smaller tents were set up beside the wagons where games were played and fortunes were read.

"Tell your fortune for a penny?" a sweet voice asked next to him.

He looked to see where it came from. A young woman with curly red hair smiled up at him. She stood beside a small round table with a crystal ball on it. Beside the sphere sat a deck of cards. Bracelets jingled on her wrists when she slipped her hand around his waist.

"Reading my fortune won't tell you anything," he said gruffly and tried to shrug her off.

"My Lord, you can't always get what you want. No matter how much you try and fashion the future. It's not woven on your whim." She steered him toward the seat opposite her.

The cheers from the rodeo drew his attention. He tried to move away from her once more, but her grip on his waist was stronger than he'd thought. Krampus eyed the fortuneteller as she sat on the other side of the table. A red scarf, the same color as her hair, hung over her shoulder and covered her ears, hiding something else.

"I'll indulge your notions, if you tell me what

you're hiding underneath that scarf of yours."

Her hand went up to the headscarf. A look of pain flashed in her eyes. Her smile flickered for a moment along with her youthful demeanor. Something more than a fortuneteller was underneath the scarf. Then again, the owner of the rodeo was a dwarf and he'd already encountered one of her centaurs. It would make sense the rest of the company was comprised of other not-so-human beings.

"Why does my Lord want to know what is underneath my scarf?"

He withdrew a gold piece from the pouch at his waist. Her eyes widened. He figured it was more than she might make in a month or more. "I can make it worth your while. You get to keep this all to yourself and not bother sharing with your bitch of an owner."

The woman giggled. "She is a bitch." She hesitated a moment and undid her scarf. She placed it on the table. "Happy?"

Small, curled horns that hugged her head. They reminded him of a goat's Krampus lifted his hood a little and then showed her his. "We both have horns. You keep them hidden so you don't scare the patrons."

Her expression darkened when she touched her horns. "Mine are a curse. I read the fortune of a god once. He didn't like what I told him. I didn't know who he was at the time, but he punished me with these and these." She stuck out her foot so he could see cloven feet.

Krampus took her hand. "You shouldn't hide what you are. You're beautiful."

"Not many think that."

Krampus placed the gold coin on the table. "When you're done here, if you like, come up to my house."

"To be your sex slave?"

"No. But I can pay you better than what you make here. If you wish other favors, we can work that out. I need a new chef. The old one has gotten a little too crumbly around the edges." He started to get up so he could go to the rodeo. The idea of watching Dallas as a bull with others on top of him as he bucked them about aroused Krampus. He shifted in his seat and tried not to think about how he would ride Dallas after. Something about this strange woman drew him. He wasn't sure why he made her the offer, but she would definitely get better being in his service. Maybe it was because he felt some sort of kinship to her.

"Master Krampus." She grabbed his hand as he got up. "My name is Emerald. I'd be honored to serve you. But know this, the one you have your heart set upon will not stay. He has another love, and a lust to make his way in the world."

She released him as he stood. Her words hurt his heart, but he couldn't dwell on them. "He's free to do as he chooses. He hasn't had that luxury before. But you already know that."

"Dallas is a good man. He deserves to be happy. You've freed him, but he still needs the release from you before he can fully be free. You have a good heart even if you can't see it. I'll think on your offer."

Krampus nodded and placed another coin on the table before he walked off. The cheers were louder and the wall of people thickened around the corral. The announcer cheered on the crowd and called out for the next rider. Krampus pushed his way around the throng and over to the main gate. A centaur grumbled something at him, but he threw him a glance and growled. The creature backed away. In his full bull form, Dallas stood about seven feet tall and must have weighed over a thousand pounds. The man on top of him held onto a rope tied around the middle of the bull. A flag man across the corral dropped a green flag. A man turned over a large hourglass and the sands ticked down.

The rider held on for dear life as Dallas bucked and kicked around the corral. He made two rotations and the crowd cheered; they were going to win money on how long they bet he could stay on. But at the last second, Dallas twisted and threw the man off. The audience seemed disappointed and happy all at the same time.

Krampus watched another man try his hand at riding the bull shifter. The man climbed some rickety stairs so he could get onto Dallas. Once he was settled, Dallas bucked a little. He scanned the ring and saw the owner flash something reflective right at Dallas. The shifter bucked hard enough to throw the man off. He landed with a thud. The crowd shouted. He understood how the woman rigged the rodeo so she could make money. He fought his way back through the crowd to the bull pen and found the owner.

"Thought you weren't coming,"

"I told you I would. How's the take been?" Krampus asked the dwarf woman.

She grunted. "He'll take home a pretty purse."

"Good. After this is over, I expect you to never set foot in my kingdom again. Is that clear?"

"Crystal."

"Excellent. Now announce the last ride of the night. Don't even think about signaling him to throw me off. "

The woman grumbled. Dallas came up to the pen. His sides heaved from all the bucking. He gazed up at Krampus and lifted his top lip in what he assumed was a smile. Krampus patted his side. Krampus climbed the stairs of the grandstand.

"Ladies and Gentlemen, who wants to see the great Krampus, Lord of the Land, ride our magnificent bull?"

A loud cheer went up in the crowd. Krampus took off his cloak and handed it to the owner. When he climbed onto Dallas he realized the bull had knelt so he could mount him. Once he got settled on top of the shifter, he wound his hand underneath the rope tied around Dallas's midsection. Once he was secure, he made sure he had his balance.

The dwarf signaled it was time. Dallas snorted. His muscles bunched.

Krampus could feel the power in the great beast he was atop. Riding him was a different sort of sport than fucking him. He wanted to tell him, but Dallas began to buck and kick, lifting Krampus off the bull's back. He clung to the rope and tried to hold onto Dallas with his knees, but it was nearly impossible with the power of the animal underneath. He gritted his teeth and told himself he was going to stay on the bull no matter what it took. The crowd cheered him on as Dallas went around the ring. Krampus threw his head back and went with the rhythm of the ride until Dallas stopped.

The bull shifter returned to the bull pen and he dismounted.

"Quite a ride, isn't it?" the dwarf woman asked.

"Yes," he said feeling exhilarated.

"Good. You got what you wanted." The woman handed him his cloak, which he put back on. She shoved a heavy purse into his hands. "This is his payment for the night."

"Pleasure doing business with you." Krampus

took the purse and weighed it. *This will see Dallas far in the world.* The idea pained him that he might lose his newfound lover. He noticed Stephen by the edge of the corral waiting for Dallas so they could be together. The bull shifter had opened his heart, but looking at the human male, Krampus knew they were suited to be together. He couldn't keep Dallas with him. It would almost be as bad as the rodeo owner. It didn't matter if he freed the bull shifter from the spell keeping him at the rodeo. Dallas had to be free to make his own decisions.

"That was magnificent, don't you think?" Stephen beamed. "He's magnificent."

"Yes, the ride was wonderful. Tell me, Stephen, do you love him or are you just infatuated with Dallas?"

The human paled. "I love him, sir. I wouldn't have risked my life coming here and looking for him for a year to --"

Krampus trailed his finger down Stephen's cheek. "I believe you. I just had to be sure. When Dallas is done, come back up to the house. I have his purse."

"I'll tell him."

He headed back up to his castle. The people were getting on his nerves and he was getting a hankering for human meat pie. He'd have the cook prepare him something while he waited for his lover to return.

* * *

Krampus stared into the fire waiting for Dallas to return with Stephen. The more he thought about it, he knew the right thing to do was to let him go. Dallas's true love was Stephen. It was obvious when he looked at the two of them together. Stephen had eyes for no one else. Krampus wished he had something in his life like that. *Maybe I'm not built to have any kind of relationship for long.*

"Sulking won't make you feel any better."

The shadows from the darkest part of the room pulled away from the wall and formed the shape of a woman. The darkness became the fabric of her dress, showing stars zooming and comets colliding, sending bursts of light over different parts of her body. Tendrils of dark hair spilled from behind her back, blending with her dress. Her vibrant blue eyes stood out against the whiteness of her flesh.

"What are you doing here, Nyx?" he asked the Incarnation of Night.

"I thought you could use a little bit of company." She stood before the fire and warmed her hands. The light in the room dimmed. Her domain was darkness and everything it touched. She was another Incarnation like him who many assumed was evil, but he never saw her that way.

"I'm not in the mood for company," he growled.

She walked over to him. Nyx straddled him and wrapped her arms around his neck. Even through his thick pelt he could feel the coolness of her flesh. It was different than his power, which called upon the cold and freezing temperatures of winter. Hers was a power that had a coldness of nothingness in it, because the darkness of the night was a nothingness. She rubbed along his length and aroused him. He tried not to be, but the few times they had coupled it'd blown his mind. Nyx pressed her lips to his in a light kiss and pushed the hair back from his eyes. He dragged his claws down her back and caught her around the waist.

"I thought you weren't in the mood for company?" she smirked.

"You always find a way to brighten my mood."

She laughed. He watched a sun blaze across her chest and blind him for a minute. The heat warmed his face. He grabbed her ass and squeezed it through the fabric of her dress. She arched her back and wiggled against his erection. "I can brighten it even more, if you like?"

"Temptress. No wonder humans think you're evil."

"Not as evil as you. I don't eat human children for dinner."

"I don't eat the children, just the stock I have in the back. The taste comes from the office I hold. I used to be human once upon a time. I don't recall much of it now."

"It's another life. I don't remember being one either."

Krampus sighed and moved her off him. She pouted. "I'd love to continue this, but not right now. Did you really come here to ride my candy cane?"

She leaned back on his couch. "No. But it would be nice. I wanted to tell you there's a new Incarnation."

"Really? Who might that be?"

"Samhain."

"I thought the office was occupied by a woman?"

"It was, but she stepped down and he stepped in. I think you and him might hit it off. Go see him when you get a chance. You might find that you have some things in common." Nyx trailed her fingers over his thigh and cupped his prick. He closed his eyes as she worked the fabric of his pants and let his head fall back against the sofa. Nyx massaged him until he was on the brink and then released him.

"You're a minx."

She got up and then kissed his nose. "I know, but

you love me for it. Come see me when you want to get off."

Krampus opened his eyes to see the shadows swallowing Nyx whole. He grunted in frustration as he adjusted himself. This wasn't the first time she had done this to him. Hearing about the new Incarnation intrigued him, but it didn't surprise him. They held offices named for the major holidays or the things that interacted with humans such as Time, Death, or Fate. Some were good. Some were evil. Some were gray. Most humans thought he was evil. Krampus didn't see it that way. He was his office, and his nemesis was the Claus.

"Master?"

"What do you want?"

"Your guests are outside. They've asked to speak to you."

He took a moment before going to the front door to meet with Dallas and Stephen. He came upon them whispering to one another. The argument seemed heated. Stephen was insistent and Dallas kept shaking his head. When they realized he was there, they stopped talking.

"Clo, we ahh… came back for the night and I --"

"Actually, sir, Dallas wanted to talk to you about something."

Dallas picked at a few stray threads in his vest and wouldn't meet his eyes. Krampus slipped his finger down the shifter's cheek so he could look at him. Those dark eyes met his and he could already see the feelings brimming there. "I --"

"Shh… it's okay. I already know what you're going to ask."

"You do?"

Krampus took the pouch of gold Dallas earned

from the rodeo and placed it in Dallas's hand. "These are your winnings from tonight. You're free. You don't have to feel beholden to me since I freed you from the rodeo. I want you to go and be happy."

"I can't leave you."

He put a finger to Dallas's lips and shook his head. "There's nothing to say. I appreciate you opening my heart once more. Go with Stephen. I know how much you love him and he loves you. Just don't blow it on stupid shit."

Dallas wrapped his arms around Krampus and hugged him. Krampus reined in his emotions and kept his face blank. He didn't want to let on how much he didn't want to let the bull shifter go. Even if it was for the best. Dallas embraced him harder. "Thank you."

The bull shifter pulled Krampus to him and kissed him hard before releasing him. He turned quickly from Krampus and grabbed Stephen's hand. Krampus stood in the doorway until they disappeared around the bend and he was left alone. Although it was the right thing to do, Krampus pushed aside his feelings. His heart didn't harden, but it still hurt. He closed the door and thought about the short time he had with Dallas. The shifter had awoken his desire and his heart. He didn't want to let that go again.

He waited there a few moments before someone wrapped on the door. A little irritated, he opened the door once more hoping it would be Dallas. Instead, it was Emerald. Her scarf was removed and wrapped around her waist. A long skirt hid her cloven feet. Her bag was slung over her shoulder.

"The cook offer still open?" she asked.

"Yeah. I wasn't sure you were going to take me up on it." Krampus stepped aside to let her come in. A whiff of flowers came to his nose as she walked by. The echo of her hooves in the hall made him smile.

"I told Lucille to fuck off. I was tired of her. What's the pay?"

He touched her arm lightly. "Let me show you to your room, and we can discuss that."

Emerald flashed him a sly smile and tossed her hair back. "I'm always up for negotiations. It seems like you are, too."

Krampus chuckled. "Negotiations might get a little rough."

Emerald shrugged. "I don't mind. I've always been told I'm a beast."

"Right this way then."

Forging Krampus

Crymsyn Hart

Krampus is busy forging bells for the upcoming holiday season when Nyx, the Incarnation of night, informs him there's a new Incarnation in town. Samhain's in the mood to meet up with Krampus and rock his world, but something's eating away at Samhain's realm.

Krampus is the only one who can discover what's happening and keep the darkness from spreading to other realms. As he investigates, an old foe rears his head, determined to take out Krampus.

Krampus must save Samhain's realm and see how thankful the other Incarnation really is. Forging bells has never been so stimulating.

Chapter One

Emerald snuggled closer. The blue teardrop necklace Krampus had given her glowed in the darkness. He kissed her between her horns. She murmured something in her sleep. Something had awoken him from a good dream. Tasty sugar plums fell into his nets and human meat pies adorned his table. Emerald danced around him naked while serving him squirming gingerbread men. Her breasts were covered in whipped cream and he had been about to lick them when something stirred him from his slumber. At first, he didn't realize it was a bell.

What in the hell? He climbed out of bed and slipped on his robe. The sound grew more insistent as he walked downstairs to the tall evergreen tree in the living room. It was decorated with bells. Each one possessed a twin in the human world. When one rang, it was because some human had gotten ahold of one of his bells. Usually a dozen bells or so rang a year. He tracked down each one and dealt with those who rang them. Krampus snapped his fingers. The bell lifted from the branch and reappeared in his palm. The design on the bell's body was of him torturing humans with his whip. He smirked as he thought about it. His power was growing as the season turned toward winter. He could feel it in the air around him. Even his tree was greener as autumn set in. Summer tried to rear her head once more. Winter dueled with her and was winning. Krampus wondered how Autumn felt being in the middle of the war.

With the bell in working order, Krampus closed his eyes, focused on the bell's counterpart in the mortal world, and sensed someone on the other end. They didn't feel human.

"Hey." Emerald's arms looped around his waist. Her fingers snuck underneath his robe. "I missed you in bed."

"I heard one of the bells."

"I didn't hear anything. Are you sure it was one of your bells?" She stroked his prick until he stirred once more.

He trailed his fingers over one of her nipples and touched the stone. "This brings out the color of your cheeks."

"I love it. Where did you get it again?"

"Found it among some old things when I was moving boxes around the other day in the forge. I thought you might like it."

"I don't plan on taking it off."

"What about other things?"

"What about the bells?" she countered.

"I'm sure there's someone on the other end ringing it. Fuck, woman." Krampus closed his eyes and thought about nothing more than how her hand slid along his cock. She pressed against him until he moaned. He closed his hand over the bell and crushed it. It dropped to the floor with a heavy clunk. Emerald worked him faster until his hips bucked forward. He was close to coming, but she stopped. Emerald went to her knees before him. She took his shaft in her mouth and sucked all of him in. Krampus grabbed her horns as her head bobbed. Emerald moved her tongue around his length. She had done this to him the other night, but only after he made her scream his name five times.

He clutched her horns as the pleasure rode up in him. The coldness of his power lingered in his fingertips. Krampus rocked his hips.

"Master?" the gingerbread man asked timidly.

"Fuck. What do you want? Can't you see I'm busy?" Krampus bellowed.

"Forgive me, someone's come to see you. "

He glanced at the gingerbread servant. It was a fresh one Emerald had made the other day. Its raisin eyes were bright. Its teeth were sharp underneath the white frosting mouth. His green gumdrop buttons glistened in the morning light. As the rays passed through the crystalized sugar, rainbows hit the walls. "Who is it?"

"Nyx. She's in the study. I was cleaning and she appeared. I can tell her to go if you like."

Emerald stopped sucking his cock and glanced up with amusement in her eyes. Her lips twitched into a smile. "Go ahead. I have to start cooking for the day to feed my furry employer. He has me slaving away in the kitchen making gingerbread cookies that come to life. How odd is that?" She stood up and kissed him, pushing her breasts into his chest.

He brushed his thumbs over her nipples. "Yes. It's horrible. I'll be in later to oversee the next batch and make sure the magic is woven into the dough. Go tell Nyx I'll be with her in a minute," Krampus instructed the gingerbread.

His servant rushed out of the room. Krampus caught Emerald by the wrist before she went off into the kitchen. "What's the matter?"

"Nyx and I have history. We, ahh --"

She put a finger to his lips. "You forget that I can see things. I already know about your affairs and some of the things that go with your office. Don't worry about it. What you do and who you do it with is fine with me."

Krampus took her face between his hands and felt his heart melt. He kissed her lightly. "Why are you so calm when you say that? Others would be jealous."

"I know you're always going to come back to me. You might fuck others, but I have your heart." Emerald kissed him back and slipped out of his grasp.

He tightened the belt on his robe. He was surprised at what he'd just learned. Krampus enjoyed finding comfort in his cook ever since she arrived from the rodeo where he met Dallas, the bull shifter he'd freed. He thought about the shifter and felt good he had released him. He missed him as much as he missed Cupid. Krampus walked into his study.

Nyx stood by the fireplace. Her dark dress showed the universe as it moved around on the fabric. She turned around when the door closed. "There you are, Krampus. I hope you don't mind the intrusion."

"You're always welcome here. You know that. What can I do for you?"

"Something's stirring among the Incarnations."

He shrugged. "I haven't sensed anything. What makes you think something's going on?"

A comet exploded on her dress and the remnants trailed over the sleeves. Her eyes glowed orange for a second. "The energy of the night is off. I can't quite put my finger on it. Let me know if you find anything unusual."

"Now that you say that, one of my bells went off this morning and woke me up."

"Do they normally go off this early?"

Krampus poured himself and Nyx a drink. He handed it to her and she took it with a shaky hand. The warmth of the alcohol slipped through his stomach. It heated him from the inside out and calmed his nerves. "Sometimes, but I can normally tell if a human's rung it. This time I felt something that wasn't mortal. I was going to explore it more, but I got distracted."

Nyx downed the rest of her drink. She set the glass down and crossed the room to him. The way she sauntered over was the old Nyx he knew. The Incarnation tugged on his belt. "I can make sure you're a little more distracted."

The thought entered his mind. He could see himself with Nyx and Emerald. He was sure the embodiment of Night would agree to it. "Maybe later. I'll let you know what I find out." Krampus kissed her before she dissolved into the shadows. Nyx never came to him with her worries. *What about the bell? Is her coming here and the bell related*? Krampus sipped his drink and wondered where this would lead him.

* * *

Another bell rang and woke Krampus. Pulling on his pants and a purple vest, he made his way down to the tree and saw another bell ringing. When he touched it, he felt the same anomalous energy he had the night before. Krampus plucked the bell from the tree to give him a direct link to the being holding the bell. Grabbing his cloak, he threw it over his shoulders, concentrated on the bell and followed it to whomever was summoning him.

The coldness of his power descended. A flurry of white surrounded him as the snow carried him away. When it cleared, Krampus stood in a graveyard. Spirits lingered by several tombstones. Their ethereal forms flickered like old movies. He paid them no mind as he walked toward the outskirts of the cemetery. Leaning against a stone pillar by a side entrance was a tall thin man in a black suit with white pinstripes. He wore a wide brimmed hat.

Krampus pulled the cloak closer. Children ran up and down the street with plastic jack-o'-lanterns, bulging pillow cases, and other containers in their hands. Candy spilled along the sidewalk and road as the kids raced from house to house and got their spoils. A cold wind scattered red and gold leaves around him. He glanced up at a full moon. Black forms dashed across the silver surface. One of the trick-or-treaters stopped before him and lifted up a plastic clown mask. Underneath the disguise wasn't a child. Instead, there was a death's head with black eyes and a skeletal grin. The creature held up his basket of treats. At further inspection, it wasn't candy.

Apples were filled with razor blades. Shiny coins that should have been money, but they weren't. He didn't know what they were, but Krampus didn't get a good feeling from it. Mixed in with the booty in the basket were nasty looking toothbrushes.

"Master, is there anything else you needed?" The trick-or-treater gave the basket to the man in the pinstriped suit.

"Very good, Charlie. Go get one of your brothers and look for some flaming bags of dog shit. Gather those up along with some rotting apples. I think the orchard is full of them. Those will make some nice tricks for the naughty children."

Krampus chuckled. "You have quite an operation going on here."

The man turned around. His face was a mixture of human, pumpkin, and some other grotesquerie. The Incarnation seemed to get tired of it and peeled his face off as if he would a mask. The appearance underneath the mask was more human, with a bright red nose and a blue painted mouth.

"Krampus." He grabbed his hand and pumped it in a tight grip. "It's an honor to meet you. Nyx's told me a lot about you."

"I take it you're the new Samhain."

"Yes. I've been dying to meet you."

"Is that why you've been ringing my bells?" he growled.

"Whoa, don't get all bent out of shape. I could've popped in, but I didn't want to alarm anyone. Word gets about faster than a vampire bat can fly around here." Samhain pulled his face off again. This time he resembled a cheesy version of some dime store vampire. Even the plastic sheen stayed on his face. "Nyx gave me the bell. There was something I wanted to show you."

Krampus ran talons through his goatee. If Nyx had given the bell to the other Incarnation, then something was definitely up. If anything was unbalanced in the world she would know because she touched every realm and world where night existed. Her counterpart Helios was the same except he was the sun and the day. Krampus had never met the man, but Nyx had told him more than a few times that Helios was an asshole. "If Nyx gave you one of my bells, then what do you want? I understand you're new at this. The one before you was a woman."

"Why don't we take a walk and I'll show you?" Samhain stepped out of the boneyard and offered his hand to Krampus. "My, what big claws you have."

"The better to swat your ass with."

Samhain chuckled as they wandered along the streets of what looked to be a small town from the 1920's era of human history. Horses and Model T's shared the roads. The buildings were brick or stone. All of them decorated for Halloween. Autumn colors adorned all the trees. Costumed children ran along the storefronts and the houses. Adults who answered gave them candy. Others carved pumpkins on their front porches. It seemed an ideally happy place to be. It felt rather homey in a sick twisted way. What looked to be strings of bats hanging on doors were in reality decapitated black cat heads. Garlands of leaves were intestines.

"You keep this place a perpetual Halloween night?"

"Most of the time. I rather prefer it that way. Don't you keep your little slice of eternity deep in winter snow?"

"No. It's not conducive to raising the human livestock. My domain has regular seasons unless I get a little bored with it. The winter does last a little bit longer."

The other Incarnation stopped him. "I find all of this as strange as it gets. I'm adjusting to the new life. I wasn't looking to become the Incarnation of the dark side of Halloween, but I'm rather enjoying it. My human lifetime seems such a long time ago. Although, I do miss the companionship." Samhain put a hand on Krampus's arm. "I've always had an inclination for big and cuddly things."

Krampus chuckled. "I don't think I'm that cuddly. I like to bite."

Samhain's plastic mouth turned up in a smile showing off his elongating fangs. "I like to bite, too. How about after this I show you exactly what I can do?" His other hand cupped Krampus's cock.

A zing of pleasure shot through Krampus. He wasn't sure he could be himself while kissing the fake vampire face. *Maybe underneath the mask is something more pleasing.* "I could go for that, but how about you show me what you wanted to show me? Before we give in to our carnal pleasures."

"Right." Samhain pulled away and straightened

his jacket. He peeled his face off again to reveal the bandages of a mummy. His nose fell off and his teeth were yellowed with age. His eyes were nothing but dark slits in his face. Krampus followed behind Samhain until he stopped in the middle of a street. The houses on one half of the street were dark with no activity. The faint scent of sulfur lingered in the air. Across the street all homes were lit up. Samhain's minions ran from house to house collecting tricks and treats. As they watched one house on the lit side of the street went dark.

A wave of dark energy washed over Krampus as he went closer to the house. He placed his hand on the bricks. When he pulled his palm away his handprint remained on the blackened bricks. The coldness of the brick wasn't from winter, but of an emptiness that now lingered inside of the house. When he sniffed the smudges on his hand, he smelled rotten eggs. "What's happening?"

"I have no idea. It's slowly taking over more and more of my realm. The inhabitants of the houses and businesses are snuffed out. The buildings crumble away. It's as if something is taking all the energy. I don't have any experience with it. Neither does Nyx. She thought you might understand which was why she wanted me to call upon you."

"Why would she think that, when I don't even know what this is?"

He shrugged. "I don't know. Come, let's go back to my crypt."

They walked beside one another as Krampus thought about what Samhain said and what he'd seen. He had the knowledge of his predecessors, but he seldom called upon their old memories. Samhain's realm was virtually being drained of power. *If this is left unchecked, then it'll spread to all the realms. Is this what Nyx was picking up on? Why did she recommend me?*

Back in the graveyard, Samhain opened the door to a large sepulcher. Krampus expected to go down some steps and into a dark, damp mausoleum filled with skeletons and coffins. Once he stepped inside, he found a homey interior. Stairs led up to another level. Samhain closed the door and looped his arm around Krampus's waist. He led him through the house and into his library.

A large coffin shaped sofa sat before a large fireplace. Bookcases lined every wall full of ancient tomes to modern day horror novels. Samhain led him to a large marble table laden with various bowls full of candy, fruit, and all other treats he might want to help himself to. Behind them were decanters of liquor and another vat which smelled like spiced apples.

"Would you like some cider? My minions made it this morning. They picked the apples and squeezed it themselves. The secret ingredient is the cinnamon we grow here. They harvest the bark and dry it." He grabbed a cup and held it out to Krampus.

When sipped, he tasted the tartness and the sweetness of the liquid. It was better than the stuff he made at his place. "It's very good."

"Do you have something like it in your realm?" Samhain asked.

"I have orchards and we trade with others, but nothing quite like this. We'll have to work out some arrangement in the future where we trade. You might enjoy some of the things that my chef cooks. I wouldn't expect you to have a hankering for human meat, but I have other traditional holiday fare."

"I'd like that." Samhain set his drink down and trailed his fingers along Krampus's arm.

"Just because I came here doesn't mean we have to be intimate."

Samhain seemed taken aback. "I find you quite attractive, and it'd be an honor." He leaned in and tried to kiss him, but Krampus moved away.

"What's wrong?"

"I get your office gives you certain powers over your holiday, but are you human underneath the mummy face?"

"Right. The masks. There are thousands of them. Anything some child ever thought up is at my disposal. Sometimes I don't even realize what I'm doing or what I'm wearing." He grabbed his nose and pulled. The mummy bandages came away and revealed a human face. His olive skin glistened in the firelight. He had deep green eyes and an oval face. His suit remained, but he took off his hat and underneath it was a shock of black hair that tumbled to his shoulders. He didn't look more than twenty without his costume on. "Better?"

"Much." Krampus traced Samhain's cheeks with his talons and left faint scratches behind.

"What about you? Is there a human underneath all this fur?"

"Only if I decide to give up the office will I return to my male form. You're going to have to deal with the fur." He pressed his lips to Samhain's and kissed him lightly.

The other man returned the kiss with a hunger like he hadn't been with anyone in years. Krampus held his face in his hands. He brushed his tongue along Samhain's lips until the other man pulled away. Krampus savored the tang of apples and spices on the other man's lips.

"I can deal with the fur. Like I said, I like to

cuddle with big furry things."

"I'm not a teddy bear. Far from it."

The other man undid the buttons on Krampus's vest and dropped it to the floor. His fingers buried in Krampus's pelt and found his nipples. He pinched them between his fingers until Krampus bellowed at the wonderful pain. Krampus grabbed Samhain's hands and moved them away. "I think we need to talk about this a little bit more before we get fully undressed."

"Right." His cheeks were red from blushing so hard.

Krampus took his hand. "Hey, I'm not putting you off. I'd feel better if we can figure out what's occurring in your realm before we get all hot and heavy. Besides," Krampus slipped his hand over Samhain's groin and felt his already hard prick. "You called me here for a reason and I intend to figure out what that reason is. How about we take a raincheck? Let me go back to my realm and think on what I've learned since Nyx seems to think I might know what's going on. I have to look back in my predecessors' memories and figure it out. Why don't you come by in a couple of days and bring some of that cider. I'd love to share it and you with my cook. I think she'd love you."

"You mean the three of us?"

"Or the two of us if you prefer? Are you attracted to females?"

Samhain's lips turned up into a grin. "I love pussy and dick. I'll take the raincheck." He grabbed Krampus's cock and squeezed it until he grunted.

Krampus laughed and let his cold power encompass him. He thought about returning to his realm and was swept away by the snow.

Chapter Two

Krampus appeared back in his house. The scent of baking gingerbread made his mouth water. He hung up his cloak and realized he'd left his vest behind at Samhain's. As he walked in to see Emerald, he felt a pang of guilt. It quickly faded as he watched his chef dance around the kitchen with her long hair bound up showing off her horns and how her hips moved underneath the apron. He could see her and him with Samhain. Without the masks, the other Incarnation was attractive. He imagined how Emerald would moan when she was being kissed. *Maybe I'll watch first before I get in bed with the other two.*

"Hey, handsome, what were you thinking?" Emerald asked him.

He tapped her cute nose and pressed his lips to hers enjoying the molasses taste of the gingerbread. "I was imagining you riding the last Incarnation I met with. I think you'd find him interesting."

"Oh, that sounds like fun. You'd be involved, too?"

"I wouldn't miss it."

Krampus shook his head.

"What?"

"You never cease to amaze me, woman."

Emerald kissed his chest, took one of his nipples in her mouth, and bit down. Krampus jumped at the sudden pain. Her fingers glided down to his cock. Her light touch made him harder than he already was. He batted her hand away and pushed her against the kitchen counter. Emerald grunted but didn't tell him no. He lifted her skirt and shoved her legs apart. Her wet pussy glistened for him. Krampus went to his knees. He pressed his face into her pussy lips and flicked his tongue over her inner folds.

Krampus grabbed her thighs and laved at her sweetness, using his tongue and his teeth to find her clit. He sucked on it and wanted to eat her all up. Her hips moved with a rhythm all their own. Each time they came back into him, his prick throbbed in time with her movements.

"Clover! Yes." Her voice rose the closer he brought her to climax.

Only he didn't let her get quite there. He withdrew when her trembling became almost unbearable. From there, he lowered his pants and slipped his shaft into her waiting pussy. Right when he entered her, Emerald cried out. He felt her clench around him. She grabbed one of his hands and sucked his fingers into her mouth. Krampus nearly lost it then as her tongue wrapped around the digit. All that mattered now was getting to come. He couldn't hold back any longer. Emerald's teeth grazed his flesh. "Fuck, baby. You feel so good." He pushed into her one more time and came with a loud roar. He rested a moment on her back before pulling out and cleaning himself up.

Emerald put her arms around his neck and kissed him deeply. He raked his claws down her back and grabbed her ass. She giggled and pulled away. "I take it your meeting went well with the other Incarnation."

"He's interesting. Something's happening to his realm. I'm not sure if it's spreading or not. Nyx mentioned something being off in the universe. She told him I could help him, but I don't know what's going on," Krampus admitted.

"If she brought it up, then there has to be some truth to it. Do you want me to poke around? I might pick up something being a psychic and all."

"No. I don't want you to get involved in this. It's part of what I do. I don't *just* antagonize the Claus at Christmas or steal children and humans from the mortal world. There are other aspects to who I am."

She smiled. "Okay. I'm here if you need me. Clo, do you think you can invite this other Incarnation over here when you're ready? I'd like to see your face while I fuck him and you're watching. Stroking that big cock of yours."

Krampus felt his cheeks flush. "Damn, woman. Sometimes I forget you can pluck things out of my head or out of thin air. Is that how your gift works?"

Emerald giggled as he left the room. He needed some time to think. He walked out to the grotto, stripped off his pants, and dunked himself down into the water. The heated pool made him feel good. Krampus settled on the natural seat and let his mind drift backward. The sum of his predecessors' lay in his memory. He didn't know how many others before him had taken up the office.

It wasn't until he waded through them, back to the very first Krampus, that he found something. He slipped further back until he could barely feel his body and was back in the moment where it all began.

* * *

Krampus stood with the other Incarnations. They were all there. The good ones like Claus and the bad ones like him and Samhain. Both were needed in order for the system to work. They created a balance in the universe. Something called them all together because that balance had been tipped.

"It's happening in my domain as well," a petite pixy dressed in pink feathers flittered around. Her high-pitched voice made him wince. This was the Fairy Queen. Although not an Incarnation, her realm touched all the others because they had their part to play when it came to the humans.

"Peace, Queen Tir, that's why we're all here. It's affecting all of us," a man dressed in a ragged cloak carrying a staff said to the fairy queen. Father Time.

"What are we going to do about it? If we don't stop him, he's going to eat all of our realms. There won't be anything else for us or the humans. The balance will shift," Nyx said as she stepped forward. "Someone has to do something."

Krampus hadn't wanted to say anything. He knew what was going on and he didn't want it to come to this. If this wasn't stopped then even his domain would be touched. "I know who's doing this and how to stop him."

All of the Incarnations looked at him. Silence surrounded him as they waited for him to say something. "It's Walpurgis. He's my brother."

"Why is he doing this?" Cupid asked.

He admired the golden winged Incarnation and thought about what it would be like to ram his cock up that tight ass. Krampus shoved the thought from his mind. "He's hungry. He's always hungry. Last time I checked he was locked up and there wasn't any way he was getting out."

"It looks like he's gotten out," Claus growled. "You have to put him back in his prison."

"I can do that, but I'm going to need some help. The last time he was put in there was by the very being who created us all." Krampus wasn't sure he could put his older brother back in the prison he had escaped from. Even with all their combined power, he didn't know if it was enough.

"What do you need from us?" Father Time asked.

"I need something you work with. Cupid, you have your arrows. I have my bells. Something that holds a bit of your power in it. I can take those back to my realm and fashion them into manacles. They should hold him."

"How do we know we can trust you to do that?" Claus asked.

Krampus held up his hands. "He might be my older brother, but if he's hungry enough, even my domain isn't safe. He'll devour everything taking a little bit at a time and leaving only ash behind. He's good at blending in so you might not even know he's there until it's too late. Be on the lookout. I understand if you don't want to trust me. Some of us have a certain ingrained animosity toward one another." He shot Santa a look. "That doesn't mean I want the lights to go out on all of us."

Nyx placed a hand on his shoulder. "I believe in him." She reached into her dress, plucked a star from the night sky, and placed it in his hand. It glowed and became a metal representation of a star.

Cupid came over next and gave him an arrow. "I do, too." Cupid whispered in his ear, "When this is all over, stud, it's you and me."

Krampus almost laughed at the comment, but he gave the other Incarnation a quick nod. The fairy queen plucked one of her feathers and handed it to him. Claus was next and produced a red sack. He grunted and also gave Krampus a candy cane. "Suppose you need something to hold everything in. Keep this."

"Thank you," Krampus replied.

The Claus didn't reply. The next one to come up was Jack Frost. His bluish skin and white hair made him stand out. Especially with his yellow eyes. He plucked an icicle from his coat and tossed it in. The other Incarnations lined up and each gave a piece of their office. By the time he was done, the sack was heavy. He hefted it over his shoulder and looked at the others.

"I won't let you down."

"How will we know if you've succeeded?" Father Time asked.

"I'll tell Nyx. She touches your realms so she can let everyone know all at once. Will that work?"

"Yes," Father Time replied.

Krampus returned to his realm and melted the objects down in his forge. He made manacles from all of the Incarnations' pieces. As he tested the shackles, he knew they would work. All he had to do then was find Walpurgis and draw him out.

* * *

Krampus opened his eyes. He jumped up with a start and realized he had fallen asleep while reliving the memory. He climbed out of the grotto and headed back inside to let Emerald know what he had figured out, and that it only left him with more questions.

* * *

Krampus searched his library for something that went back to the first Krampus. He found the diaries of the ones who came before him, but nothing from the original. He slammed his fist down on the desk and growled.

"Damn it, what the hell is going on?" Krampus asked no one.

"Master!" One of the gingerbread cookies burst into his study trailing crumbs behind him. A zigzag of white frosting held on his left arm.

"What?" he snarled.

"Come quickly."

"I'm in the middle of something. What is it?"

The gingerbread soldier pointed toward the door. "One of the tin toy soldiers. I found him in pieces by the corrals of humans. Several of them are also dead. I've never seen anything like it. You have to come."

"Fuck." Krampus followed the gingerbread cookie into the back of his estate where he kept his human livestock. The gardens were being tended by the tin soldiers. When it came time for Christmas season, they'd be walking around the house and doing drills to make sure his prisoners didn't get away. A group of gingers and soldiers gathered around something on the ground. They parted when he got closer.

"Master, we found him like this," one of the tin soldiers said. The top of his black hat came up to Krampus's knee.

Krampus turned his attention to the remains. He'd assumed the soldier had stopped working like they did sometimes. They froze in mid-step with no more magic to animate them. When this happened, he melted them down in his forge to use once more. This one's arms were ripped off. Rust spread over the red painted jacket even as he stood there. Krampus touched the soldier and it crumbled in his hand.

Shit. Walpurgis is here. He searched around to see if he could catch him. He didn't see any other evidence the darker entity was around. The human stock lingered around something. He walked over and they scattered. All were mute. Several body parts were arranged in a pattern in a readable message.

Hello, Brother.

"Master, what did this? What are we going to do?" a tin soldier asked him.

"Bury the humans. Gather the rest of the soldiers and the gingers. I want the patrols doubled. No one is to be by themselves at any time. Including Emerald or me. Even if I yell and scream at you to get the hell out, someone must be in the room. Make sure you tell the others. This is not a drill."

"What are we looking for?"

He let out a snort through his nose. "I don't know, and that's what I hate. Do this for now. Understand?"

The tin soldier saluted and hurried back to the rest of his battalion and the other gingerbread cookies. Krampus rushed into the house. He found Emerald in the kitchen rolling out more gingerbread dough on the long table. Various sizes of cookie cutters ranging from two to three feet long were laid out. She wiped sweat from her brow. Her cloven hooves poked out from underneath her long skirt. His heart hitched. He didn't want anything to happen to her. She was a good thing in his life. He didn't want to lose her.

"You okay?" Emerald asked.

"Yeah, it's fine."

"Liar. What's on your mind?"

"Something or someone has come onto the grounds. They've killed some of the human stock and one of the soldiers. They're going to be watching us at all times. No matter where we are. I want to be sure that you're safe."

"I can take care of myself."

He took her hands. "I know you can. I'm sure you did that for years with the rodeo. You're living here under my protection as my employee."

Her eyes narrowed and she broke away from

him. "Is that what I am? I'm your employee that you're fucking when you need some relief for the night?"

"No. That's not what you are. I was pointing out that you work here and so do a few other servants. You don't see me screwing them, do you? You're not *just* an employee. I think you know that."

"Do I?" She crossed her arms over her chest.

I don't need this right now. "Damn it, woman! Don't you know I care about you?" He took her face between his hands. "I love you. It's not easy for me to say. I'm sorry if I don't come off that way, but maybe I'm not built for it. I've never had a long lasting relationship. It's true. I like putting my dick into different holes. Occasionally the people attached to the holes tug on my heart, but you've stuck."

Emerald's expression melted and she uncrossed her arms. "I believe you. And I love you, too. I know you like to put your dick in other holes besides mine. Like I said before, you come back to me. I don't mind it but hearing you say those words is wonderful. I'm sorry if I overreacted. I'll be careful."

He kissed her forehead. "Thank you. I have to talk to Nyx. I don't know when I'll be back. Be careful." Krampus left the kitchen and part of him couldn't believe he told her that he loved her. She opened something in his heart that made him question his sanity. He pushed all that out of his mind for now until he could figure out how to find Walpurgis and put him back in his prison.

In the study he placed his hand on the wall. The coldness of his power stretched along the wooden wall until it formed into a lacey archway. Krampus knocked three times on the center of the archway. If he was going somewhere else, he would pop over. Since he was going to see Nyx, he announced himself. When the doorway changed into the threshold of darkness, he knew his invitation was accepted. Once he crossed into the dark realm, the portal closed.

A light fluttered toward him, appearing to be a small sun as it kept spinning and shooting small solar flares from its center. One of the tendrils looped around his wrist and tugged. This was one of Nyx's minions. He followed the sun deeper into the darkness. Pinpoints of light burst around him. Sparks fell down around him and singed his fur as a meteor dashed across the sky. In the distance swirls of galaxies went on into eternity.

"I was expecting you to visit." Nyx's presence appeared from the dark landscape.

"I need to talk to you about something."

"Would you like something to drink? Something to make you more comfortable?" Nyx waved her hand. The darkness became fluid and formed around him into a house. The stars became torches to light the room. The sun flew into the fireplace and rotated. A black velvet settee appeared and Nyx sat on it. She patted the space next to her for him to sit down.

Krampus perched on the edge of the sofa. Nyx ran her hand along his leg. His flesh tingled where she touched him. The caress aroused him as she rubbed his prick. His dick hardened. She always had that effect on him. At any other time, he would have enjoyed her touches and let things go, but he needed answers. Krampus grabbed her wrist.

"You're no fun," Nyx pouted.

"It's not that I don't want it, but I need to discuss what's been going on in Samhain's realm. You told him to come and see me because I might know what it is. Well, I need some information. Since your realm touches everything, I have a feeling you know more than you're telling me."

"That's true." Nyx pulled back. "What do you think's going on with Samhain? He described it and it sounded vaguely familiar. It popped in my head that you might know something about it. I don't know exactly what's going on. What did you find out?"

"Apparently, it's my brother. Or the original Krampus's brother, Walpurgis. He's escaped the prison he was in. He's draining the energy from the realms. Where he touches it turns to ash. The shell remains, but it withers away. Back when the first of us were here, all the Incarnations gave me--well the first Krampus--parts from what gave them their power. I fashioned manacles to keep him contained using the pieces of their power. It seems he has escaped."

"Damn, that's something. Why do you need me?"

"Because I can't find anything about it in my realm. You can't remember anything about it. Someone wiped this event out of everyone's minds. I need to know where his prison is."

Nyx stood up and moved her hand in a circle. A black hole formed. A star floated over it and settled into the center of the hole until its light was almost sucked in. It stretched to the edges of the hole creating a mirror in the space. "If this has been wiped from our minds, then I'm going to need your help in finding the prison. Are you up for that?"

"Anything you need."

She took Krampus's hand and guided him over to the edge of the black hole. "Call up the memory or however you learned about Walpurgis. I need a reference point. Something that has his energy so I know what I'm looking for."

"Okay." He thought about the memory. It drifted

to the edge of his consciousness as though he were remembering a dream. He tried to hold onto it long enough for Nyx to do whatever she was going to do.

"Come on, Krampus, I need a bit more than that," she told him.

His arm and forehead tingled. His flesh grew heavy as her magic worked up his arm and snaked into his brain. He held onto the image for as long as he could and felt the heaviness pierce his thoughts. He grunted when the magic left him and the pain ceased.

"Got it."

He stared into the pool and saw the hazy image of what he'd remembered the night before. Nyx fast forwarded to him holding the manacles and then it all went dark. She passed her hand over the pool. "Do you know where it is?"

"I'm not sure. The memory is clouded. Even I can't hold onto it for long. I think I have something." She pushed the black hole away from them so it joined the night sky. The fabric of the room changed back to the darkness Krampus had walked in to. Nyx grabbed something out of the air. She didn't like it because she released it back into the universe. Nyx drifted around her realm until she came back to him. "I think I found something."

The darkness around him spun until he looked at a different set of constellations. She expanded a particular constellation that reminded him of a crescent moon. Nyx pointed to the top star. "This shouldn't be there."

"What is it?"

"It's a black hole. It's older than anything I've seen before, but I haven't noticed it until now."

"It'd make sense if we were supposed to forget about Walpurgis that this would be wiped away from your memory, too. Then you wouldn't notice it. Can you sense anything about it?"

"I can do better." She grabbed his hand and touched the black hole.

The air rushed around him. Solid ground fell away from underneath his feet for a second and then he was on firm ground again. They appeared in a darkened room. Pinpoints of light expanded until they could see. It was a round room made of black stone. In the center was a metal loop and through the loop was a long chain that led into the corner. Krampus followed the chain to its end and discovered the manacles he saw in his memory. A link was broken in the center of the shackles. They had to be together in order to keep Walpurgis imprisoned.

"Thank you, Nyx, for bringing me here. Do I have your permission to return on my own?"

"Of course, as long as you make it up to me. Maybe you and your new cook can let me have some fun with the both of you."

Krampus chuckled. "I think we can arrange that, but after I deal with this situation." He brushed his lips across hers and used a little bit of his power so she could feel his cold bite.

"Oh, no fair to tease me like that."

Before he could answer his power took him back to his realm and left Nyx wanting more.

Chapter Three

Krampus reappeared back in his domain. The tin soldiers and gingerbread cookies were patrolling the grounds as ordered. He went to his study, where there was a guard by the door. He found Emerald curled up on the sofa reading a book. She smiled as he came in and sat down next to her. She kissed him and pulled him down into her lap. He started to protest, but she put a finger to his lips.

"You can take a minute to rest your horns and hooves before you go running off to your forge. I missed you while you were gone."

"I apologize, love. I hate I had to leave you alone for a few hours."

"It's been a few days, Clo."

"Days?" He hadn't realized his journey to Nyx's and the prison had taken so long.

"It's okay. Everything's been quiet. There's been nothing for you to worry about." She rubbed his horns right at the base. He shuddered and closed his eyes as it instantly relaxed him. The tension drained from his body as her fingers eased the strain he didn't realize he was under.

"You always know the right thing to calm me down," Krampus murmured.

"Of course I do, little brother," Emerald's voice grew raspy. Her grip on his horns tightened so he couldn't get away. His eyes snapped open. Emerald's eyes were completely black. Her face grew pale and wizened. Her eyes sunk into her face and her teeth grew long and pointy.

"What have you done with Emerald?" Krampus roared.

"I'm using her for a bit. I see you discovered my

prison. Everything's changed in the world. You're my brother and yet you're not. How strange. Too bad. I'm still going to eat everything up. You never should have put me in that hole in the first place," Walpurgis was chuckling.

Krampus thought about struggling, but he didn't want to hurt Emerald. Instead, he called upon his power and touched her arm. Emerald screamed in her voice and returned to herself. The sudden cold threw Walpurgis out of her. Krampus got up and held her to him. Her face and skin returned to normal.

"Are you okay?"

"I-I'll be fine. Just have to get warm."

"How did he take you over?"

She shook in his arms. "I don't know. He's evil, Clo. He's hungry and evil. A bottomless pit that wants to be fed. He wants to destroy all of it. You have to stop him."

"That's what I'm hoping to do --"

Emerald put a finger to his lips to stop him from speaking. She looked around the room. He followed her gaze and saw a distortion of energy by the fireplace. He sent a jet of cold after it, but it went around the distortion.

"You can't get me that way, little brother!" Walpurgis's voice echoed in the room.

"Look, I don't know you or why you've broken out, but you can't eat everything in sight."

"You know nothing of the torment I've been through because of what my real brother did, locking me away. I was promised more than being stuck in some hole."

"If you want all that you say you do, then why don't you show me what you look like?"

"Why? Don't remember? Did they make you

forget about that, too? Oh yeah, I figured it all out. I've had a lot of time to think. I was able to get the one weak link in the chains broken. Nothing's going to stop me from taking what is yours even that little filly over there. I need me a good piece of ass before I devour her, too." Walpurgis's sinister laugh filled the room, but the distortion exited the room.

Everything in Krampus wanted to go after Walpurgis, but he had to be prepared to meet him. He hugged Emerald closer to him and wiped the tears from her eyes. "It'll be okay. I won't let him hurt you."

She didn't respond.

"You don't believe me?"

"It's not that. I'm not sure how you can stop him. He's so strong. All those years sitting in the darkness. He's already taken in more than he did before. There's more energy for him to feed from. I don't really understand all I've seen because I'm not like you."

"I understand what you mean. There's more energy because there are more people in the world than there was before. He has more sources of energy to feed from. Each Incarnation is shaped by those energies and those beliefs. We don't change much, but sometimes we do. Does that make sense?"

"Yes. Should I expect you to change any time soon?"

"I don't think so. Look, I have to get these manacles fixed and then go hunting for him. I put him in the prison before and I'm the one who has to do it again. No one else remembers anything about him. Even my memory is a little fuzzy. I can hold onto it because I'm dealing with him right now. After all of this is over, I have a feeling it's going to be wiped away again. Whoever did the magic to clear his memory from the existence is pretty strong. I want you to be with one of the tin soldiers or gingerbreads all the time. I'm going to order them to keep you locked up if they see you acting funny. Okay?"

"I understand. I'll be careful."

Krampus brushed his lips across hers and headed out to his forge. He found the tin soldiers had followed his instructions and remained on his tail, but they didn't interrupt him while he started working. He loaded the wood into the furnace to get the fire nice and hot. Krampus sat at his workbench while he waited and examined the broken link in the shackles. It was worn smooth from time. Once it had broken, the shackles had opened and he was freed. *I have to make something for Walpurgis to wear that doesn't have any links*. He took out a piece of paper and sketched out a few ideas, but scrapped each of them. He needed a failsafe. Even if Walpurgis broke free from one, he needed another that would keep him imprisoned for all time. He glanced at his supply of bells he'd made throughout the year He would need more metal than what was already in the manacles.

"Go to the tree in the main hall and gather all the bells from it," he told the soldier guarding him.

"But, Master, won't that eliminate the bells in the other realm with the humans?"

Krampus wondered the same thing. There were still a few more months before Christmas and he wasn't yet at his full strength. He needed to utilize what he had. "Maybe. This is more important. I need all of them and I want you to bring some soldiers who would be willing to step into the forge."

The painted features on the tin soldier paled. "Y-you want to melt us down?"

The fear in the tin soldier's voice would have made him smile under different circumstances. "I don't *want* to. I'm going to have to so I can have enough metal. The ore you and the gingers mine for the bells and making soldiers will take me too long to perfect for what I need. I need five volunteers. Will you ask the others for me, please?"

The solider saluted him and hurried off. This was the only way Krampus could see of having enough metal. The mine was near the edge of his domain. He visited there a few times a year to bring new workers and pick up the ore they dug out for him.

Krampus added a bit more wood to the fire. He was already sweating from the heat. He took his favorite hammer and hefted it making sure the weight was still perfectly balanced. Forging metal items was something that came with his office. He knew how to work metal and that was how he shaped the bells and other things in his house when the mood struck him. *When this is all over, I'm going to make something for Emerald. Something gold. I'll see if the gingers can find me some stones.*

"Master, I've found the volunteers." The soldier reappeared with seven other tin soldiers behind him. Each also had a bag full of bells they dropped at his feet.

"I know this wasn't an easy decision for you, but it's important or I wouldn't have asked," Krampus said to them.

"Is this about getting what killed Reggie?" another tin soldier asked.

He knelt down so he was on their level. "Yes. If this monster goes on, he's going to destroy everything. All realms will cease to exist."

They all saluted. "We are happy to give our lives to stop this monster."

"Thank you."

Krampus added the manacles to his smelting pot and all the bells. The soldiers marched up to the hot metal and jumped in. The last one nodded at him before he dove in. They dissolved quickly into the molten liquid. Krampus dug around his workshop looking for the manacle molds, but couldn't find them. He delved back into his memory and searched. Nothing came to mind. Then something caught his eye. The small space behind the forge where the fire charred the bricks black. He called upon his magic and cooled the flames down so he could stick his hand in the back of the forge. He pounded the bricks to loosen them. They fell to the floor and revealed a large hole. He reached into the darkness and the fire jumped. The flames singed him until he wrestled them back under control. The heat against his magic wore him down because he wasn't at full strength. Krampus gritted his teeth and focused on keeping them under his control until he could retrieve what was in the hole.

An ancient wooden box. He opened the latch and found the molds inside. His fingers tingled when he touched them. They possessed a more powerful and ancient magic than his. He set the molds on the table. The clamps that held them together disintegrated. Krampus inspected the inside of the molds and found them to be perfectly usable. Once he finished the first set he could make a second. Each one he fashioned, he would set his intention into keeping Walpurgis captive. He hoped he possessed enough magic in the metal from the manacles, the bells, and from his soldiers.

He clamped the molds back together. Krampus checked on the metal. The golden orange metal had a silver sheen over the top of it. The magic was infused into them. He closed his eyes and summoned his power. It left him winded as he gathered it between his palms. It floated around like snowflakes in a snow globe after being shaken. He forced all that he could into his hands and added it to the metal. The top of the hot liquid froze over. After a second, the thin ice melted and the magic was absorbed. His head spun from the effort. He tried to summon his power again, but it was beyond his reach. Hopefully, it would be there when he needed it to go against Walpurgis.

He poured it into the molds and waited for them to set. In the meantime, Krampus cooled the fire and set the metal back over the flames to keep it hot to pour it again. He sat on a pallet of old blankets and closed his eyes.

* * *

When he opened them, he found himself looped in another memory. Walpurgis had already wiped out the fairy realm. The queen barely escaped and was recuperating under Cupid's watchful eye. Krampus melted down all the objects, but each time he tried to pour it into the molds, they broke. This was his fourth go around. The others were counting on him. The longer his older brother was out in the world, the more he would eat. Nothing would stop him from moving into the human realm. A knock sounded on the door. He wasn't in the mood for his cookies to interrupt him.

"Go away or I'll throw you into the fire until your buttons fall off and your raisin eyes shrivel up," he growled. The knock came again. He pinched the bridge of his nose, got up, and yanked open the door. "What?"

Outside a figured cloaked in white stood there. The hood was pulled down over the being's face. However, he caught a glimpse of bright red hair against the white material. "I understand you're having some trouble with the molds to make the shackles that will hold Walpurgis."

Krampus didn't know what Incarnation this was. Then again there were some obscure ones who hadn't come to the gathering. The aura around her made his skin prickle and his hair rise up. She stepped into the workshop and walked over to where the molds where cooling. Dumbfounded, he watched as the woman took both molds and placed them back into his smelting pot. The fire flared when she waved her hand and swung the pot back over the blaze. The flames took on a silver and blue hue, burning hotter than he had ever had them.

"What are you doing?" he finally got out.

"Doing what I can. I can't have your older brother going around eating everything. He's a disgrace."

"But your hands. The fire, it should've burned you."

"We have an understanding. It's not going to do anything to me, but I still have to manipulate things. Do you have the molds for your bells?"

Krampus pointed them out against the wall. The woman took the molds and grabbed one of the small delicate hammers he used when he was carving the bells showing the scenes of him eating children and sneaking up behind the Claus and taking him prisoner. Of course that scene was one of the ones that played over and over again in his imagination. *One of these days, the big, jolly, fat man isn't going to be so jolly. He's going to be down on his knees begging me to release him from what I have planned. Or I could have one of the cookies go after him. That's an interesting thought. Having the food attack the humans I bring. I'll have to start baking them with teeth and imbibing them with a little bit of taste for human meat or their own kind.* The evil thought made him smile. Although, the better picture was having Santa tied up. His hands behind his back. The horrified look on his face as Krampus forced the fat man to suck his cock.

"Are you done with your fantasies about cannibal gingerbread men and the things you want St. Nick to do to you?"

Her voice brought him out of his musings. "Sorry. I've had a long, aggravating day. The slight diversion made me smile. What are you going to do with the bell molds?"

"I've already done it. I've reshaped them so they will take the metal. And I made an extra one so you can make the chain. All the extra magic was what was making it so they weren't setting right. I should've foreseen that. When you pour the metal, you shouldn't have any problems. There is enough in the smelting pot to form the chain as well."

"Who are you?"

The woman turned back to the forge. The flames died down. She touched the pot full of metal as though it had no heat to it at all. "Give it about five minutes and you can pour it. Wait twelve hours for the molds to set. While you're waiting, you can forge the links to the chain. I have a place all set up for your older brother. He'll never be able to escape from this place."

"What happens if he does?"

The woman moved the hood off her face. Red hair cascaded over her shoulders and fell to her knees. Her eyes were pale blue. She had a heart shaped face and a button nose. When her gaze met his, Krampus's knees buckled underneath him. He understood -- this woman was God. He fell to his knees before her.

She touched his shoulder. "No, Krampus, I'm not who you think I am. I'm like you in a sense. I am an Incarnation. I'm a little bit older. Let's pray that Walpurgis doesn't escape from his prison. If he does, then you will have to deal with this again. I'm doing what I can to help."

"Why can't you put him in the prison?"

"Because he grows more powerful with each domain and life he takes. You have the combined magic of all the Incarnations in those chains, plus a touch of some older magic that's long been forgotten. If I were to go against him alone, I wouldn't be powerful enough to trap him and hold him long enough to get these on him. You are."

He was a little confused. "How can I be powerful enough to trap him, if you've already said he's grown powerful enough he can defeat you? He'll eat me up then, won't he?"

She withdrew something from around her neck and held it out to him. It was a necklace with a fine gold chain. On the chain was a blue stone. "Not with this. This will give you the power so you can stand up to him." She placed it around his neck.

He glanced at the blue stone. It was cool in his palm and yet the power in it made his body sting. "What is it?"

"It's a single tear."

"From who?"

The woman pulled her hood back over her face. "Remember what I said about letting the molds cool and forging the chain."

"How do I bring him back to this prison when I don't know where it is?"

"You will when you have him. Good luck, Krampus. If all goes well, we won't ever meet again."

* * *

When Krampus opened his eyes, it hit him. Using all his magic had knocked him out for over twelve hours.

He checked the molds and saw they were set. When he pulled the clamps off the molds fell apart. The cuffs were cast perfectly in silver, but he could feel the embedded magic emanating from them. He pulled each of them apart and made sure they clamped. The fire blazed hot enough to heat the metal so he could pour the second set of manacles.

He looked around for the chain molds and found them shoved in the very back. Then he had another idea instead of the chain. Walpurgis wasn't going to be getting out as easily as he had before.

Chapter Four

Krampus put the completed set of shackles on the workbench and stretched. He tested the key once more and made sure it fit into the holes and turned to lock them. All of them worked with one key. He slipped the key into his pocket. He gathered up the four cuffs and headed back into the house. Emerald was baking a meat pie. A soldier stood in the corner to watch over her. Dark circles had formed underneath her eyes. She looked up and flashed him an uneasy smile. The blue pendant hung around her neck. He pulled her away from her baking.

"Are you okay?"

"Rough night. I didn't sleep well. Every time I did, I thought I felt Walpurgis near. When I investigated, there was nothing. I didn't want to disturb you. One of the gingers checked on you and you were sleeping. They couldn't wake you up and you were murmuring in your sleep. Did you get everything done that you needed to?"

"I did." He touched the pendant between her breasts. "I need to borrow this for a while."

She frowned. "Don't you want me to have it?"

"Of course I do. There was a reason I was asleep for so long. I had to go back in my memories and figure out how to capture Walpurgis. This is important. I didn't know that when I gave it to you. Can I borrow it for a little while?" He kissed her quickly and waited for her to do something. He wasn't going to take it off her, but if he was going to confront Walpurgis then he needed it.

"Of course." She handed it to him.

"Thank you, Emerald." He opened the clasp and slipped the key onto the chain. He then put it around his neck. Warmth flowed over him when it touched his fur. The feeling passed quickly and he returned to normal.

"You're going after him?" She twined her fingers through his pelt.

"I can't let him loose upon the world. You said you saw what his plans were. You know what's going to happen."

"I know. Please be careful. I love you, Clover."

Hearing his true name on her lips made him smile. "I love you, too, Emerald. When I get back, I'm going to prove it to you over and over again."

"When you get back, I hope we can get Samhain over here so I can fuck him while you watch before you join in."

"Don't tempt me to stay here and take you up on that offer right now."

"I know you can't stay. Be careful. He knows you're coming."

"I'll be on guard." Krampus gathered the manacles and put them into his sack. He normally used it to stuff naughty humans into it. It could be any size he wanted and hold as much as he wanted. He wouldn't feel the weight of any of it. He hooked it to his belt. Krampus put on his cloak and felt it add to his power. There was one last thing. He needed his whip. He wrapped the cloak around him and thought about Samhain.

A flurry of cold enveloped him as the snow carried him away. Krampus reappeared in the center of the graveyard. All of the houses and the businesses were dark. The scent of sulfur lingered around him. The grave markers didn't shine as they had before. Even the full moon had a lackluster appearance. Nothing fluttered across it. A whimper came to him from somewhere in the cemetery. Krampus followed it until he came to another crypt. Hiding behind it, he found one of Samhain's minions. This one looked like the quintessential ghost in the white sheet with big black eyes drawn with black marker. Large inky tears leaked from its oval eyes.

"What's the matter? Where are all your friends?" Krampus asked.

It sniffled. "All dead. He came in here and sucked all of them into his big mouth. I ran and hid. My master locked himself in his vault. He's safe there, but I don't know for how long."

Krampus sensed something off about the skellee. "I'm not going to be fooled by your antics, brother. I know you can be other things. Why don't you show yourself to me instead of possessing others or looking like something else? Are you afraid of me?"

Laughter erupted behind him. He turned around. A tall, thin figure leaned on one of the graves. The skellee rushed out from behind the tomb and wrapped its ghostly arms around the man's legs. "Master, I thought it had you."

"Hush, little one. You don't have to worry about anything. I'm going to make sure the scary man doesn't hurt me. Go ahead. Give me a hug," he said to the skellee. He enveloped the ghost minion. The scent of rotten eggs emanated from him. The white sheet fluttered to the ground and the minion inside of it was no more.

"You're Samhain?" Krampus asked.

Samhain peeled off his mask and off his mask and underneath was Krampus's brother, Walpurgis. "You fell for it hook, line, and sinker, little brother. 'Oh, Nyx, I'm new here. I've heard so much about Krampus, I want to meet him. Nyx, thank you for helping me.' You all fell for it."

"I guess we did. How did you break out of the prison?"

"I've been calling out for years and finally Samhain, the former Incarnation, heard me and came to my aid. She accepted my story of being wrongly imprisoned. As soon as she got close enough and touched me, she sealed her fate. I absorbed her energy and all of her knowledge and power. I didn't realize how much time had passed being trapped in that godawful prison. No light. No sound. Nothing. I was completely isolated."

"If there was no sound or light, then how did your cries get out? How did she hear you?"

Walpurgis chuckled. "By that time, I'd worn down the link on the chain. The power that held me weakened. So had the power around my prison. Once I took her and learned how much time had passed, I knew all of you were going down. The funny thing was when I went back in her mind, she had no recollection of me. I was forgotten. I hadn't figured that would happen."

"Well it did. You've had your fun. It's time to go back in the box, brother."

"You're not putting me back there!" When he lashed out, his form wavered. Gone was the form of Samhain, and in his place was a wraith like being with an elongated face. It had black holes for eyes. Its mouth was full of small needle teeth. The robe was tattered so he could see the emaciated form underneath. The strength he felt coming from his brother made him pause. Walpurgis had been hiding underneath the guise of Samhain.

Krampus didn't know how not having Samhain around would affect Halloween. Halloween was the lighter Incarnation of the human holiday and Samhain was all the dark and negative things associated with the festive day. Krampus grabbed his whip and snapped it at Walpurgis. It wrapped around his leg. Krampus pulled and Walpurgis fell to the ground. He snatched the whip and yanked it from Krampus's hands. He dove to the ground to get it, but Walpurgis stood over him. His needle sharp teeth grew as did his mouth.

"I'm going to eat you up and then fuck that sweet woman of yours." His mouth distended more. The power of the creature pulled in the energy around him, but the pendant he had underneath his vest burned cold against his pelt. Energy flared over him and strengthened Krampus so he didn't feel Walpurgis's influence. Walpurgis seemed to notice and growled.

"Having a little bit of trouble?" Krampus got up, but Walpurgis stepped backward.

Walpurgis pulled out a short dagger and swiped at him. The point of the blade caught Krampus diagonally across the chest. It stung, but it didn't deter him. Krampus snatched the whip back from the ground. Walpurgis rushed him and backed him up against the larger gravestones. Krampus clutched his brother's wrist to keep the dagger from being plunged into his chest.

Walpurgis possessed a greater strength than he had anticipated. Krampus twisted Walpurgis's wrist until the dagger fell to the ground. Krampus brought his knee up and got the other Incarnation in the stomach. Walpurgis doubled over. Krampus took the opportunity and reached into his sack. He pulled out one of the manacles and went after Walpurgis. But he twisted out of the way and ran from Krampus.

"You won't put those things back on me again."

"You're not getting away from me that easily. You're going back in the cage."

Walpurgis darted behind a mausoleum. Krampus held the manacle and the whip as he moved around to the other side. Walpurgis wasn't there. The chill in the air came over him. Krampus noticed a distortion in the air. It moved, trying to slip past him. Krampus dove and tackled the hazy form. He fumbled for the cuff. Walpurgis struggled underneath him, but Krampus had him pinned down. He wriggled around, but managed to secure the handcuff. Krampus pulled out the long chain with the key, shoved it into the lock, and turned it. Once it clicked into place, Walpurgis reappeared. Krampus turned him over and felt him trying to draw on him again.

"You think these are going to hold me? I'll get out once more."

Krampus quickly fastened the three other bracelets. Walpurgis stopped his struggles and his face grew sallow. Nothing remained of the scary monster ready to eat the world except a broken being, but Krampus wasn't going to let that fool him. "These aren't like the manacles fashioned by the previous Krampus. I've put my own spin on them. Even if you get one off or two, the others will compensate. And I have the only key. You're not going to get out again."

Krampus hauled Walpurgis up and returned him to the prison he had escaped from. When he appeared in the black, circular room, he found the woman in white waiting for him. Her hood remained over her face, but her hair burned scarlet against the pure white material of her cloak. Walpurgis screamed when he saw her.

"No. You can't make me."

"I can make you do anything. I made you, my dear son. I can unmake you."

"Then why don't you or has he forbidden it?" Walpurgis asked.

"We all have our purpose. You know that." She walked over to Krampus and took Walpurgis. A chain appeared in her hand. She touched it to each of the cuffs. A loop appeared at the end of each one. The chain wound through each one and then connected to the ring in the center of the room.

Walpurgis stared at him. "Be careful, brother. This might be your fate if you step out of line. Mark my words, I'll be seeing you again."

"Maybe. Maybe not."

The woman flicked her wrist and Walpurgis was thrown backward. "You've done enough damage. I have to rebuild Samhain because of what you did." The woman turned and faced Krampus. "You did a good job at fashioning the manacles and using your magic to strengthen them. Although, it wasn't necessary."

"Are you sure about that? Because I needed more metal to make the handcuffs and the key to go with them. How can you remake Samhain?"

The woman touched his shoulder. The world spun around him and they were no longer in the prison. They returned back to Samhain's domain. Everything was dark and cold. "Walpurgis is going to be stuck in the prison for a long time. You did well, Krampus."

"Thanks, what did Walpurgis mean about you being the one who made him?"

"Because he's right in some way. I was the one who created him. At least part of him."

"So you're God? Or some kind of goddess?"

"No, I'm an Incarnation like you. I think you know that from the memories you have from the original Krampus. I'm a little bit of everything. Let's keep it at that. You have your circle of Incarnations and I have mine. It all depends on who you interact with. I'm assigned to those who work with humans. Therefore, Walpurgis thought of me as Mother, but I'm not. Does that answer your question?"

"Yes. What about Samhain?"

"He'll be fine. I have a human in mind who can take over where Walpurgis left off. I'll modify his memories some so he won't know about what Walpurgis did to this realm or the office. He'll have all the memories of your meeting him. I suspect you won't treat him any differently."

"But if I know he's different, and what Walpurgis did, it's not going to be the same."

She smiled. "After this conversation, you won't remember any of this. If there comes a time you need to recall them, like before, then you will. For all intents and purposes, he'll be the same Samhain you met. Nyx and anyone else he encountered won't recollect this. Don't worry. You'll know you've saved the day, but maybe not from exactly what."

It all sounded well and good. "Why erase all this from our memories?"

"Because if no one remembers Walpurgis, then they won't go looking for him. Do you want him loose upon the world again?"

"No."

"Okay then. You should get back to your lady. She's waiting for you. I'll send Samhain your way. It was nice to meet you, Krampus." She kissed his cheek. A zing of warmth enveloped him. The world moved and he reappeared in his own realm once more.

* * *

Krampus stood by his forge and focused on making bells. No one knew why all his bells had disappeared from the tree along with his stock he worked on for the upcoming year. He poured the molten metal into the molds he set out and waited for them to cool. He filled all twenty of them. Another off thing was he didn't recall having twenty molds. Yet as he thought about it, all seemed normal. *Maybe I did and I hadn't noticed it before.* He wiped the sweat from his brow and dunked his head in the barrel of water outside the door to cool down. When he came up, he shook himself dry.

"My. My. Don't you look handsome today?" Emerald carried a large stein down to him. "Thought you could use this."

He took it and swallowed half of the contents before realizing it wasn't beer. He licked his lips and tasted the sweet-tartness of the liquid. "Apple cider?"

"Samhain brought it. Don't you remember you invited him over so we could have a little bit of fun together? You told him to bring some of his cider. It's very good. I don't think I've had anything like it." Emerald pinched one of his nipples.

He growled and kissed her hard and fast before pulling away. His thoughts turned toward the other Incarnation. Underneath all the masks he wore was a fine specimen of a man. "I recall inviting him. I didn't think it'd be so soon. How much of the cider did he bring?"

"A couple of barrels. I showed him over to the grotto. Thought he might want to cool off while I got you. You look like you could use some cooling off too after being in front of the forge all day." Emerald walked her fingers along the waistband of his pants.

"I could use a dip. The molds are set. I'll have to be in here for several weeks to get each of them remade. I can take a break for now. Are you going to be joining us?"

"I have to finish making dinner since we're going to have a guest. I didn't think he wanted human meat pie. That's only your taste. I'm not a cannibal. I had to whip something else up from what we had in the pantry."

"Are we running low on supplies? You know you can always go into town and get whatever you need if we don't have it here." Krampus was concerned about her whipping up something.

She giggled. "No, silly. It's fine. I go weekly anyway. My employer likes specific things we don't have here. Last time he didn't give me enough money, so I had to pay the shopkeepers by other means." She ran her fingers down her thigh and hiked up her dress a little to show off her legs and her cloven feet. Seeing even the least amount of flesh made him hard.

"I bet they got the ride of a lifetime. I'll have to talk to your employer. Can't have you whoring yourself out to everyone. You're *my* whore. Don't you forget it." He slapped her ass and pulled her closer.

She smacked him on the cheek, which was really more of a small tap. "How dare you!"

Krampus smiled. "I can't help it. You make me horny every time I see your ass wiggle. Sure you have to finish dinner?"

"Yes. Go see to our guest and then I'll service you both after."

He pinched her ass as she walked off. Krampus took another swig of his cider and headed over to the grotto. He found Samhain with no mask and no clothes. His black hair curled around his shoulders. Samhain's frame was slighter than he realized, more lean than muscular. His olive skin glowed in the torchlight. Krampus set the stein down on a natural shelf next to some towels he realized Emerald must have brought down. Samhain leaned back in the water and smiled at Krampus.

"There is the horned god himself. I've been looking forward to this." Samhain licked his lips. The slow movement of his tongue over Samhain's bottom lip made him bite his lip. He shifted his cock in his pants. "Are you going to take those off or are you coming in here with them on?"

"You want a show?" Krampus teased.

Samhain cocked an eyebrow. "Only if it gets me lucky."

"You're going to get lucky anyway and dancing isn't one of my strong suits." Krampus unbuttoned his pants and shimmied them down a little over his hips.

"You're a tease."

He chuckled. "Emerald says the same thing." He dropped his pants the rest of the way and kicked them out of the way.

"That's an impressive prick. Come over here and let me play with that thick cock."

Krampus slipped into the water and let the warmth of it embrace him. He settled next to Samhain on the stone seat. The other man raked his hand up Krampus's thigh. He shivered from the contact of Samhain's fingers as they caressed his balls. He let his head fall back. A grunt left his mouth when his lover's hand caressed his prick. Krampus reached for Samhain's dick and found it to be plump. He drew Samhain to him and tasted those luscious lips. He got the tang of apples and smoke like burning leaves.

Krampus walked his fingers along his lover's face using a little bit of power to cool him off.

"What was that?" Samhain moaned.

"A little taste of what I can do. I'm sure you have similar powers as well. It all depends on how you use them. Focus." Krampus thrust his lips forward and his control faltered.

"Like this?" he whispered close to Krampus's ear.

A blast of energy rode his nerves. His back arched off the seat as he pressed himself into Samhain. He lost his grip on Samhain's shaft and squeezed his eyes shut. He bit his lips as the other man sent another jolt of power through him. Krampus moaned and couldn't hold onto control any longer. It didn't matter they were in the water. Samhain's mouth enclosed his cock. Krampus shivered and opened his eyes. His lover had gone to his knees and his head was underneath the water.

Samhain's lips wrapped around the very root of Krampus's dick. He wanted more. He needed to come. He couldn't hold on much longer as Samhain sent his power through him. His heart slammed into his ribcage. Seeing him underneath the water and not coming up for a breath made him lose it. Krampus thrust forward and came. He pressed his nails into Samhain's shoulder and cried out as the last of the pleasure left him.

The other Incarnation lifted his head with a smug smile. "Did that satisfy you?"

"Very much. What about you?" Krampus reached under the water and grabbed Samhain's thick shaft. "It's not fair that you come here and pleasure me. What do you want?"

Samhain's lips twitched into a smile. "I want that

furry ass of yours. I thought I could wait, but you are something else. Whatever you zapped me with, I feel like a bunny that could keep on going. Turn around, baby."

Krampus chuckled. He gripped the edge of the pool and wiggled his ass. "This what you want?"

His lover spread his legs and slid his arm under Krampus's arm. He grabbed his nipple and twisted it. Krampus groaned. Samhain pushed him over until he was leaning on the edge of the grotto. "God, you have a great ass. Now you're going to get a taste of your own medicine."

Krampus tasted cider on his tongue and smelled burnt leaves at the same time. A warmth grew from his chest and spread through his body. It ignited his nerves until his legs shook. He nearly lost his footing, but Samhain had him pinned to the edge of the pool. He tightened his hold on the edge as his lover's power flashed through him. Krampus's cock surged to life with a mind of its own. All his feelings went directly to his prick. All he could concentrate on was relieving the building pressure inside him. It hurt, and yet it was so pleasurable.

"What is this?"

"Trick or Treat," Samhain teased.

"Treat."

"Sorry. You get a trick for this one."

Chapter Five

More of Samhain's power flooded him. Krampus hadn't experienced anything like it. He realized this was what the others felt when he blasted them with cold. Krampus ground his ass against Samhain. The desire riding him made his knees buckle. He bit his tongue to keep from screaming and yet it kept on inflaming his desire. Without warning, Samhain shoved his prick into Krampus's ass. This finally made him cry out at being taken by the other Incarnation.

"Yes. Fuck me. I need it."

Samhain chuckled in his ear. "Yes, you do. Your ass is so tight. I love it."

Krampus couldn't hold it in. He went with the rhythm created by his lover. Krampus hung his head to keep up with him. Samhain grabbed his horns. He couldn't take it anymore. He itched from the inside out. It felt as though he were going to go out of his skin if Samhain didn't give him release. Just as he thought he was going to lose it, the other man screamed. His power faltered and Krampus came.

They lay locked together for a minute until Samhain slid back into the water. Once Krampus regained his feet and his legs weren't wobbling anymore, he sat next to him. He let his head fall back while enjoying the tingling sensations of the aftermath from his orgasm. Samhain rubbed his thigh and sighed.

"That was something."

Krampus looked over and flashed him a contented smile. "It certainly was. It's a shame we had so much fun here. Emerald really wanted to join us."

"Who said we're done? Emerald is very fetching and I hear you have a wonderful bed."

Krampus caught him by the nape and drew him forward until their mouths met. He tugged on Samhain's lower lip with his teeth before plunging his tongue into his mouth. Samhain moaned and pushed against Krampus. They broke apart. Samhain gasped for air.

"I sure do." Krampus slid from the seat and dunked under the swirling water and let it caress all of him. The weightless feeling made him push everything from his mind. The pleasure tingled his flesh with anticipation. He wanted to feel it with the three of them. Krampus came out of the water and wrapped a towel around his waist. He threw one to Samhain. "We should go up to the house. Emerald hates it when I'm late for dinner. She gets on me sometimes, then I have to take her over my knee to spank her. It's fun to hear her squeal."

Samhain chuckled. "We shouldn't keep her waiting. I'd love to see her bare ass wiggling. With your permission of course."

Krampus clapped him on the back. "We'll see how it goes. I can attest to her ass being marvelous."

They went up for dinner. Emerald was bending over the table. Her naked ass welcomed him. Krampus's cock stirred again.

"Holy Mary. What a moon," Samhain whistled.

Emerald giggled and wiggled her backside while looking over her shoulder and giving them an innocent look. "I thought you might want to see what you're in for. Not all of me is perfectly human. She lifted her leg to show her cloven feet. Most of her was human except the horns on her head and the cloven feet that started at her ankles.

Samhain went down to his knee and caught her foot. He kissed the underside of it and flicked his tongue along the flesh. Krampus watched with amusement as Emerald shimmied to get away from the other man. She glanced at him.

"Clo, save me," she whimpered.

The Incarnation glanced at him. Krampus winked. "I don't know, love. He brought us all the lovely cider. I want to be sure he gets payment for what he brought."

She twisted as she tried to stay balanced on one leg. She gripped the edge of the table. "Ganging up on me isn't going to get you lucky."

Krampus came up behind her, caught her when Samhain released her, and spun her around. His love for her blossomed with the surprised look in her eyes. "I'm sure your dinner is great and you're a tease. Wearing nothing but an apron. You really want to push the envelope don't you?" He nipped her earlobe. He slid his fingers under her apron to her thatch of curls and found her clit. He rubbed it a moment until she squeezed her thighs together.

"We should," she moaned, "save that for later. Dinner'll get cold and I'm hungry."

"Fine." He released her.

"Sam, why don't you sit down?" Emerald told him.

Samhain sat in the chair across from Emerald. Krampus sat at the head of the table. Emerald made plates for all of them and passed them around. Krampus started eating when Emerald slid her hand along his thigh and underneath his towel. When she touched his cock, he jumped. The devilish look on her face only made him want to shove everything off the table and fuck her right there, but he was trying to be polite.

"You must be getting ready for All Hallows

Eve?" Krampus asked Samhain.

He nodded. "My minions and I are getting all geared up for it and for Devil's Night which is the night before Halloween. I also get to party on *Dia De Los Muertos*. That's when all the ghouls come out to howl. You should come out, too. We could all have some fun."

"I'm not sure the humans would appreciate my looks," Krampus replied.

"What would they care? They'd think you were in costume. You get to be yourself. I can show you the best parties all over the world if you like."

"Can we, Clo? I've never been to the mortal world," Emerald asked. The anticipation in her eyes made his heart skip a couple of beats.

"We can work something out. It sounds like fun. We'll make a date of it."

They finished eating and Emerald brought out dessert. Instead of placing it in the middle of the table, she set it down in front of Samhain. Emerald climbed into his lap, put her finger in the whipped cream on the pie, and offered him her finger. Samhain's gaze flicked to him. Krampus nodded for him to go with whatever Emerald offered. Watching her with the other man was already getting him hot and bothered. Samhain's lips slid over her finger. His hands trailed up her back. Krampus sat back in his chair and watched as they kissed one another. Their lips locked in a hungry exchange. Samhain cupped Emerald's ass. Krampus ran his finger over the whipped cream and tasted the sweetness of it. He sucked on his finger and glanced at Samhain kissing his cook. For a moment, he had a flash of Samhain being someone else. Before he could lock down the vision, it floated away. He shook his head.

"Are you going to join us?" Emerald batted her

eyes at him.

Samhain had a stupid grin on his lips and a lovesick puppy expression as he stared at Emerald. She tossed her hair over her shoulder and winked at Krampus. That was all it took. "Coming."

He followed behind them as they went upstairs to the bedroom. Emerald pushed Krampus into the chair by the bed. He grabbed her apron and pulled her down on him. She struggled to get away from him.

"You're not going anywhere before I taste some of you."

"You're being rude to our guest."

"I don't care." He ripped her apron string around her neck so the top fell away revealing her breasts. Krampus flicked his tongue over one of them while twisting the other one between his fingers. He nibbled on the firm bud until she cried out.

"Harder."

Krampus obliged her and he took more of her breast into his mouth. Samhain came up behind her. He kissed Emerald's neck and licked a line down her throat. Krampus reached over Emerald and drew Samhain to him. Their mouths joined together and their tongues danced. Emerald bit at his throat while she slipped her hand down to his cock. He broke the kiss when she rubbed him. Samhain's eyes were glazed with pleasure. Emerald breathed hard. Krampus's prick throbbed in time with her breathing.

"Sam, take her onto the bed," Krampus ordered.

The other Incarnation led Emerald over to the bed. He dropped his towel and removed the rest of her apron. Samhain pecked at Emerald's neck and slid his fingers down to her thatch of curls and slid his finger inside of her. Krampus removed his towel and stroked his cock while he watched his two lovers. Emerald ground against Samhain, but his eyes were on Krampus.

"What do you want me to do?" Samhain asked him.

"Shouldn't you be asking me?" Emerald purred.

"He's the boss here. I do what he says. Next time you come to my realm and he does what I say," Samhain answered.

"Deal. What do you want, Clo?" Emerald trailed her fingers over her body until she held onto Samhain's hand. The other Incarnation continued to finger her until Emerald writhed. Krampus couldn't take his eyes from them. It took a second for him to come up with the words as he listened to her soft moans. He knew those sounds. She was ready to come.

"Lay her on the bed and eat her pussy. Emerald, suck his cock. His ass is mine."

Samhain withdrew from Emerald right before she orgasmed. Krampus couldn't wait long before he would come again. The foreplay got him hard enough he had to hold onto his control. Emerald lay on her back. Samhain bent over her and nestled between her spread legs. His firm ass faced Krampus. His cook and the other Incarnation found a tempo of their own. Samhain thrust forward as Emerald raised her hips and rocked back and forth. Even as Emerald sucked on Samhain's cock, Krampus heard her small moans of pleasure. The muscles in his legs tensed. Krampus couldn't wait any longer as he took in the display of limbs while they pleasured one another.

He licked his palm and stroked his cock to lubricate it. His prick needed to find a home in Samhain's ass so he could claim it for his own. He spread Samhain's cheeks and buried himself inside of the other man. Krampus gripped Samhain's hip with one hand and looped the other around Samhain's waist until he found Emerald's breasts. Krampus fingered her nipple as he thrust into Samhain. His lover's mounds clenched. He clutched his lover's hips as Emerald screamed.

"Don't stop." Her cries became unintelligible. Krampus shoved into Samhain once more. He moved his hand from Emerald's nipple to Samhain's cock. He stroked the slick member as he rode the other man. Samhain continued to pleasure Emerald. The pleasure unleashed his power as it poured into Samhain. The coldness spread from his male lover to his beloved. All at once, it reached a crescendo.

They all came as the ecstasy drove them over the edge.

* * *

Krampus checked his bell molds. He had two hundred of them ready to go for the season. He still had more to finish, but he had time to get them done. Halloween was approaching in the mortal world. Samhain had been pulled back to his domain so he could focus on his duties there. As the fall marched into winter, Krampus's powers grew. He looked forward to facing up against the Claus this year. Something dark had awoken within him and his hunger for human flesh grew. This time of year he noticed how much he wanted to eat, fuck, and act out his fantasies. Emerald was more than happy to oblige him when it came to the bedroom. This year, he would face the one the little children called Santa Claus and claim him. They always did a dance being the opposite sides of the same coin, but this year would be different. Jolly Saint Nick would be on his knees sucking Krampus's prick and enjoying every minute of it.

The image brought a smile and made him hard.

"Looks like someone has something naughty, naughty on the brain."

The deep tenor voice made him look up from the molds. Leaning against the forge was a slight man in a green velvet suit. His hair was spiked into a blue Mohawk. His flesh had a white gleam to it as though he had been stuck in an ice cream freezer too long. The fire in the forge froze over when he waved his hand across it. The temperature in the room plummeted. The worksheet iced over with a thick coating of ice crystals.

"Jack, I wasn't expecting to see you here this early in the season." Krampus walked over to one of the barrels of cider Samhain had sent over. He pounded on the top of it. "Would you mind unfreezing this for me?"

"Of course."

The cider unfroze. Krampus offered his guest a stein of cider and one for himself. Jack sipped at it. "From Samhain. Best cider there is."

"I agree. Now tell me why you're here, Jack Frost. It isn't your time to be terrorizing the humans yet."

He shrugged. "I needed a change of scenery. You haven't come to see me lately. I hear you have this new woman in your life. I wanted to come and check her out. Maybe give her a little go around on the frosty candy cane."

Krampus slammed down his cider stein. "Emerald isn't a whore. She's mine." He sent a blast of power at the mischievous Incarnation which blew him across the room.

Jack put up his hands. "My bad. I've never seen you this smitten with anyone before. I was saying I missed you." He wound his fingers through

Krampus's dark brown pelt.

Krampus shivered from the sudden cold over taking his body.

Jack pouted. "You and me go way back, K. You've always liked my ice pop."

"I still do. I've been busy, and Emerald's here. I figured when it got closer to winter we could figure something out." He trailed his fingers down the white cheek of the man before him. "You've always taken my breath away. Give me a month. Come around then and I'll introduce you to Emerald."

Jack slid his hand over Krampus's. White frost laced through his pelt up to his elbow. "I'd like that. I guess I'll get going. Next time I come by, we can discuss how to make the jolly fat man sing. I'd love to see him in leather ass-less chaps."

Krampus chuckled at the image. "Maybe. Although, I think he needs a taste of his candy canes flogging him senseless. I'll see you around, Jack."

Jack Frost winked and blew away in a flurry of snow. Emerald walked in as the ice crystals dissolved from the room and the fire unfroze. She rubbed her hands over her arms. "Brr. What was that?"

"Just Jack paying me a visit. He's getting a little lonely." Krampus grabbed Emerald around the waist and pulled her to him. He gripped her ass, kissing her hard, and inflaming his desire.

"You're frisky."

"You don't know the half of it. Bend over my knee. I'm going to spank you until your ass is red. Maybe I'll even give you a few stripes and call it a candy cane."

She winked at him. "Whatever my employer desires."

Krampus to the Rescue

Crymsyn Hart

When Jack Frost appears at Krampus' house asking for help to save Santa, Krampus knows with his arch-enemy gone, Christmas could be his for the taking. But Jack is willing to sweeten the deal, so Krampus goes to help Jack on his mission.

What they find is the Elves running amok in Christmas Town and Mrs. Claus held prisoner. Racing against time, Krampus must face an even darker energy to rescue Santa.

Chapter One

"Jingle balls. Jingle balls. Swinging all the way. Oh what fun it is to squeeze…"

Krampus followed the sound of Emerald's off-key singing into the kitchen. He stood in the doorway and watched the cook. Her scarlet hair was bound up between the two curled horns on her head. She once told him she got the horns and her hooves from a god who cursed her because he didn't appreciate her psychic predictions.

Krampus adored every bit of her -- except her singing.

She rolled ground meat between her hands and set the finished ball into a pan. From the smell of the cooked ones, he suspected sausage and ground turkey. They weren't made with the human meat he enjoyed more. His taste for long pig was an acquired one. It came with the office. Still, his stock had thinned during the winter and he needed them to fatten up. He listened to a few more bars and cringed before he went into the kitchen.

Emerald glanced up from her task. Her smile dazzled him. "You're back early. Dinner's not ready yet."

He nuzzled her neck. His forked tongue flicked along her flesh until she shivered. A small moan escaped her lips as his hands slipped underneath her apron and skirt and over her luscious thighs. "I needed a break. And then I smelled this wonderful aroma and heard your god-awful singing." Krampus bit her throat and rubbed her clit.

Emerald quivered as he pleasured her. "You need to stop doing that or I won't be able to finish these. The ones in the oven will burn. The meat…"

"What about the meat?" Krampus took a couple of her fingers covered in raw meat and sucked on them, savoring the taste of the mixture of herbs. His hunger for all things was amped up this time of year because it was nearing Christmas. He scraped his sharp teeth along her flesh until no tidbit remained. Emerald shook as she came. He nearly spread her legs and thrust inside of her, claiming her right there. His cock ached at the thought of it.

"Clover, you have to stop. I gotta make dinner. We have guests coming over, remember? We need to save our energy for later," she said between pants.

Krampus buried his face in her hair and unwound from Emerald. "You're right. I forgot. Where would I be without you?"

"Lost."

Krampus grabbed a warm meatball and plopped it in his mouth. "Yes. Lost is the word for it. No more singing. It hurts my ears."

"Sorry. I sing when I roll my balls around. Jingle balls, all the way."

"The humans sing *Jingle Bells*. The song has nothing to do with balls. Although, I don't mind when you roll mine around."

"Really? I hadn't heard that one. Mine is from a werewolf. He said he got it from a cousin who fell in love with a human chief or something like that. He traveled with the rodeo for a couple of seasons. It's quite a catchy tune."

Krampus smirked. "This werewolf sounds like an interesting fellow."

Emerald washed her hands. "He was very interesting. Taught me a few things. Maybe if you're good, I'll show you later."

"Have you been holding out on me?"

She gave him a quick peck and dried her hands. "Go take a bath. You stink. I have to get this made. Samhain and Nyx are coming over tonight. We've been planning this for weeks. I don't want to ruin it."

"God, I love you, woman."

"I know. Remember what I said. I don't care who your dick goes into, because your heart belongs to me." She winked at him.

Krampus chuckled and went upstairs to get cleaned up for dinner. Emerald was correct. They had tried to get Nyx and Samhain over to the house for weeks. Emerald wanted both of them in bed. Sometimes her requests surprised him. Jealousy never darkened her feelings for him when he told her about his most recent foray with another Incarnation or creature. Sometimes her appetite was nearly as insatiable as his.

Dried off and clean, he straightened his purple vest and ran his fingers through his goatee. This was the only free night he'd had for weeks. He spent his spare time in the forge casting bells.

Krampus looked forward to the night ahead. Samhain, Emerald, and he had already shared one another before this. Nyx was the newest addition into the mix. He and Nyx had been intimate in the past, but she had never participated with Emerald before. The anticipation of the coming night aroused him. Then again, Emerald's wiggling ass turned him on.

He forced the image from his mind and let his gaze move across the room. A small box lay hidden in his dresser. He thought about getting it, but decided to wait for a better night.

"Master, your guests are here." A tin soldier entered his bedroom. The two foot tall soldier looked freshly painted. The soldiers and his gingerbread servants also looked forward to this time of year. They painted one another while the gingerbread cookies whittled out the weakest among them by eating one another. Those who survived were stitched back together with frosting. They called it the Ginger Rumble.

"Thank you. Frank, isn't it?"

The red circles on the toy soldier's pale cheeks grew larger. "Y-yes, sir. You remembered my name."

"You have to forgive me. You all look alike; it's difficult to remember. Especially during the holidays when I have other things on my mind. Please go down and escort the guests into the library."

The tin soldier left the room. Krampus clipped on his pocket watch. It was painted red like a Christmas ornament. When he opened it, the inside was a regular clock face. The engraving read, "To Clo, love you -- horns and all. Em." She had given it to him as an early Christmas present. He straightened his vest once more and went to join their guests.

He walked into the library to find Samhain, the Dark Incarnation of Halloween, relaxing on the couch. Emerald sat on his lap. They were kissing. Nyx, the Incarnation of Night, rested in a chair across from them and watched. Her black skin lightened so he could easily make out her features. Her entire dress reminded him of a sun, the way it flared in oranges and reds. Her hair spun down her back in silver waves.

"It's about time you got down here." She got up from the chair and dragged her fingers through his pelt, stopping to play with the silver buttons on his vest.

"Sorry."

"It's not a problem. I've been watching these two. Krampus, she's lovely." Nyx nibbled his lips, then walked over to Emerald. She broke Samhain's kiss and claimed Emerald's mouth. Nyx cupped Emerald's breast and kneaded it.

Krampus drew in a slow breath to stay focused. "I didn't think we were going to jump directly into bed." He poured a stein of Samhain's cider and downed it.

"What's the matter, Krampus? Getting a little jealous watching the lovely ladies?" Samhain's husky voice sounded next to his ear. The other Incarnation cupped Krampus' cock and squeezed it.

Krampus nearly dropped the stein but set it back on the desk. He turned and grabbed a shock of Samhain's hair. He pushed his mouth against the man's, catching him off guard. Samhain groaned as he kissed him. His fingers raked down Krampus' arms until he could feel the points through his thick pelt. Krampus thrust his tongue between Samhain's lips and tasted the sweetness of the honey in the cider.

All Krampus wanted was to fuck. His base animal desires came through stronger as it grew closer to Christmas. Samhain returned the kiss with the same ferocity until he broke away to catch his breath.

Emerald moaned. Krampus focused on her. Her head was thrown back on the sofa. One of her legs rested on Nyx's shoulder as the Incarnation kissed the inside of his beloved's thigh. Nyx spread Emerald's legs wider and buried her head between them. Emerald jumped and groaned. Krampus broke away from Samhain. He couldn't hold back and tore at Emerald's blouse, revealing her breasts and pert rose colored nipples.

"Oh, Clo," Emerald cried out.

He took one of her nipples in his mouth. His tongue curled around her areola as the skin puckered.

Her quick gasps told him her blood nearly boiled. Krampus stuffed as much of her breast as he could into his mouth. Samhain came behind him slipping his pants down around his waist. Krampus didn't object. The Incarnation shoved his cock between Krampus' ass cheeks and thrust against him.

Emerald's cries rang in his ears. Krampus needed to be inside of her but that would come later. Instead, he bit down on her nipple and twirled the other one between his fingers. Samhain grabbed onto Krampus' dick. He grunted as the male Incarnation and worked his prick. Krampus lost control of his power. He clutched Nyx's shoulder and the cold left him.

Emerald screamed. Nyx let out a sigh. Samhain also came. Krampus grunted and the heat of the orgasm took him as well. He slumped against the floor with Samhain on top of him. Samhain grabbed his nipples and twisted them. Krampus growled but enjoyed the pain.

"That was unexpected," Emerald panted.

Krampus chuckled. "At least before dinner. Speaking of which, I'm hungry."

"How about we go down to the grotto, then eat after? Unless the lady of the house objects?" Samhain suggested.

"That's fine with me. I could go for a quick soak," Nyx replied.

Emerald unwound herself from Nyx. Krampus shredded the rest of her clothes. Her bare ass whizzing by him was invitation enough to follow her wherever she went. Krampus took off his clothes and followed. Down in the hot springs hollow, Emerald was already in the water. Droplets glistened on her skin. The chill in the air signaled it would snow later. It was about time. He sat on the seat and Emerald came over to him.

"Did Nyx please you?" Krampus asked her.

She straddled him and slowly slid down onto his cock. He grasped her hips and moved deeper into her. Her eyes fluttered shut and she smiled. "She's good, but you're better. Not that I'm complaining. The mix with your power sent me over the edge. I could feel all of us together. It was wonderful." She ran her hands up through her hair. Krampus buried his head between her breasts. He flicked his tongue over her sweet flesh and thrust into her again. Emerald wrapped her arms around his neck and rode him.

"Look at you two. Starting again without us." Nyx settled into the water.

Krampus glanced at her, but his attention was drawn across the grotto to a thin man leaning against the cave wall. Emerald increased her rhythm. He kept his gaze locked on Jack Frost. The full lips of the pale white man curled into a big grin.

Emerald drew Krampus' attention by kissing him once more. He couldn't hold on any longer. He shut his eyes and let the orgasm take him. Emerald turned to see what he was looking at. Nyx and Samhain settled next to them. Krampus got up and waded over to the edge of the grotto.

"What do you want Jack? I'm a little busy."

"I can see that. Hey, Nyx. You're looking good."

"Hey, Frosty. What are you doing here?" Nyx asked.

"We have a problem," Jack Frost replied.

* * *

"What problem do we have?" Krampus grumbled.

"Can we talk in private?" Jack Frost asked.

"Anything you want to discuss can be said in

front of all of us, Frosty," Nyx said. She teased her fingers down Krampus' back.

"Fine, but you might need to cool off first." Jack placed his hand on the cavern wall.

White lacings of frost raced along the stone and hit the pool, freezing it to solid ice. Emerald cried out. Krampus tried to get over to her, but he couldn't move. Her skin started to turn blue. "Jack, release your power. Emerald isn't like us. She's mostly human. If she dies because of your antics, then I swear there will be hell to pay. You wanted my attention, you got it."

"Happy?" Jack released his power.

The ice melted away. Krampus raced over to Emerald. Her teeth were chattering and she was shivering. He wrapped his arm around her and led her out of the water.

"I'll take her back inside the house. Sam, come on. Let them talk. Jack's being a party pooper." Nyx placed a towel around Emerald. Nyx's dark skin flared orange and a small red sphere appeared in her hand. Heat permeated the small space. She placed it over Emerald's head as they walked away. She led her back up to the house with Samhain in tow.

Krampus put a towel around his waist and dried off his head with another one. "What is this problem?"

"Claus is missing."

"Why should I give a flying reindeer if he's missing? We don't get along anyway. If he's gone, then I can slip in and take over. I'm sure the good little children of the world would love to find coal and entrails in their stockings instead of sugarplums and candy canes."

"It's a big deal. Unlike you, I'm stuck in the middle. I have to get along with you *and* him. I went for our weekly chess game and I found the workshop in disarray. Petunia -- Mrs. Claus -- is also missing. She has the best cookies. The reindeer were still in their stalls and beating on the doors to get out. The Elves were in the workshop, so I think they were okay for now. Rem's been gone for three days."

"Rem?"

"Sorry, Claus. Santa's real name is Remington. I call him Rem. Anyway, I don't know where he is. He's not at the North Pole. Without him or his wife around, the Elves are going to start running amok. You are the only other Incarnation I knew of who can withstand the cold of the North Pole. Your magic is similar in certain ways. I wouldn't have come to you if I wasn't desperate. I need you to help me save Christmas and Santa. Will you do it for me?"

Krampus wasn't sure he heard Jack Frost correctly. The thin Incarnation, with the pale white skin and the blue shaded Mohawk, was asking him to save his arch- enemy. It took a moment for him to process. He laughed. The echo reverberated in the cavern. "Is this some kind of joke, Jack? Seriously, when do the others come out and start pulling my leg?"

Small snowflakes flitted down from the ceiling. A cold blast of air chased them away as Jack sat down on the bench and hung his head between his hands. His blue nails scraped over his face. His hands shook as he looked back at Krampus. "This isn't a joke. This isn't like other times when I've told you a snowman's eating your townspeople. Or when you rushed out to find Rudolph getting it on with one of your goats. It's one thing to pit you guys against one another. If you do this for me. I won't pull any practical jokes on you for a century."

Krampus' eyes widened at the statement. Jack

Frost was the ultimate trickster. It was part of his office, along with bringing the first frost to the world. Lacings of thin ice on windows at night or on leaves after fall was all about him. Jack took pride in painting the world with ice and snow. If he was saying he wasn't going to pull anything on Krampus for a hundred years, that was big. They were friends and at times lovers, but Jack had never once asked him for something so big. "Okay, Jack. I'll help you find Claus, but swear to me on your office: no shenanigans for a hundred years."

Jack put both hands over his heart. Krampus' breath came out in a white blast. "I swear. No tomfooleries for a hundred years, if you help me." As he said the words, they crystalized in the air and glowed. The power of the promise hung in the air for a second before it broke apart and flitted to the ground. "Satisfied?"

"Yes."

"Great. Go get dressed so we can leave."

Krampus rolled his eyes. "Do you know how hard it's been for me to get Nyx and Samhain here?"

"You didn't invite me, so get your furry ass up to the house and get some clothes on. We need to leave. Chop. Chop. Next time, you'd better invite me to the orgy. I do miss our time together. That little filly of yours has kept you too busy to ask me over and we're getting into our seasons."

"Fine. Next time you can come to. You're such a whore."

"I know. You love it." Jack made a kissy face at him and winked.

Krampus shook his head and went back up to the house. His company sat around the table eating. He went over to Emerald and pulled her away. "I have to go out for a little while."

"What's the matter? Does it have something to do with Jack?"

"It does. Claus has gone missing and Jack wants me to help find him."

"He's your archenemy. Why are you going to help look for him?" Her concern for him hitched his heart. He didn't want to leave her.

"I know, but I promised him I would go. I'm uniquely suited for it because I can withstand the environment of the North Pole. Speaking of, are you okay after Jack froze over the grotto?"

"I'm fine. Whatever Nyx put over my head dried me off and Sam's cider warmed me up. You have to go now, don't you?"

"I do."

Emerald bit her lip and looked at the others. "Do you mind if they stay?"

Krampus chuckled. "You minx. No. I don't mind if they stay. Have your fun." He pinched her ass and nipped at her earlobe. "Just tell me all about it when I get back. Or you can show me."

"I can do that."

He let a bit of his power flow over her flesh until she shivered and groaned. Emerald pressed herself against him. Her skin flushed and her breath hitched. Krampus loved seeing her reacting to him whether it was his power or from his touch. As long as she enjoyed herself. It took all of his will to pull away from her.

"You are such a tease," she panted. "Give me the pleasure, but not your cock. It's not as much fun."

"Sorry, love." He kissed her quickly and addressed the others. "Nyx. Sam. I have to head out with Jack. Something's come up at the North Pole. I promised I'd help. Will you stay and keep Emerald company?"

"Of course. As long as you don't mind," Nyx replied.

"Not at all. We'll get together some other time. Maybe after the new year so the four of us can enjoy one another's company." Krampus went upstairs to get dressed. He came back down and donned his cloak. His whip hooked onto his belt. He grabbed his sack and went into a back room where his gingers and tin men were gathered. "I need a few volunteers to come with me. Who is up for an adventure?"

Several hands raised from the tin men. A couple of gingerbread soldiers stepped forward. An aged nutcracker about three feet tall with an eye patch over his left eye shuffled forward. A few tufts of white remained on his beard. Krampus didn't use the nutcrackers much. He'd always preferred the cookies and the soldiers, but the nutcrackers did come in handy when he needed more man power to patrol the grounds when it got closer to Christmas.

"I'll go with ye, sir. These old bones could use some adventure. Where ye taking us?"

"Get into the sack and you'll see when we get there." He laid his red bag on the ground and opened it. Each of the eight volunteers climbed into the darkness. The sack magically shrunk as he secured it to his belt. If he needed something inside of it, he could summon it with a word.

Emerald met him at the door with something in her hands.

"What's this?"

"Something to snack on. I know how hungry you get. It's pretty rare too."

He sniffed the package. "You made me long pig

calzone. I can smell the cheese."

"I did. The tin soldiers butchered this morning."

Krampus stuffed it into his bag. "Touch the food and I'll eat you or melt you down. Understand?" He heard the muffled echoes of agreement from inside. "Thank you. I should go."

Emerald kissed him quickly. He went outside and joined Jack.

"Took you long enough," Jack grumbled.

"Let's get on with this."

Chapter Two

Jack held out his hand. "Take my hand, and I'll bring you to the North Pole."

"I know how to get there."

"I'm sure you do, but I know a short cut. This way you don't have to deal with any of the security Rem has put up for those who try and kidnap him."

Krampus rolled his eyes and took Jack's hand. "Fine. Let's go."

Cold enveloped Krampus. It sucked the air from his lungs and froze his insides. Jack's power had a harsher bite than his did. Krampus could bring the snow and the cold. He could freeze the body, but Jack's power went down to the soul. It layered over him until it felt as though he was inside of an icicle and could never get out. Right as Krampus thought he wouldn't be able to stand it any longer, the cold broke.

They emerged inside a large log cabin. The sweet scent of candy and chocolate assailed Krampus' senses. It made his teeth ache. With the dozen differently-decorated Christmas trees and the model trains running along the ceiling, it looked like Christmas had puked over every single surface. Candy cane sculptures hid in the corners. A two-foot-tall snowman slid along the floor, leaving a trail of water in its wake. It nearly made Krampus lose his lunch. He wasn't sure he could take all this Christmas cheer.

It made him cringe.

"Keep your hood up. I'm hoping the melts and the Elves don't raise the alarm seeing you here. It would only make this worse," Jack instructed.

"The melts?"

"Sorry. It's what he calls the snowmen since they melt as they move inside. They're not really his permanent servants."

Krampus nodded. "Lead the way. Show me what you saw to make you think he's missing."

Jack led Krampus into Claus' study. Krampus figured he would find a place full of scrolls with lists of naughty and nice children. Shelves stacked with toys and maybe even some lumps of coal for bad kids. But he found the place in shambles. Papers were scattered everywhere. The room smelled like rotten apples and whiskey. The fire had burned out to ashes, and something dark stained the gray slate hearth stones. Shards of porcelain were scattered near the fireplace. The chair behind the desk was toppled over. A pedestal lay on its side with a large book spread out on the carpet. Chess pieces in the shapes of Elves and reindeer were scattered everywhere.

"Do you see what I mean? Rem is meticulous when it comes to order. I mean to a fault. It gets annoying. If I don't remember to put my hot cocoa on a coaster he flips out. What do you think?"

Krampus looked around the room once more and checked behind Santa's desk. His curiosity got the better of him. He searched through several of the stacks of scattered papers and saw lists of names. He opened the middle drawer in the large antique desk and pulled out a leather-bound book. The leather seam was ready to split. Krampus opened it. Each page had a date on it and some handwriting. He glanced over the entries and realized he was holding a day planner. He flipped toward the back of the book and saw an entry in neat looped handwriting.

Dinner with S.

"Jack, come look at this." He handed over the day planner. Jack glanced at the page. "Do you know who S is?"

"No. Never heard of him."

"How do you know it's a him? Could the perfect Santa be having an affair on the Missus?" Krampus sneered.

Jack flipped through the book a few times and didn't seem to find anything. He dropped it back onto the desk. "He wouldn't. I mean he could, but he and Petunia are like you and Emerald. They love each other. It's all ooey and gooey like a melted marshmallow. It makes my teeth hurt. They're all over one another."

Krampus couldn't see the Jolly Fat Man pawing at Mrs. Claus with his shirt off and him in nothing but red boxers. He shook the image from his head and tried not to retch. "I might love Emerald, but she knows I'm horny. As she says, 'I put my dick in a lot of people', so Claus could be doing the same thing. Who knows what their relationship is? He could be a total sadist. He could tie up his Elves and do all kinds of things to them. You never know."

"This is true, but I don't think that --"

"Did you hear that?" Krampus listened harder.

"No. What is it?"

"Someone screamed."

"Maybe it's one of the reindeer squealing."

"Don't think so. I know a scream when I hear one. It's coming from upstairs. Come on." Krampus walked out of the office and into the main foyer. Two large spiral staircases curved up the sides of the walls and led upstairs. As he looked up at them, he realized they were in the shape of candy canes.

The shriek came again. Krampus rushed up the stairs and went to the end of the hall. He tried the door, but it was locked from the inside. Jack shoved his shoulder into the wood. Krampus tried also, but it wasn't budging. Another cry came from behind it.

"Screw this." Jack rubbed his shoulder. He pressed his hand against the door. Thick ice formed underneath. Once the entire door was a solid sheet of ice, he tried pushing it again. It wouldn't budge.

Krampus added his magic to Jack's. The cold left his hand and the ice grew denser. A little colder. With one good kick, the ice cracked and the wood splintered, leaving a hole large enough they could enter through.

Once he entered, it took him a minute to process what he was seeing. Eight two-to-three-foot tall creatures dressed in latex and leather were gathered around someone suspended from a sex swing. The walls were striped red and white like a candy cane. Every manner of whip, flogger, handcuffs, rope, paddles, different sized dildos, butt plugs in the shape of Christmas Trees, nipple clamps fashioned after ball ornaments, were in the room. All the instruments needed to torture or pleasure a person in this dungeon were Christmas related.

"Holy shit!" Jack whispered.

"Merry! Oh! Christmas!" A woman's voice echoed from behind the Elves.

The thwack of a paddle hitting skin sounded in the room. He cleared his throat loudly to get the Elves' attention. They parted to reveal a buxom woman in the sex swing. She was spread eagled with an Elf between her legs. Krampus spied two more behind her each with a paddle in their hands as they took turns slapping her ass. Another a step stool adjusted a nipple clamp with a reindeer suspended from it. The other on the left side used a riding crop to tease her nipple.

"Oh, Holy Night!" she cried out again.

Krampus couldn't help but be turned on by the show. He coughed this time. The remaining Elves, who were masturbating to the performance, turned around. They froze with their hands on their cocks. Their mouths fell open as they grasped who he was. One was about to scream when Krampus put a finger to his lips to shush him.

"Ahh, forgive the intrusion, but I was looking for Santa. Have any of you seen him?" Jack asked.

The moment was broken. Mrs. Claus's torture ceased. She opened her eyes. "Jack, oh thank gods you found me. I've been telling them to get me out of this thing, but they won't. Would you be a dear?"

Jack helped Mrs. Claus out of the straps until she was on her feet. Her legs wobbled so Krampus lent her a hand as well. Her white hair curled and fell down her back. Looking at her, he might have picked an age anywhere between forty and sixty. Not that it mattered. She appeared sweet one minute, and the next she was as sexy as a fox.

"Are you okay?" Krampus asked.

She gazed at him as he helped her sit down on her bed. Jack covered her with a blanket. His hood had fallen off while they were walking her to the bed. Fear burned in her eyes as she realized who he was. "Jack, why did you bring him here? Is he the one who took Rem?"

"Calm down, Mrs. Claus. I didn't kidnap your husband. Although I've thought about it many times."

"Demon!" she yelled, and pulled away.

"Petunia, enough. Krampus isn't here to hurt you or Santa. I asked for his help. I came by the other night and found his study in disarray. You were gone. The Elves seemed occupied. I got a little worried. What happened? How did you get locked in your candy cane room?" Jack handed her a glass of water.

"Rem was working late checking his lists twice. I went to bed and left him with a cup of hot chocolate. I woke up in the swing with the Elves... ahh... torturing me." Her cheeks turned rosy red.

"It looked like you were enjoying it," Krampus stated.

"Krampus, I don't think now is the time to ..."

He held up his hands. "Hey. I'm just going on what I see."

Someone knocked on the bedroom door. "Mrs. Claus, is it true that...?" The Elf's eyes widened when he saw Krampus. The bell at the end of his hat started ringing from his shakes. His fingers were all covered in bandages. His brown eyes got huge and then he passed out.

"Is he going to be okay?" Krampus asked.

"That's Clover. He's obsessed with you. Santa had to demote him to mistletoe and holly picking. All he asks about is you."

Interesting.

"Petunia, we came across Rem's date book. Do you know anyone by the name of S? It seems he had dinner planned the day before our weekly chess game," Jack asked her.

"He didn't mention anything to me. Then again, I'm not allowed inside his study once he locks the door. I've always assumed he was going over his lists." Mrs. Claus shrugged.

"Could he be having an affair?" Krampus inquired.

"He's not like you. I've heard the vile rumors of you screwing anything with legs. How could anything want to fuck a demonic creature like you?" Petunia spat.

Krampus bit his forked tongue on what he wanted to say. Instead, he placed a hand on her knee. "Ma'am, I don't know what you've heard about me. It's true that I like to get around with certain individuals. I'm open about my sex life. The woman I love is okay with it. And, not to be rude, but even I don't have a sex dungeon. I think you've both read *Forty Shades of Purple* one too many times."

"That's not the name of the books, Krampus," Jack interjected.

"Whatever. But you get my point. Look, I don't care what you and Satan do -- sorry, Santa -- behind your closed doors, but don't judge me until you get to know me. Okay, chickie?" Krampus walked out of the room. He needed some air and to get away from Mrs. My Perfect Husband Could Do No Wrong. He curled his talons around the wooden banister and stared down into the foyer.

"Why did I ever agree to come to fucking Christmas town? I won't hear the end of it." His power shot along the wood until it groaned from the weight of the cold penetrating it.

"Um… excuse me, Mighty Krampus, sir." Someone tugged on his cloak.

Krampus glanced down. Clover the Elf had regained consciousness. His green and white striped socks clashed with his purple vest and black pants. "What do you want?" Krampus glanced down at his vest and pants and realized the Elf and he were wearing the same outfit.

The Elf cringed. "Please don't eat me."

Krampus rolled his eyes. "I'm not going to eat you."

"C-can I have your autograph?" The Elf reached into his pouch and drew out a book and a felt tip marker.

"Why do you want my autograph?"

"You're my hero."

"Hero? I'm nobody's hero."

His hands shook while he held out the pen. "You're mine. I've been following you for years. I dress like you and I even told them to call me Clover." The Elf looked around and lowered his voice. "Because I know it's your real name."

"You're cracked for an Elf. Why don't you worship the Claus the way all the others do? Hell, why weren't you in on the orgy with the missus?" Krampus signed the book and handed it back to him.

"Ehh... the orgies get boring after a while. And Santa is sooo nice to the children when sometimes I just want to smack them. And you... you eat them if they get on your nerves or are naughty. Everyone knows Elves are insatiable when it comes to sex. That's why Santa has us working all the time. If not, we'd be whacking off to every little thing. Just the curve of a snowball gets me hard."

Krampus laughed. "Well, Clover, it was nice to meet you." With his mood lightened he headed back into the bedroom, but the Elf stopped him by calling out:

"Wait! I know who Santa had dinner with."

Chapter Three

"What do you mean you know who Santa had dinner with?" Jack came back out of the bedroom.

"I was outside cleaning out the window boxes and getting ready to stuff them full of holly and mistletoe. I saw the whole thing," Clover told him.

"Had you ever before seen this person that Santa was with?" Krampus asked.

"No. He kinda looked like a younger version of Santa. He had reddish brown hair and a long red coat. He was jovial and he brought out a wineskin full of some kind of alcohol. He and Santa got to talking and laughing. He offered Santa some of the drink. They kept on all night. They got rowdier and rowdier. At the end of it, they were singing lewd carols. I don't know what happened after that because I finished the window boxes and had other duties in the shed. Then I had to go deal with the reindeer. I didn't notice anything was amiss until I came into the house and Santa's door was still locked the next morning. I usually put fresh holly in all the rooms in the morning. They love everything to be festive all the time. It gets rather boring." Clover toyed with his pen and drew a picture of Krampus.

The Elf was fairly good at drawing. "It sounds like Santa got a little drunk and went off with his friend on a bender. We just have to figure out where his friend went."

"You should be able to use one of the reindeer to find Rem." Mrs. Claus came out of her room dressed in a robe.

Jack hit his forehead with the back of his hand. "I didn't think of that. Thank you, Petunia. If I go into the stables with Krampus, the reindeer are not going to react well to his presence. Will you come down with me and ask the reindeer?"

"I can do that. I'm as worried about him as you are."

"Didn't you enjoy the time you had with your Elves?" Krampus asked.

She shot him a glance. "It wasn't unpleasant. Come on. Let's go into the stables."

Krampus and Jack followed her out of the house into a connecting breezeway to the stables. Every inch of the house or wall space was done up to celebrate the holiday. Krampus took pride in his side of the holiday, but this was a bit much even for him. He cringed and prayed Emerald would never go off the deep end and insist they do this to his house. The stables were colder, but his cloak and pelt kept him warm. Mrs. Claus rubbed her arms as she went into the stalls.

"Oh dear. I didn't realize it was this bad," she commented.

Some of the reindeer were rooting around in the hay. Others were outside. Once they saw Mrs. Claus they came over to her. Every reindeer had a bell around their necks. Each bell had a name engraved on it. Krampus stood off to the side as the reindeer gathered around her and rubbed against her. It was clear they seemed to care for her. Then something poked him in the ass. He growled and turned around. One of the reindeer speared him again. *Vixen* was written on the bell. The brown eyes of the deer widened. The reindeer screamed and charged him. Krampus put up his hands.

"Whoa! I'm not the enemy here. Stop stabbing me in the ass. Go bug Jack."

"Guys, I need you to listen," Mrs. Claus said. "Santa's gone missing. I wasn't able to let you out because I was detained in the bedroom. The Elves should've known better. Jack Frost and Krampus are here to help. I need one of you to go with them and find Santa. Can one of you sniff him out?"

The reindeer gathered around one another. Several of them pawed the barn floor until one of them stepped away from the group. "Cupid, I appreciate you going with them. No, Krampus didn't hurt me." Mrs. Claus patted the reindeer on the head. "Cupid will go with you. He already knows what Santa smells like. Reindeer noses are better than bloodhounds."

"If that's the case, then let's get going," Jack said. "Cupid, lead the way. We'll follow your trail." Jack held out his hand for Krampus.

Jack's power flashed through him once more chilling him to the bone. Cupid raced off into the flying snow, but it didn't blind him. They went along until Cupid descended. They landed outside of a large igloo-shaped house. Cupid stomped on the ground and motioned with his head toward the entrance.

"Thank you, Cupid." Krampus opened his sack and summoned all the soldiers who had come with him. One of the gingerbread men had broken in half. He offered the top half to the reindeer. As Cupid crunched on the gingerbread man's head, Krampus divided the legs and torso among the other servants. He summoned the meal Emerald had packed, and munched on the calzone.

"You have to eat now?"

Krampus shrugged. "You don't tell Rem to stop eating his cookies and drinking milk, do you? I get hungry this time of year for everything."

"Fine. Just tell them to be quiet. Why did you bring them anyway?" Jack gestured to the backup Krampus pulled from his sack.

"Hey guys. I need you to go inside the house and find Santa. Can you do that?" he ordered his men.

The tin soldiers saluted. The nutcracker was already heading toward the door with the gingerbread men. Cupid plucked one from the snow and started munching on its head. Krampus caught the last of the ginger's screams as the reindeer devoured him. He smirked and went over to the reindeer. "You like them?"

Cupid snorted.

"You come work for me, you can have all the gingerbread you want."

"Stop trying to bribe the reindeer. They belong to Santa. The song wouldn't make any sense if he didn't have all of them, including Cupid. There's a reason why there isn't a Jorge mentioned anywhere in the song about Rudolph." Jack tugged on his arm. "Come on. We don't know what's in there and you might be sending them on a suicide mission."

"That was one of the reasons why I sent them in. Anything dangerous and they'll get the first round of fire." Krampus finished his meal. Long pig had the best tang to it of any meat. His hunger was satiated. If only Emerald were here, he'd throw her down on the ground and fuck her until she couldn't walk, but duty called. He followed Jack into the large igloo. Rugs were thrown around to cover the ice floor. The aroma of cinnamon and peppermint lingered in the air. He didn't find his soldiers anywhere but heard groaning coming from down the hall. Jack had started to go up the ice steps.

"Jack, this way." Krampus gestured toward where he heard moaning.

They went down the hall. His soldiers were gathered outside a half open door. The nutcracker's mouth had dropped all the way down to the floor. Krampus chuckled as he peeked in. A rubberized version of Krampus was naked and squeaking. Jack went to go in. Krampus stopped him and slowly opened the door to watch the whole scene. He couldn't tear his gaze away. Santa was having sex with the Krampus doll. It was bent over the couch and Santa was going to town with Krampus' rubber ass. The other man who sat on the sofa resembled a younger version of Santa. He drank a flagon of beer as he watched.

"Fuck the bastard," the other man shouted.

"Oh, yeah. I'm fucking the horny bastard," Santa slurred. "Fuckin' Krampus."

Jack elbowed the real Krampus while suppressing his laughter.

"Shut up," Krampus mouthed back at him.

Jack's grin went from ear to ear as he continued to watch the train wreck which was happening right before his eyes. Krampus' arch rival, his nemesis, Santa was having anal sex with a Krampus sex doll, horns and all. The other man in the room kept cheering him on. One of Krampus' gingerbreads hit the door and it creaked open. Santa groaned and looked over. His eyes widened, but then he flashed them a jolly smile.

"Jack, where ya been?" Santa hiccupped. "I've been looking all over for you. I finally took your advice and got away for a while." The words came out slurred, but Krampus got the gist of them. "Who's yer friend?"

"I should be asking you the same thing. I was worried sick when I found your study in a shambles. I brought in Krampus to help look for you. Petunia was being abused by the Elves. We should get you home." Jack went over to him, but Santa pulled away.

"No! I'm having fun! I gotta show him who's boss." Santa tottered over toward Krampus.

"What did you give him?" Jack asked the stranger. "And who the hell are you anyway?"

The man rose and gave him a low bow. "Hello, Jack Frost. And the real Krampus, I never thought I'd meet you. I'm Saturnus, winter god of festivities. I've been after Santa to get over here so he can relax. He's under so much stress all the time."

Krampus dodged out of the way as a naked Santa chased him around the room. Every time he would get to a safe spot, Claus snatched at him. The last time he grabbed his fur and pulled him forward. Krampus tried to get away, but the Jolly Fat Man had him. Santa pulled him down and pushed his puckered lips onto Krampus'. All he could taste was peppermint. Krampus shoved him away again so he landed on Saturnus. They both went onto the couch. He dragged his arm across his mouth to wipe away the tang of the mint.

"What the hell is he on?" Krampus growled.

Saturnus winked at Krampus. Santa tried to get up and fell back into the sofa. "Just a little bit of spiced peppermint rum. It's a specialty of mine. I added a little bit of my secret ingredient so he could loosen up."

"Well, you've loosened him up enough. He needs to get home or the Elves are going to start tearing apart the North Pole. They can't be left alone. Rem, come on. Stop antagonizing Krampus. We need to get you dressed." Jack tried to coax Santa to come with him.

"No! I don't wanna. I'm going to stay." He crossed his arms over his chest.

"When is this stuff going to wear off?" Krampus asked Saturnus.

"Who said anything about it wearing off? Santa is staying with me. All he needs to do is give in a little bit more to his base desires. A couple more hours and then everything he is will be mine." Saturnus's smile twitched. His younger visage melted away to reveal the creature underneath the human façade. Krampus saw cold and ice. Black voids for eyes and no nose. His long, sharp teeth were from some nightmare creature. He waved his hand and a blast of cold hit Jack.

Jack turned into a human ice sculpture. Krampus glanced at his friend. "How in the hell can you do that? Jack is made of ice."

Saturnus touched Santa. He calmed down immediately. His face went slack as though he was nothing more than a zombie waiting for instruction. "As the Incarnation of Jack Frost, he is made up of the natural element of winter and the frost of cold and snow. I'm just cold. I come from the void where there's nothing but ice. It looks good on the outside, but once you get past the exterior, then you see the true cracks. I can turn him to ice because I am cold at heart. For so long I've wanted to be warm. For years, I've been going to Santa. I finally got him here, and then you come along. I won't let you take him." Saturnus waved his hand, but Krampus was faster.

He grabbed his whip. He unfurled it and wrapped the end around Saturnus's throat. Saturnus tugged at the whip, but Krampus wasn't about to let go. Cupid rushed inside. He flipped Santa over his antlers until he landed on his back. The reindeer trumpeted. The air stirred. Three other reindeer, including Rudolph, materialized in the room. They surrounded Saturnus.

"No. Get them away from me!" Saturnus wheezed.

Krampus released the whip. "Return Jack to his normal state."

He didn't do anything. The reindeer got closer, until Rudolph's nose was inches from Saturnus. "Fine. Fine." With a flick of his wrist, the ice that held Jack cracked. His friend wilted but Krampus caught him.

"I'm okay."

"Woohoo! Ride 'em, Santa. Giddy-up, horsey!" Santa kicked Cupid.

Krampus couldn't stand seeing that big, fat, white ass mooning him anymore. He took off his cloak and wrapped it around Santa. He patted Rudolph. "Thanks guys for coming in and saving the day. Keep him pinned down until we can get out of here."

"Rudolph says he has to pay," Jack told Krampus.

"Okay, what did you have in mind, Rudy?"

"Cover your eyes." Jack shielded his eyes.

Krampus did the same. Intense heat blasted against his pelt until it felt like he was on fire. He could see red even through his closed eyes. A strangled cry filled the room and died away. The heat faded and so did the red glow. He opened his eyes. A black smudge on the ice floor was all that remained of Saturnus.

"I knew that schnoz was powerful, but damn." Krampus felt like he'd been sitting in front of a fire even after the glow had disappeared.

Rudolph nodded his head up and down. The bell around his neck went off.

"He wants to know if you want a ride back to the North Pole."

"That would be an honor." Krampus climbed onto Rudolph's back. Jack mounted one of the others. Krampus glanced around for the soldiers he'd brought with him. All he saw were the burnt and melted remains of the tin soldiers and a charred stick left over from where the nutcracker was. *Guess the heat was too much for them*. Rudolph left the igloo and started to run. Krampus leaned over his neck. The reindeer jumped into the air and flew off back to the North Pole.

* * *

Santa snored on Cupid's back. It took both Krampus and Jack Frost to lift him up and drag him into the house. They were out of breath by the time they got him into bed.

"Where did you find him?" Mrs. Claus followed after them.

"With an entity who called himself Saturnus. He was hell-bent on taking over the operation and claiming everything for himself. Not sure exactly what he was, but underneath the handsome exterior was a being who thrived off base desires and tricked people into giving into them. Once that happened, I guess he could take them over. He seemed to be afraid of the reindeer. Rudolph and a couple others cornered him. Then Rudolph blasted him with his nose. He melted away."

She threw her arms around him. Krampus stiffened, but then returned the hug. "Thank you. I never thought I'd be thanking you after… well after everything that I've heard about you."

"I get it. Believe me. Santa and I aren't on the best of terms, but we have to help one another out when the time comes. We may inherently be rivals, but that doesn't mean I want him dead. Although, I could think of a few things I'd like to see happen to him."

Jack elbowed him in the stomach. "What Krampus means is that we're glad Rem's okay. Now that he's safe and sound, we're going back to our realms. Once he recovers, let him know I plan on beating his ass at chess."

"I will. Thanks again," Petunia told them.

Jack led Krampus outside. Krampus patted down his pocket vest. "Shit."

"What is it?"

"I lost my pocket watch."

"We can get you a new one," Jack chuckled.

"No, you don't understand. Emerald gave it to me. I can't lose it."

"Ahh. It will turn up. Come on. Let's get you back to your beloved. I'm sure she's pissed at me for keeping you away all this time."

Krampus touched his pocket again. "Yeah. Time to get home."

"No. No wait. You can't leave yet." Clover, the Elf, ran down the steps towards them.

"What do you want?" Jack asked.

"I want to go with you." Each time he took in a breath the bells on his shoes rang.

Krampus chuckled.

"I'm not sure that's going to work out. Wouldn't Rem miss you around here?" Jack ran his fingers through his Mohawk to spruce it back up.

"They won't miss me here. They hate me already because Krampus is my idol. They won't know I'm gone." The Elf fell to his knees and wrung his hands. "Please. I don't belong here. I'll do whatever you want me to do."

Krampus couldn't stand to see the Elf groveling. "Get up. If you come with me, I'm not calling you Clover. What's your real name?"

The Elf looked down and mumbled something.

"Sorry, I didn't catch that."

He looked up. "I said my name is Peppermint

Patty. You can call me Pat."

"This place and all their fucked-up names. Why can't you just be Frank? Yes, I can call you Pat. You want to be in my service, then take my hand." Krampus offered his hand to the Elf. He let his power take him away as Jack's mingled with his own. The whiteout of snow and frost washed over them.

All three arrived outside of Krampus' workshop. Snow blanketed the landscape. A chill ran through him and he felt stronger than he had all season. He ran his hand over the air and released the coldness. Flakes floated down from the clear sky. The Elf chuckled and flopped down in the nearest snowbank and started making a snow angel.

"Thanks for the help. I'm sure I could've done it without you, but --" Jack laughed.

Krampus pulled his friend into his embrace and planted a kiss on the other Incarnation's lips. When he broke away, Jack still had his eyes closed. "You're welcome. Now go play some pranks on someone else. We'll catch up after the season is over."

Jack opened his eyes. "Are you finally going to let me have a chance at that woman of yours?"

"That's up to her. I'm not going to auction her off. Pat, come on up to the house." Krampus motioned for the Elf to follow him.

When they entered, the mouthwatering smells of Emerald's cooking permeated the house. His stomach growled. Pat looked around with a bit of awe. Krampus chuckled. "Come on. You need to meet my cook. She's the lady of the house so whatever she tells you to do, you do it, understand?"

"Yes, Master," Pat whispered. "Will you eat me if I misbehave?"

"No. I'm not going to eat you. I'll make sure the

gingerbread men don't either. They have a bit of a cannibal streak in them. I've known them to eat my human stock. The tin soldiers patrol the castle and the nutcrackers are backup. I don't use them much anymore."

"Is it really true that you eat little children and the people you bring here?" Pat asked as they got into the kitchen.

"At times. It depends on how hungry I am." Krampus lifted the Elf onto one of the chairs so he could see the table and Emerald. She wiped her hands on her apron and rushed into his arms. Krampus kissed her lightly before letting her go. His heart warmed at seeing her. Everything about her made his soul sing, and he couldn't imagine being without her.

"I missed you. I was afraid that you weren't coming back. You've been gone for a week."

"I'm okay. I'm sorry I was gone for so long. It wasn't my intention. Time moves differently when traveling between realms. I didn't mean to worry you. Do you forgive me?"

"I can think of a few ways you can show me how sorry you are." Emerald squeezed his cock and he grunted.

"We can certainly catch up later. First, I want you to meet Pat." Krampus gestured to the Elf.

"Hey, short stuff. I'm Emerald. Nice to meet you."

"You're so pretty." Pat squeaked out. "Can I kiss you?"

She looked at Krampus. He shrugged. Emerald brushed her lips over Pat's, but the Elf took her face and stuck his tongue down her throat. Krampus grabbed the over-enthusiastic Elf and pulled him off her.

"Pat, if you do that again. I *will* eat you," he scolded.

Emerald giggled and rubbed the Elf's head. "Oh, leave him alone, Clo. He's so cute. If you do that to me again, I'll chop your dick off and make it into a little kabob. Understood?"

Pat nodded.

Emerald patted his cheek. "Good. Just so we are on the same page. You might be a groupie, but you don't touch what's his without permission. Got it?"

"Yes, Ma'am. What do you want me to do around here?"

"I'm sure we can think of something," Emerald said. "For now, can you watch the bread in the oven? The timer is on the counter."

"I can bake you some cookies," Pat piped in.

"Sure. Cookies would be great." Krampus took Emerald in his arms and nibbled on the side of her neck. "We're going to be a while. If I catch you peeking in the room, then I'll throw you to the gingerbreads. Got it. I'm not like Santa. I don't like an audience unless you're invited. I don't want to catch you whacking off to our private time. Got it?"

"Won't happen. Promise."

"Good." He picked up Emerald, threw her over his shoulder, and headed upstairs to make up for lost time.

Chapter Four

It was two days before Christmas Eve. Krampus examined the bells on the tree in the living room. Five had gone off so far, but he expected another dozen or so to sound before the New Year. Once January 1st went, he declared the season over and got ready for a couple of months off and then began the whole cycle again.

He paced the living room. The humans he'd captured so far were being guarded by the gingers. Every once in a while, he heard their screams as the gingerbread soldiers looked in on them. Compared to him, the humans were tiny. When he brought them into his realm, they were only inches tall. Everything in his realm towered over them. He could make them normal size if he wanted, but it was easier to keep them the way they were. Even if they got out, there was no way they could ever escape unless they somehow found a way into his sack. Then out of it again once they returned to their reality. The sound of their screams made him happy.

"Are you going to keep them back there?" Emerald asked.

"I told you before. This is who I am. If you don't like it, then you're free to leave at any time."

"They're innocent lives that you've stolen away."

He set his hands on Emerald's shoulders. Normally, her distress would have wrung his heart. Right now, at the height of his power, he was more beast than man. Krampus wanted to punish those who rang the bells, fuck anything that moved, and eat as much long pig as he could. Pat and Emerald had been cooking for the last week and it still wasn't enough to satisfy him. He'd made love to her every night since he'd gotten back and he still couldn't get enough.

"They're not innocent. My bells don't go off for anyone. They have to have done something. I take them because they warrant punishment. If I get one who is innocent, I throw them back. I apologize if it makes you uncomfortable." He didn't want to see her go, but he understood if she did. Not many were okay with his lifestyle.

She shook her head. "No. I'm just overly sensitive. I can see their lives and feel their fear. One of the joys of being a psychic. When I touch the human stock in the back, they're nothing more than base emotions. I feel the difference. I know it's your job. And I --"

"Excuse me, K. There's someone at the door for you," Pat announced.

Krampus hung his head. *Always interrupted.* "Tell them to go away. I'm not in the mood."

"Ahh… you might want to come and greet them, boss," Pat said. The Elf had taken off the bells, which made Krampus a little disappointed because he couldn't hear him coming.

"Fine." He walked to the front door and stopped when he saw who was in the foyer.

"Santa," Emerald's amazed whisper came from behind him.

"Well, hello young lady. Emerald, isn't it?" Santa's jolly voice made Krampus cringe. He took her hand and shook it before brushing a kiss along her cheek. "You've been a good girl this year."

Emerald nodded.

"Hello, Claus, what can I do for you?" Krampus asked. He stayed near Emerald to make sure she didn't fall under the spell of the Jolly Fat Man.

Mrs. Claus stepped forward and held out a

swath of red fabric. "You left this behind after helping Rem. We wanted to be sure you got it back."

Krampus took the fabric and realized it was his cloak. He had completely forgotten about it after giving it to a naked Santa. "Thank you, Petunia. I was looking for this."

An awkward silence stretched between them. Mrs. Claus elbowed her husband's round belly. He dug into the pocket of his red coat and held out his hand. "Also, I found this in our candy cane room. It must've fallen out when you were assisting Pet."

His pocket watch. Krampus rubbed his thumb over it and smiled. "Thank you. I appreciate that. Emerald gave it to me. I thought I had lost it for good."

"You didn't tell me you lost it," she chided him.

He kissed her quickly. "I'm sorry, love, but I didn't want to worry you. It slipped my mind after I got back."

"Is there anything we can get you?" Emerald asked.

"We have some of Samhain's cider. I'm not sure if you trade with him or not considering he's one of the Dark Incarnations," Krampus offered.

"T-that would be nice. We like apple cider," Petunia chimed in trying to break the uncomfortable silence.

"Or I could make you some hot chocolate so you guys can talk," Pat added in.

"That'd be great. Why don't you come into the study and sit down?" Emerald tried to lead them away from the door. Pat hustled into the kitchen.

"Actually, there was something else I wanted to get off my chest before we do anything. I guess going into the study is best," Santa said.

Krampus shrugged and they walked into the

library. Whatever it was he wanted to get off his chest it was something he wanted some privacy for. Krampus closed the door. "Okay. We're alone. What did you want to talk about?" He figured it was the state he'd found him in with Saturnus, but he wasn't going to bring it up.

"I wanted to thank you for rescuing me. I never knew Saturnus was so evil. I couldn't see it. He and I were friends for years. He always wanted me to loosen up before the season started. I figured this once I could let my guard down."

"It wasn't a big deal. There wouldn't be Christmas without Santa Claus."

"True. Without you rescuing me and Petunia, we would've succumbed to our carnal desires."

"We all have fantasies." Krampus poured himself a brandy and drank it down. He turned his back on his guests. He felt a hand on his arm. He turned around and saw Santa there. Krampus poured him a drink and handed it to him.

"There was another reason I came here." He swirled the alcohol around in the glass.

"What would that be?"

"I can't get it out of my head. It's driving me and Petunia insane."

"Get it off your chest."

Santa walked his fingers along Krampus' arm. "I want to suck your cock. I want to watch as you fuck my wife."

"Whoa! I mean, we all know that I have relations with a lot of Incarnations, but I'm not just going to --"

Santa fell to his knees and wrung his hands. "You have to. I know we're natural rivals. Think about what you saw when I was at Saturnus's lair. I was fucking a sex doll in your guise. Deep down I want this. I don't know if it's his lasting influence, but I need it. I can't think about anything else. I can't look at my lists. The Elves have even picked up on it. I can't eat. I haven't been able to sleep. Petunia has to wear a pair of horns so I can make love to her."

Krampus glanced at Emerald. Her mouth had dropped open, but she closed it again.

"It's true. Not that I mind the horns, but he's been very distracted. You don't know how long it took me to get him to admit it and then come over here. I wouldn't mind it. I've always thought you were fetching." Petunia winked at him.

I'm not hearing this. But oh, I've wanted this for so long -- to see him on his knees, begging me. It feels so good to see him like this. I wonder if he'll taste like peppermint. "We can do this, but Emerald's involved and only if she approves. And you don't leave her out when you make your rounds because she's with me."

"Fine. Whatever you want," Santa agreed.

Krampus offered him his hand. Santa took it, and they all left the library. Pat came out with the tray of hot chocolate. He shook his head and indicated later. Pat nodded and hurried back into the kitchen. They got into their bedroom. Emerald slid into the chair and patted the seat next to her for Mrs. Claus. It was large enough for both of them to sit comfortably.

"Strip. Both of you," Krampus ordered.

Santa and Mrs. Claus both undressed. Krampus slid out of his clothes slowly. Rem's eyes grew bigger. Santa kissed Krampus' pelt until he came to one of his nipples. The Jolly Fat Man bit down. Krampus grunted as his lips moved further down his chest. He couldn't help but be aroused as Santa surrendered to him and went to his knees. Krampus glanced at Mrs. Claus. Her eyes were wide as she watched the show before her.

Santa flicked his tongue over Krampus' cock. "Oh yes," he whispered.

Krampus watched as Emerald circled her fingers over Mrs. Claus plump breasts. His lover winked at him as Mrs. Claus took pleasure in Emerald's embrace. Santa's mouth slipped over Krampus' prick and drew him into his mouth. Krampus shook at the pleasure of it. One of his fantasies was coming true. Santa's hand slid lower as he clutched Krampus' cock. His head bobbed up and down while he took all of his dick into his mouth. Krampus grabbed hold of Santa's head weaving his fingers through the silver white hair. Mrs. Claus whimpered as Emerald pleasured her. The sight aroused him even more. He watched the two women until he came. Santa sucked Krampus' dick until he stopped thrusting into his mouth.

"Oh, Rem," Mrs. Claus cried out.

Santa didn't pay her any attention. Instead he stayed on his knees. He glanced back at Krampus. "Take my ass. Fuck me."

Krampus ran his talons over Santa's ass and slapped each cheek several times. Each pass Rem grunted. He did it until each mound was the same shade as the fat man's cheeks. Santa wiggled his ass. Krampus slapped him one more time on each cheek. "I could get used to this."

"Petunia, come over here. Let me taste that pussy," Santa begged.

Emerald released Mrs. Claus so she could be pleasured by her husband. Emerald returned to the chair and opened her legs so Krampus could see her. Santa went down on his wife and began to pleasure her. Emerald rubbed her clit. Just seeing her kept Krampus hard. He focused on Santa's ass because the Jolly Fat Man wanted Krampus to claim him. Krampus slapped Santa's ass one more time until he spread his legs. Krampus slid his cock between Santa's ass and thrust upward. Santa jumped, but he didn't tell him to stop. Instead, Krampus kept his eyes focused on Emerald and how she touched herself.

"Oh baby. I want to fuck you." Krampus kept the friction going between him and Santa. All he needed was the view of Emerald masturbating. Mrs. Claus writhed on the ground from Santa licking her pussy. He drove up and could feel himself losing control. He gripped Santa's hips thrusting until he got Santa into a rhythm where he was riding him. Krampus closed his eyes and surrendered to the pleasure of the moment.

Petunia cried out once more. Emerald's breathing hastened. Krampus knew she was ready. He thrust against Santa one more time and stepped over Santa and his wife. They were locked in their own world. Krampus scooped Emerald up and impaled her on his cock. They fit together perfectly. She claimed his lips and ground her hips against his as he moved inside of her. He shoved his tongue into her mouth. Emerald caught his tongue with her teeth. He grunted and plunged inside of her one more time. The ecstasy of the moment took him. He set her down on the chair and nibbled on her neck.

"I love you," he whispered to her.

"I love you, too," Emerald replied.

"What do you think about them?" Krampus asked her against her ear.

"I don't think they're right for us," she murmured so they wouldn't hear.

"I agree. It was something I've always wondered about, but no," Krampus replied.

"Oh, Santa. Jingle balls…" Mrs. Claus cried out.

"See, I'm not the only one who sings *Jingle Balls*,"

Emerald giggled.

Krampus shook his head. He sent a jolt of his cold through her. Emerald jumped and squeezed her legs together. She bit her lip, but he could see the pleasure rising in her eyes. He urged a bit more magic in her as he walked his fingers down her stomach until he touched her clit. With one more blast, Emerald rose up from the chair and groaned.

Santa looked up with a glazed expression. He winked at Krampus. "That was worth it."

The couples dressed in silence as the awkwardness returned. Something in Krampus was placated. Because he'd indulged in one fantasy with Santa, he wasn't about to see his white ass again anytime soon. They left the room. Before he went out, Krampus grabbed a small box from his nightstand. He caught Pat on the way down and whispered a quick order. The Elf's smile was enough of an answer. Pat bounded off to do Krampus' bidding. Downstairs, Santa and Mrs. Claus straightened up.

Claus held out his hand to Krampus. "I think we're good. Thank you for the invigorating night. It won't be something easily forgotten. I'll make sure to stop by Christmas Eve as promised."

Krampus took his hand and shook it. Santa kissed Emerald's cheeks and squeezed her ass. She jumped and giggled. Mrs. Claus grabbed Krampus and planted a kiss on him. He responded, but she wasn't going to let go until Krampus pried her off him. Santa flashed him a proud smile.

"She's a bit of a minx. Krampus, thank you for this. I know it doesn't change the rivalry between us, but I'm sure we'll be back at it next year. I'll keep Emerald on the good list though."

"Thanks, Rem. Santa."

The Jolly Fat Man winked. He and his wife blew away in a light snow storm. Krampus locked the door. Pat rushed back in.

"Are they gone? Did they want to take me back with them?" Pat asked.

"No. Nothing like that. Take the rest of the night off, Pat. Emerald and I are going to be busy. Anyone comes to the door or even if a bell rings, I'm going to be busy."

"Okay, boss. Have a good night." Pat skipped off to his room in the back.

"Come with me. I have a surprise for you." Krampus led her through the house and out into the grotto. Snow blanketed the landscape. Candles lined the outside of the grotto, thanks to Pat. The flames illuminated the crystals in the cavern's ceiling making them wink each time a candle flame was blown by the wind. Steam from the water made it hazy and warm in the small space.

"What are we doing out here?"

Krampus got down on one knee. He plucked the ring from the box and held it up to her. He had fashioned the circle out of the gold. The diamond and emeralds the tin soldiers had pulled from the mines. The last time he went to the mine, he instructed them to look out for the specific items he wanted to make the ring. He didn't know what she would say, but he prayed it would be yes.

"Emerald, will you marry me?"

Her eyes widened. Her hand went to her mouth and her eyes teared up. "Oh, yes. I'll marry you."

His heart warmed. He slipped the ring onto her finger. She threw herself into his arms. Krampus picked her up and spun her around. She was all he wanted. His world was complete.

"Thank you. I'm never going to let you go. I'll always be there for you. I swear it. I love you."

"I love you, too."

"So what do you propose we do for the rest of the night?"

Her hand rubbed over his cock. "I have a few ideas. You think you're up for it?"

"I'm always up for you."

Krampus, Bah Humbug

Crymsyn Hart

When Krampus gets called to help find a missing Incarnation, he finds himself in over his head. It takes a little bit of magic and help from a couple of friends to win the day. More than one surprise looms that will turn his whole world upside down. Krampus has to get with the holiday attitude or lose all he holds dear.

Chapter One

"Harder, Clo," Emerald murmured as she bent over. Krampus slid his hands over her appealing ass and squeezed her cheeks. She grunted and shot him a look. He flashed her an innocent smile as he leaned over her and nibbled her neck. He raked his claws along her side and cupped her breasts, fingering her nipples until they firmed against his palm. She pressed her ass into his hard-on and groaned. This only made him pinch them harder until she panted.

"It looks like I've interrupted something."

Krampus glanced up over Emerald's horns into the dark form of Nyx, the Incarnation of Night. Her black dress illuminated in a starburst pattern. The remains of the comet flew across her chest and down her dress until it disappeared. Her silver hair hung in waves around her back. She took a seat on a kitchen stool and picked up one of the undecorated gingerbread men. Nyx broke off one of its arms and a muffled scream from the dough filled the kitchen. "These are good."

Emerald straightened up and wiped her hands on her apron. Krampus slung his arm around her and kissed her, tasting the nutmeg and vanilla on her lips. He trailed his fingers through her hair and over her small horns until she squirmed. He couldn't get enough of her no matter where they were or what she was doing. If he didn't need to prepare for his holiday duties, he would've spent every moment he could fucking her. Krampus broke the kiss, leaving his wife breathless as Emerald moved out of the way for him to get at the dough. She was having a rough time rolling out on this batch. Krampus rolled up his sleeves and latched onto the wooden handles of the two-foot marble rolling pin. The brown dough quivered as it tried to get away, but he pressed down and rolled it into submission.

"What do you want, Nyx?" Krampus asked.

Emerald went over to their guest and sat on her lap. Nyx -- along with several other Incarnations -- had been welcomed into their bed over the past few months. Nyx slid her hand along Emerald's face and met her lips. Krampus tore his gaze away from them making out. Knowing that Emerald enjoying being with others in their bed made it all worthwhile. She didn't get jealous when he slept with someone else. She knew he always came back to her.

"Your lips taste like cinnamon, Em," Nyx crooned. "How about we get upstairs and take advantage of the alone time?" She skated her hand under Emerald's dress.

"That'd be nice."

"What alone time? Nyx, you're not here just to enjoy our flesh. Why are you here?" Krampus pounded the rolling pin down on the dough.

His wife moaned when Nyx stopped her caresses. "Right, business first. Pleasure later. Your help has been requested."

He rolled his eyes. "Not this again. It's getting close to Christmas. I have things to do and a lot of new bells to forge. A lot of naughty children have cropped up this year, and I'm particularly hungry for flesh that doesn't come from my farm. The human meat I have here is a bit lean for my taste. The children are all fattening up while they wait for the Claus and baking him cookies." He gritted his teeth as he thought about his arch nemesis. He might have rescued him and the Mrs. one time, but that didn't mean all things were kosher between them. Although, he did make Claus promise to visit Emerald since she had nothing to do with their rivalry.

"Sorry, Krampus. They asked for you specifically. They've done me a few favors in the past. I couldn't turn them down." Nyx got up.

Emerald came back behind the counter and began mixing up another batch of gingerbread, so they could fix some of the older ones whose crumbs littered the house. Sometimes the older ones got a bit ornery and hungry and ate the newer ones. The cannibal gingers were a part of his special creation, but they listened well and got along with the tin soldiers and nutcrackers who kept guard on his property.

"Come on, Clo. You enjoy helping people. You just hide behind that gruff exterior. Big and scary with the horns. The clomping around of your hooves as you chase those poor children," Emerald joked.

He licked his lips when he thought about the children he would catch. "It's not just children, love. You know I bring back men, too."

Emerald made a disgusted face and poured the flour into the mixing bowl. "That's all you. I'm not into eating human. Remember, I was human until I was cursed because a certain god didn't like what I told him in the cards."

Krampus slapped her ass. "You are beautiful with horns or without. Nyx, who am I supposed to be helping now?"

Darkness swallowed the kitchen. His wife slipped her arm around his waist and held onto him. The only thing visible in the room was the glow of the coals in the oven as another batch of gingerbread men baked. The Incarnation of Night touched the kitchen door. It creaked open on its own, and two figures floated through the doorway. One was dressed in an oversized green robe with a wreath of flowers on top of his head. Red curls floated around his shoulders. He had a golden cornucopia under his arm. The other ducked as he entered the house, clothed in a black cloak that flowed behind him. Emerald's grip on Krampus tightened. She trembled against him as a cold blast of air filled the kitchen. A dark blue light surrounded the black-robed wraith as he drifted over to Nyx. A dark hood covered the spirit's face.

"Who are they, Clo?" Emerald whispered.

The blast of power from the second specter brought a cold with it that chilled even his soul, but Krampus had become accustomed to dealing with all sorts of entities. The power made him draw in his own magic and stand against the spirits. The closer it got to Christmas, the more powerful and menacing he became. It also meant he wanted to eat and fuck all the time, too.

"Enough with the theatrics, boys. No need to whip it out and measure how long your dicks are." Nyx stepped between him and the dark-robed spirit.

Krampus bared his teeth at the presence. He didn't like how the wraith intimidated his wife either. The other one floated over to the counter and picked up one of the cooling gingerbread man. The two-foot-tall ginger didn't move in the phantom's hands. It let out a muffled scream when the man took a sizable bite out of its head. Krampus watched while he devoured the first cookie and went for another one.

"These are excellent. Do you have any jam to go with it?" the green-robed spirit asked Emerald.

"Cornelius, this isn't the time to be thinking about food," the phantasm in the dark robe grumbled. He lifted his hood. His eyes and face were nearly skeletal. He had long, thin fingers with blueish-purple stubby nails. He squeezed his companion's shoulder and glanced at Nyx. "Night, thank you for bringing us here. We can speak with this creature from here." He threw a murderous look at Krampus.

Nyx stood on tiptoe and brushed a kiss across the hooded man's cheek. "Fine, but be nice. Krampus and Emerald are special friends of mine. I don't want to hear you've been misbehaving. Just because you asked for his help doesn't mean he's going to give it to you. He has a bad reputation -- but underneath it all, he's a big, cuddly Christmas demon."

She grabbed Krampus's goatee and planted her lips on his. A bit of her power flashed through him until his rose up and met hers. The energy slammed into one another and created frozen silver sparks. She tasted like earth and peppermint. When she pulled away, the room had lightened. Nyx kissed Emerald the same way and then whispered something in her ear. His wife grinned. They were planning on something. Jealousy instantly gripped him because he wanted to be in the middle of whatever they were scheming. Then Nyx faded out, leaving them alone with the two spirits.

"Now that you've successfully insulted me in my home and scared my wife with your theatrics, I suggest you tell me who you are. What do you want? Get it over with so I can shove it up your ass and get you the hell out of here," Krampus growled.

The gaunt phantasm drifted closer, but Cornelius stepped between them, wringing his hands. "Oh please, Mighty Krampus, we've heard of your magnanimous deeds, and how you saved Santa. I know we are lowly Incarnations compared to you, but we are begging for your help."

"This was not my idea," the dark-robed wraith

told him.

Cornelius shot his tall companion a look. "Shut up, Yeti. If it hadn't been for you, then none of this would've ever happened."

"Couples argue all the time. I don't know why you've gotten your robe in a bunch. She's taken off before and always come back. Women. You know how they can be."

The other man wiped the crumbs from his robe. "She's never been gone this long so close to the season."

"Guys, what's going on and who are you talking about?" Emerald asked. She opened the icebox and pulled out a container she handed to Cornelius. She then gave him a knife. "Why don't you sit down, both of you?"

Yeti grunted and followed the other man to the table. Krampus watched the two, making sure they didn't do or say anything to upset Emerald again. He leaned against the counter as Emerald brought over some biscuits. Cornelius nibbled at his second gingerbread man.

"Em's right. What do you want?" Krampus asked them.

Yeti took a biscuit and smothered it with plum jam. Cornelius dunked a piece of cookie into the container and swallowed it. "Our partner, Persimmon, the Ghost of Christmas Past, has disappeared. I'm the Ghost of Christmas Yet to Come and Cornelius is the Ghost of Christmas Present. We've heard gossip among the Lesser Incarnations of the things that you've done."

"I take it you want me to help find your partner?"

Yeti looked up. "I don't necessarily agree with --"

he gestured toward Krampus and swallowed his disgust --"your station. However, Corny seems to think you can help us, and I'm not about to let him down. He's been eating like this now for a week. To be honest, I'm starting to get a little worried about Persimmon, too." He glanced back at Cornelius who had finished the gingerbread man.

He burped and blushed. "Excuse me. Do you have any milk to wash those cookies down with?"

Emerald patted his arm, led him through the kitchen, and down into the pantry. She shot Krampus a look that only meant one thing. She wanted them both out of the house. Other Incarnations had interested him, but nothing about this pair turned him on in the least. It was hard to say that because Krampus had been with a lot of the other Incarnations: Samhain, Jack Frost, Cupid, Nyx, to name a few. Some were regular bed partners and others were an on-and-off thing.

"Now isn't the best time for me to go looking for someone. It sounds like you're associated with Christmas as I am. You must know I have preparations to make for the coming holiday."

"We do, too, but we act as a trio. Without Sim, we can't do anything." Yeti pulled apart the biscuit and kept breaking it into smaller and smaller crumbs before he shoved the plate away. "Look, we're more than just a trio of ghosts who show people the error of their ways. We're together… if you know what I mean. I love her. You must understand that even with your blackened heart." Yeti met Krampus's gaze. In those dark eyes he saw the man really cared about the woman he told him about.

Krampus sighed and straddled the chair across from Yeti. If he ever lost Emerald, he would go crazy. Never before had he thought he could love a person as much as he loved her. It didn't matter to him a god had cursed her with horns and cloven feet. It just made her all the more beautiful to him. At first, he had hired her to be his housekeeper, but then their relationship had blossomed into something more than he ever thought possible. He put a hand on Yeti's shoulder and squeezed it.

"I get what you're going through. And yes, if I lost my wife I wouldn't know what to do. Tell me what you know and I'll see if I can help you. I can't promise anything."

Hope sparked in Yeti's eyes. "Does that mean you'll end up helping us?"

"I'll look into it, but first you have to stop with the black-hearted demon bullshit. I am who I am made, by the office of my Incarnation. As you are with your office. As Nyx said, we can't be whipping our dicks out to see whose is the longest. We are each a part of the Christmas cycle and do what we are charged with. Agreed?"

"Agreed."

"Good."

Emerald came back in with Cornelius, who carried a long stick of pepperoni. The smile on his face reminded Krampus of a kid who'd found heaven in a candy store. She glanced at her husband. Krampus nodded that he would help them.

Chapter Two

Yeti leaned back in the chair as Cornelius munched on the pepperoni stick and the plate of cheese that Emerald set before him and one of the herbed breads they bought in the village. Emerald had had a craving for them lately. The last time they went to the bakery, he bought them out of the basil-and-cheddar-braided loaves. By now, the villagers were used to him coming down into the town to buy things. At first, they weren't that comfortable with him because they all knew what he represented. Normally they left him tribute at the gates at every moon so he wouldn't prey upon their children. However, he never took children from the town. He farmed his own humans, but they weren't like the normal townspeople or the wicked humans he brought back with him from the mortal realm. He only took those naughty ones he picked up on Earth that were unredeemable. Sometimes he even let them go.

"Are you going to come with us?"

Krampus sipped on the mug of mulled cider Emerald brought to him. It was tarter than normal. "I told you I would. I'm waiting for you and your friend to stop eating me out of house and home."

"Corny, give it a rest," Yeti said to the other spirit.

He belched. "Sorry. I eat when I'm nervous. I've been eating everything in sight. We really need to find Persimmon. I won't feel better without her."

"Before she disappeared, did she say anything to you?" Emerald pulled out a hunk of bread.

"We'd gotten into an argument about how we were going to be doing our Holiday routine. We always find the most unChristmaslike humans who no longer have the spirit and appear to them over the course of twelve hours. Persimmon wanted to change things up. It does get a little bit old to do this every year, but we help people. She wanted to be more modern with things. Using some technology to reach the people we help. All the mortals have cell phones, tablets, computers, or some other form of phone they stick their noses into and never take them out. But --" Yeti stopped as his voice filled with emotion. He looked away and coughed. He wiped his sleeve over is eyes and looked back.

"She wanted to update the process and maybe do a few visitations before the official start of the season by herself. We thought it was too dangerous. She likes to watch the mortals in our viewing pool. It's how we see into the hearts of those we pick," Cornelius told them and set down then drank the tankard of the cider.

"Have you looked in this viewing pool to see where she might be?" Krampus asked.

"Of course. Do you think if we were able to find her that we'd be coming to you?" Yeti seethed.

"Hey, I have to ask. I wouldn't want it to be obvious that she got lost in some shopping mall or something and you couldn't find her. Do you think she's in the human world?" Krampus questioned them.

"If she is, then someone has made it so that we can't see her. No matter where she is, we should be able to spot her in the pool," Cornelius told them.

Emerald came up behind Krampus and massaged his shoulders until he uttered a contented growl. "Guys, maybe she needed some girl time. Being around men all the time can take a toll on a girl even if you are her lovers. Any place where she might go to relax?"

"We already checked her usual places. Now is the time of year she likes to go shopping when they start to put out the Christmas decorations. She has quite the collection of ornaments. We have ten different trees she puts up. We all have our eccentricities." Cornelius gestured to the pepperoni stick in his hand. "I like to eat. I might be the Ghost of Christmas Present to show off plenty and fulfillment, but sometimes it seems like I can never get enough."

"And I show others the bleak outcome of what their lives will be. I'm drawn to the shadows and to death. I'm good friends with the Grim Reaper. We go way back. We are what we are, the same way you are. The office has molded us into the beings we are, but we have kept a grip on some of our human interests. Persimmon has only been the Ghost of Christmas Past for a century. Clementina, the Ghost of Christmas Past before her, only stepped down a century ago. She was a spitfire who found someone to step into the role and here we are," Yeti told them.

"But --" Krampus had more questions to ask them. What Yeti said was true. Krampus had once been human and stepped into his current role. It seemed so long ago he barely remembered being human.

"Clo, why don't you get your things and help them? Why are you so reluctant?" Emerald murmured in his ear.

"Gentleman, excuse me. I have to talk to my wife." Krampus led Emerald into his private study and closed the door. The fireplace popped to life as he entered. On a long table in the back were bells he was working on, plus, he had parts of toy soldiers to paint. Several of their two-foot-tall bodies stood by the side of the bench waiting for the finishing touches by him.

"You've helped others before." Emerald picked up one of the bells and ran her fingers over the intricate carvings in the metal.

He snatched it from her hands. "You shouldn't play with those."

"What the hell has your horns in a bunch? I've touched them before and even helped you smelt them. If you're going to start getting all possessive, then we don't need to be... planning the rest of our years together. Is marriage something you didn't think it was going to be?" Emerald sniffled, and tears glistened in her eyes. Her top lip trembled.

"Em, that's not what I meant. I'm sorry." He went to console her, but she shook her head and dashed out of the room.

As she did, one of the gingerbread men stood in the doorway. His left arm had a bite taken out of it. Crumbs trailed along the floor as he dragged his right foot behind him. The burnt irregular edges showed he had been left in the over a bit too long. White frosting stitches held the leg onto his baked form. The raisin eyes were dried up, as were the gumdrop buttons down his middle. "Master, someone's at the gate insisting they see you."

"Send them away. I'm not in the mood," he snarled. He glanced at the bell in his hand as his thoughts played over the argument with this wife. He flung it at the ginger. It struck the side of his face, leaving an indentation and crumbs on the rug.

"They said to insist and to interrupt you. And they said to give you this." The ginger came forward on shaky legs and held out whatever he wanted to give Krampus.

A piece of pale blue fabric with a streak of red on it. He lifted the cloth to his nose and smelled it. Vanilla, like that of a cookie, with the faint spice of nutmeg and apples clung to the fabric. The coppery perfume of blood stayed within his nose and made his mouth water. He flicked his tongue over the smudge and caught the sweet and spice like a mulled wine. It made him hunger for more than just blood. He wanted meat and he wanted to fuck.

"W-what do I tell the one at the gate, Master?" the ginger's quivering words brought him back to reality.

Krampus shook off the beast. "Bring them into the foyer."

The ginger bolted from the room as fast as his half-broken foot would take him. Krampus balled up the cloth and went back into the kitchen. The two specters stood up when he entered. He held out the piece of blue fabric. "Does this belong to Persimmon?"

Yeti took it from his hand and sniffed it. He glanced at Cornelius and handed it to him. The other man paled even more and sank back into his seat. "It's hers," Yeti answered. "Where did you get this? Were you the one who kidnapped her and now you're stringing us along?" A blast of cold power hit Krampus that made him bristle.

He nearly called upon his own magic, but he held back, telling himself the man was reacting to the thought the woman he loved had been kidnapped. "No. I didn't take her. The one who brought this here is on the way up to the house. I was going to ask them a few questions but figured you might want to be there when I do. How about you come along?"

"Sorry. I just want to find her. I-I didn't mean to accuse you of --" Yeti stammered.

"It's fine. Come on."

Krampus motioned for them to follow as he

walked into the foyer. Waiting behind the ginger was a waif-like man dressed in a tweed suit holding a hat in his hands. He had short red hair. His intense blue eyes betrayed the façade that was supposed to make him human. Krampus could sense the quiet power underneath the mortal façade.

"Can I help you?" Krampus asked.

"No, I think that I can help you. I understand you're looking for someone. You got my little present that your cookie brought up to you," the stranger said to him.

"I did, but again, who are you? I would prefer to know your name and why you're here," Krampus repeated.

The man chuckled and fluffed his hair out with his fingers. "Aren't you going to invite me in so we can talk about this like gentlemen?"

"You took her, you son of a bitch." Cornelius tackled the stranger and knocked him to the floor.

"Corny, what in the hell are you doing?" Yeti grabbed the other man and pulled the Ghost of Christmas Present off the stranger. Krampus shook his head as the other man dusted himself off. Yeti kept the other ghost in check as he struggled to get out of his hands.

"I'm fine. I said I'm fine." Cornelius pulled away from Yeti.

"Well, Krampus, I've heard your hospitality is better than this. I thought I'd be safe under your roof. It appears you aren't interested in hearing what I have to say. Good day to you." The man set his hat back on his head and turned on his heel.

Krampus waved his hand and gathered the cold. A wall of ice blocked the man from leaving. "I don't know what you've heard about me, but I don't like threats. You came here with information these two need, and you're not going to leave without giving it to them. You can stop with the human disguise because I know you're something else. Reveal yourself before I make you into a Popsicle. You're in my land and my house. Trust me when I tell you that you won't be melting any time soon."

The skin sagged around the man's eyes, dribbling down his cheeks. "If you decide to do that, then you'll never find the pretty little thing these two want." The man wiped away one of the melting globs of flesh. It hit the stone file floor and sizzled.

"Krampus, we have to know where she is." Yeti put a hand on his arm.

He looked at the gaunt man and saw the fear in his eyes. Even if Krampus didn't like him, the love Yeti had for Persimmon was the same he had for Emerald. He pulled the ice back and let the cold power dissipate. "Fine. We'll play it your way."

Chapter Three

They settled in the living room where he entertained guests in front of the large stone fireplace. He'd recently had it redone so the hearth looked like the mouth of a dragon. One of the large tin soldiers tended the fire. The black hat shone in the light since he had painted this one. However, Krampus could see where he'd missed a few spots on the red coat that needed to be touched up. The scruff of the white beard seemed to be longer than he remembered. The tin soldier turned, saluted, and waddled out of the room. Another came in carrying a tray filled with drinks. The stranger took one and sat back in the chair. A smirk spread on his lips. Behind those thin lips, he caught the glimpse of thin, razor-sharp teeth.

"This is very good. Do you make it on your estate?" he asked Krampus.

"No. It's a gift from one of the other Incarnations. We trade between one another." Krampus stood behind one of the chairs and felt the tension rising in the air. Yeti and Cornelius tried to keep their emotions under control. The Ghost of Christmas Present kept wrapping and unwrapping the cloth the stranger had given him around his hands.

"Must be nice to be able to actually socialize with the other Incarnations. I don't find many to be nice on my end of things, but I've never really been into the Christmas Spirit and all that. 'Bah, humbug,' is what I have to say." He set the cider down as Emerald walked into the room. His gaze went from Krampus to her and his smile widened. "My, what a lovely wife you have, Krampus."

Krampus shook his head to tell her she didn't need to be with them. She smiled. "Thank you. I thought you might like some refreshments. Is there anything else you need?" Her eyes were still red from crying, but she seemed better.

"No, that'll be fine. Thank you. Close the door on your way out," Krampus told her. She left the room and closed the doors. He got into the face of his guest but held back his power. "If you even so much as bat another eyelash at my wife, I promise you won't be leaving here."

The man didn't blink. "If you hurt me, then you won't find Permission. Your wife is lovely despite the hooves, but the horns do give her a little something extra. And those breasts." He dragged his tongue across his thin lips.

Krampus gnashed his teeth at the visitor. "Fine. Where is she?"

"He's not going to tell us," Yeti said in a grim voice. "He's a Scrooge. I should've seen it before. They're good at hiding. They're our natural enemies."

The man touched his nose. "Very good. I was wondering when you'd get it. Score one for the Ghost of Christmas Yet to Come."

"I thought the story was that the three ghosts appeared to Scrooge to show him how bad his life had been up until that point. You show him the error of his ways. In the morning, he wakes up a changed man and casts off the chains of his sins." Krampus thought about the Incarnations in the room that made up the Christmas story he knew about from the human world and wondered how the story truly is. It seemed obvious they were older than the actual written tale that Dickens had set to paper.

"That's how the human author wrote the story as we told it to him, but it's not exactly right. We are far older than the tale told in the human realm. I'm sure you realize that with how you are portrayed in the mortal world. Half demon/half goat who preys on naughty children, stealing them away in the night back to his lair where he cooks and eats them," Cornelius said to him.

"Yeah, sounds about right," Krampus said to him and looked at the Scrooge. "Where is their companion?"

Scrooge crossed his legs and relaxed now he had all the attention. Krampus decided the sooner this character got out of his house, the better. He made him uneasy and that was very hard to do considering he had seen and done a few things over the years. "How about we set the parameters of our negotiation?"

"No negotiations. Where's Persimmon? What have you done to her?" Cornelius asked. Yeti had to hold him back once more.

"I'll tell you that she's safe. Lovely lady didn't know what hit her until she woke up tied to my bed," Scrooge grinned. "She tastes so sweet -- like her namesake." He licked his lips again. "Just like honey."

This time it was Yeti who nearly tackled him, but Krampus grabbed him instead. "This is getting a bit old. Clearly, you want your woman back. He wants something in return for getting her back. What the hell do you want, Scrooge?"

Scrooge sipped at his cider. "You are absolutely correct. This $is@ getting a bit old. I came here with a good faith offer. We -- the other Scrooges -- want you to leave us be this year so we can spread our kind of cheer among the mortals. We have a right to speak or influence the humans as much as you do. Plus, we want some of the perks that you have." He reached into his pocket and pulled out a list.

Krampus snatched it from his hand and glanced

over it. "None of these are outrageous, but I don't think you had to kidnap their companion."

"What are your demands?" Yeti asked.

Krampus handed him the list. Yeti started laughing. "You want to spend some time with Persimmon? Not on your life."

"She's ours!" Cornelius protested.

"This is where I beg to differ. She isn't yours. She is her own person and just because she falls into her little triad of goodness doesn't mean that's what she wants," Scrooge said to them.

Krampus looked between them and something clicked. "Yeti and Cornelius, look over the list and see if you can come to some compromise to some of these things." He grabbed Scrooge up and hauled him into his study. Scrooge's human disguise wavered when Krampus let him go. The creature underneath had a dark, thin body, but there was also some humanness to him.

"That was uncalled for. I told you if we were going to work things out, then I wasn't going to be manhandled."

"I pulled you out of there so I could talk to you without the others around. Tell me straight, did Persimmon send you here?"

Scrooge sagged. "Is it that obvious? Then again, I thought the others would catch on. They're taking it harder than she assumed they would." He leaned back against the wall. Some of the dark disguise fell away and Krampus felt a little more at ease with him.

"Is she really tied to your bed?"

"No. She's shopping in the mortal world. I gave her a medallion, so it keeps her from their view. Persimmon is an amazing woman. She cares for them, but we're in love. They wouldn't understand that because of what I am and what she is. Hell, the others don't believe it either. It goes against our very nature, but her companions think they can rule her every move. If they knew…" Scrooge ran his fingers through his red hair and looked up at him with sad eyes.

"It's more than that. Both of them are in love with her. I'm not sure if it's their station or if it's how they feel. It's more than being possessive. They truly love her and are distressed she hasn't returned. Look at how they attacked you. Although you did provoke them."

"I was playing a part. Persimmon said to put it on a little thick to see how they would react. I guess I went a little too far. At least it shows that they do care for her. She doesn't know how to tell them she's in love with me. We have to meet secretly because the other Scrooges frown upon our love." He hung his head in his hands and his shoulders slumped forward. He reminded Krampus of a man in the throes of his first love.

"It sounds like you've gotten yourself into a pickle, but you don't need me for anything."

"But we do. You're an advocate for other Incarnations. They were right about that. You have to help us. I saw how much you love your woman. You can't tell me that others haven't objected to you marrying, given your position and what you represent?"

Krampus rolled his eyes. "Don't make this about me. The best thing for us to do is to go find your girl, bring her back here, and then the four of you hash something out. No more of this fucked-up nonsense about her being kidnapped and you making ransom demands. Why don't you take me to her?"

"You're going to leave those two here? Won't

that be a bad idea?"

Krampus waved his hand. "I'm not worried about them. The gingers and my toy soldiers will make sure they don't get into trouble."

Scrooge stood up, and he once again looked like the overdressed Englishman who'd showed up at his doorstep. "Aren't you going to stand out in the human world if you go looking like that?"

"What wrong with what I'm wearing? Short pants and a vest are rather fashionable. Wearing long pants is not feasible when I'm in the forge and I rather like the vests." He tugged on the end of the vest to pull it down some. His talons caught on the chain of his pocket watch that Emerald had given him for his wedding. He smiled when he thought about his wife. Their marriage had been a grand affair with all the Incarnations they were friends with and Nyx officiating over the ceremony. Even his arch nemesis, the Claus, had come with his wife, and they had a truce for the day. Krampus was surprised when Cupid and Dallas -- the bull shifter he had a fling with -- attended too. They each promised to come back when they could spend some time together.

"You won't blend in with the mortals in the mall. They'll figure out that you're... not one of them. Don't you have a disguise?"

"Ahh... Wait here." Krampus walked out of the room and into the foyer. The smell of gingerbread permeated the kitchen as he found Emerald cutting out a gingerbread man and laying it on the large cookie sheet to bake once the other pan came out of the oven. It was an arduous process to make them because she could only cook two at a time since the cookies were two feet tall and they cooked at a higher temperature because they weren't your ordinary gingerbread men.

Emerald met his gaze. "Did you need something else, Master Krampus?"

He put his hands up. "Whoa! Hey, I don't want to be making any more waves. I'm sorry for whatever I did."

She crossed her arms over her chest as a strand of her hair fell into her face. She tried to blow it away, but after several tries Krampus brushed it out of the way for her.

"You don't have to treat me like I'm some servant when we have guests. You might've hired me to be your cook and housekeeper when we first met, but I'm not your maid anymore."

He pulled her close to him as his heart melted. "I wasn't trying to treat you as my servant, Em. Those clowns came bursting in here expecting me to help them and then this Scrooge fella was looking at you funny. I didn't want to put you in any danger, that's all."

"I can hold my own." Her voice rose with the stubbornness he loved.

"I know you can, but not with other Incarnations. They all have different powers than I do. I'm stronger here because this is my domain, but even I don't know what they can do. I've never met them before. Can't you forgive me for not wanting to see you get hurt?" He lifted her chin and kissed her lightly. Krampus put a little bit of his cold power in the gesture so it would chill her. She deepened the kiss and finally broke it off with a moan and let out a cloud of breath.

She rested her forehead against his chest as she shook in his arms. This wasn't like the woman he knew. Something still bothered her. "It's fine. I'm sorry. I shouldn't have overreacted." Emerald turned away from him and sniffled. He caught her wrist.

"Hey, what's the matter?"

"Nothing. Forget it."

"It's not nothing. Em --"

"Um… Krampus. Sorry to interrupt, but if we are going, then we have to go now so we don't miss her." Scrooge popped into the kitchen.

He gritted his teeth since he had gotten sidetracked. "I'll be right there. I'm sorry, Em. I have to go."

She pulled away and her face went blank. "Don't worry about it. Go and help them. I'm used to it." She went back to putting the finishing touches on the cooled gingers.

Krampus left the kitchen, grabbed his cloak in the foyer, and went back to Scrooge who met him there. He threw the cloak over his shoulders and pulled the hood over his face. "The humans won't even see me. If they do, it won't register in their memory. The cloak makes me invisible in the human world. I show myself when I want to. Lead the way."

Chapter Four

They appeared in the middle of a shopping place crowded with humans and their children. Some of the little children ran past them. He loved the pudgy ones who didn't want to listen to their parents and were unredeemable. Those were the ones who made the best meat pies. His stomach growled loudly as another one bumped into him. The little boy must have been approaching his teen years, but he still had the roundness of a child not quite yet turned into a man. His head was buried in his cell phone with white wires coming from his ears as he listened to music so loud Krampus could hear it. The boy tried to walk through him, but then realized something was in his way. He mumbled something, but when he couldn't get past the roadblock, he looked up. Krampus didn't hide his appearance from him. The boy's expression went from one of not caring to true horror as it reached his brain at what he was looking at.

"Excuse me, sir," the kid blubbered.

"That's right. Take your face out of your phone the next time you decide to run into someone so you can see what's going on around you. Pay more attention to the world, young Timothy, or you might find one of my bells on your Christmas tree. Once it rings, I come calling and you become dinner. Understand?" Krampus flicked his tongue over Timothy's cheek.

"Eek." Timothy dropped his phone and ran along.

Krampus chuckled.

"Was that necessary?" Scrooge asked.

"Why not? He needed someone to put a bit of fear into him. Why not let it be me? If not, I'm sure he'd end up on my list. He's already been naughty enough that the Claus no longer considers him to be of any use. Where is Persimmon among the sea of humans? I'd rather not spend much time among them. They make me hungry."

"Follow me." Scrooge wove through the throng of shoppers as they went into store upon store and came out with bags on their arms. Mothers yelling at children. Fathers who lost sight of their kids. Then there were a few couples he could see were truly in love with one another, and it made him think of Emerald. Something was off about her today. Come to think about it, she had been a little more withdrawn in their normal lives for the last couple of weeks. Although she'd been a hellion in the sack, sometimes tiring him out, which was unusual.

They stopped outside a store that carried all different kinds of lotions, candles, shampoos, and other smelly things humans used on their bodies or in their dwellings. Scrooge went inside, leaving Krampus to mingle. He picked up a few things that smelled like vanilla and thought Emerald might appreciate them. He slipped a few candles and other products into the pockets inside of his cloak, feeling the extra weight. Standing on one of the tabletop displays was a stuffed reindeer toy. It reminded him of the Claus, but he pushed past his dislike and swiped that as well. Scrooge came back over. He was paler than normal.

"She's not here. This is where she should be. I don't understand."

"What is it that females do? Is she in the bathroom? Or maybe she went to another store and found something else? Clothes. Shoes. Something sparkly. Maybe she was hungry."

"No. The medallion I gave her kept her and I

linked so I would know where to find her."

Krampus looked around the store. Something gold caught his attention by a basket of hand soaps. He walked over to it, brushing past a woman who kept spraying different types of scents on her arm. As she sprayed one that reminded him of a dead skunk mixed with burnt cedar, it made him sneeze.

"Bless you," the woman said.

"Thank you," Krampus replied.

The woman looked over and her smile turned to terror. Her eyes grew wide and she staggered back into a display of candles and soaps. The items toppled to the floor and several of the assistants rushed to help her up. Krampus swiped the gold chain with the medallion on it, along with a few of the smaller soaps. The necklace was covered in blood. He offered his hand to the woman, but she screamed again.

"What is it? Are you having a heart attack?" the saleswoman asked.

The customer shook her head and pointed at Krampus, but no one else could see him. "Don't you see it? The demon dressed in a plaid vest and red pants. H-he has a pocket watch."

"I think she's hallucinating. Call an ambulance," a salesman yelled.

"You just had to make a scene, didn't you?" Scrooge asked him.

He shrugged. "All I said was thanks." He held up the necklace. "This what you're looking for?"

Scrooge grabbed the necklace and the expression on his face darkened. "This isn't good."

"Could something have happened to her? Do you have any enemies?"

"No. I mean the others know about our relationship. They don't approve of it, but they wouldn't hurt Permission. We don't get along, but that's the nature of our holiday interactions. We go back and forth with it, but we don't harm one another. We've pulled pranks. We all try to influence humans to go our way. Sometimes we get the same ones, but other times we have different ones. I don't think it would be one of the other Scrooges."

"Are you sure about that?" Krampus asked. He pulled his cloak a little closer around him as he kept getting side looks from the humans in the store. His nose twitched again, and he suppressed the urge to sneeze. They had taken the hysterical woman out so the doctors could work on her. Sales associates picked up the scattered items. He pulled Scrooge back into a corner so they were out of the way.

Scrooge clutched the medallion and shook his head. "I-I don't know."

"There's only one way to find out. Let's go back to your place and see if there's anything there."

"Well, I don't really have a place. We have a shared space."

"Where can you go? When can you go to the head of your order and ask around?" Krampus grumbled. He eyed a gold candle and swiped that as well for Emerald.

"Don't you think they're going to notice you've been pilfering goods from their shelves?"

"Not really. Let's go."

Scrooge put out his hand and Krampus took it. They whooshed away and a feeling of disinterest swept over him as though nothing about the holiday season excited him. He realized it was the power that Scrooge gave off. As they came back into view, two other Scrooges rushed past him trailing a roll of wrapping paper. The place smelled like spoiled eggnog and dried balsam. Red and green lights blinked, strung up haphazardly on the walls. One set looked to be in the shape of a tree. Wrapped presents were scattered around the room. Another Scrooge dashed by them, naked, as they listened to slow versions of Jingle Bells on a gramophone, a naked angel ornament on the horn.

"I thought you all hated Christmas? This doesn't look like that you do."

Scrooge scratched his head. "We don't $hate@ it. At least the youngest of us don't. The older ones don't really enjoy it. They're stuffed shirts. This place is where we stay to see if we're going to make it. If not, then we return to our human lives. I've been here twenty years, and I know the others are getting ready to find a permanent place for me. If I don't pass my final test, then they send me back to become human again. I don't want to go back to all that. It'd be nice not to have to deal with these idiots. I don't hate Christmas. I find this time of year to be refreshing. However, look at what Christmas has become. It's all about the merchandise. People buy one another's happiness. The spirit of the season has gone out of the holiday. We were created because of this."

"Okay. Good to know. Where would Persimmon be?"

Another Scrooge ran past them. His Scrooge grabbed his colleague. "Dude, you see a chick come in here? Long red hair carrying some bags."

The other man glanced around as his eyes deglazed. "No, bro."

Krampus shook his head. $These Incarnations are nothing more than frat boys.@ He walked around the room and ducked under some low-hanging holly boughs. Shoved in the corner was more crumpled wrapping paper stuffed between some half-crushed boxes of presents. Something hit him besides the scent of stale beer and ripe old vomit; he caught the overwhelming aroma of vanilla and citrus along with the same blood scent he had from the cloth Scrooge gave him. He followed his nose and swiped the mess away that was shoved in front of a closet door he hadn't realized was there. Krampus opened it and discovered a woman tied up in ropes of blinking Christmas lights with a ball gag in her mouth. Her eyes grew wide when she saw him. Persimmon fidgeted to get out of the closet.

"Hey. Whoa, it's okay. I'm not going to hurt you."

She kept gesturing with her head and her eyes widened. She screamed through the gag as he got closer. Krampus understood his appearance could be shocking, but this woman was having a downright fit. He raised his hands again.

"Calm down. I'm not going to --" Then something hard came down on the side of his head and he went down like a Christmas angel toppled off the top of a Christmas tree.

Chapter Five

The back of Krampus's head throbbed where someone had clobbered him. He opened his eyes. The green and red flashing Christmas lights gave him a headache that was enough to make his teeth hurt. Or that could have been from the knot next to his horns. Someone snapped their fingers in front of his face. He focused back on them and tried to move. His hands were tied behind his back. He struggled against his bonds but found he couldn't break them.

"Hey, Krampus, over here."

A bright flash went off in his face that blinded him temporarily. Once the stars disappeared from his eyes, he saw the woman from the closet and Scrooge kissing one another while the female snapped a picture of the two of them. "This is going to be so great! None of the others are going to believe that we pulled this off. And I couldn't have done it without you, Sugar Muffin."

"I think I just threw up a little bit in my mouth." Krampus grumbled as he tried to get free from his restraints.

"That won't work. Those manacles are specifically made so you won't get out of them." Scrooge untangled himself from Persimmon and walked over to Krampus.

"We'll see about that. Scrooge, what the hell is going on here? I found Persimmon stuffed in the closet, and then you hit me over the head. Free me and we'll call it a day," Krampus said to them. He tried the restraints again and found that the magic holding them was strong and he couldn't break them. However, he slowly called upon his power of cold and pulled it into his hands. His fingertips tingled. He concentrated his magic into the metal of the cuffs and felt them getting colder around his wrists. It would only be a few minutes before he snapped them.

"Dude! You did it." Another Scrooge appeared next to him.

"Told you I could. Does that mean I'm in?"

Another slim figure who barely looked human appeared out of the shadows. "Well done, my boy. No one has ever been able to snag Krampus. This is a momentous occasion. You have earned your place among us, Scrooge #1313. Ghost of Christmas Past, you have also done well and proven you are willing to help us even when it goes against your being."

"Capturing me was just a hazing ritual to make sure that he got into your club?" Krampus asked. The metal on his wrists was cold enough his flesh was nearly numb even through his pelt. He twisted his wrists again and felt the metal give. Almost there and he would be able to break them. He put a little bit oomph behind his concentration while he tried to tune out all the others who were high-fiving one another. He rolled his eyes and thought about getting back to Emerald and letting the others know about their precious Persimmon.

"You're not going anywhere," the head Scrooge said to him. "You're going to stay here while we take over your spot. We can use your power to --"

"Yeah, I don't think so. All this is a load of bullshit." Krampus snapped the manacles and stood up. The Scrooges backed away. Persimmon took another picture of him. He growled, flung his cloak around her and held her to him. Cold enveloped him as he moved with her through the realms back to his place. He faltered a bit using so much magic to get the chains off. It had taken a lot out of him, along with the bump on the head as his body tried to heal it.

"What the hell?" Persimmon said to him as she stepped away.

Krampus grabbed the wall to keep himself upright and to use his magic over the house, creating a no-fly zone so no one could come in or out. Persimmon dashed toward the door, but he caught her. "I don't think so, sweetheart. Hey, guys, guess who I found."

Her expression fell. "No. You can't make me go back with them. You don't understand what it's like. They smother me. They expect me to fall in line. They keep going on and on about loving me and..." She shivered. "I just can't. It's not who I am."

"Then why did you agree to take the office?"

"I didn't have much of a choice. The woman who had it before me told me it was an opportunity of a lifetime. I needed to get out of a bad situation. I had no idea what I was stepping into."

"Those two men love you. They want to make you happy. If you set some ground rules with them --"

"I've tried. And then I met Scrooge. He makes my heart skip a few beats. He loves me."

"He used you to get to me. Think about it."

Yeti and Cornelius came to the door and nearly came in at the same time. Their dark expressions lightened when they saw her.

"Simmi." Yeti took her into his arms and pressed her into his chest.

Persimmon looked at him with a panic-stricken expression. He laughed. He wasn't going to get into the middle of this one. "You guys need to have a serious talk with your companion. This whole disappearance was a ruse to capture me for some initiation that Scrooge was part of. Apparently, if they were able to kidnap me, then her Scrooge would become one of them permanently. They thought they could hold me, but their restraints didn't work out too well."

Cornelius's expression dropped. "Simmi, how could you do that? How could you run off with him? Don't you know how worried we were about you? We came here to have Krampus look for you."

"I never told you to do that. I love Scrooge and he loves me."

"We love you, too," Yeti proclaimed.

"You smother me. All the time you want to know where I'm going and what I'm doing. You never let me get a chance to do something alone. I get we have to do certain things because of what we are, but in the meantime, I need you to step off. Scrooge listens to me. You don't."

Cornelius took her hands and kissed them. "We love you. I'd do anything for you. If you need space, we can work it out. Don't say you're going to run away with Scrooge. You'd slowly lose who you are and become one of them. It's happened before to several others in your position. If we seem a little suffocating at times, that's the reason why. We don't want to lose you. Please, don't let him pull you away from us. You're not like so many of the others. We can change."

"Corny is right. We can do better." Yeti took her other hand. "Please give us another chance. I don't want to see your heart shrivel and you become one of those husks that the Scrooges have become."

Persimmon looked over at Krampus. Her expression became troubled, and she smiled. Her eyes were damp as she looked back over to them. "After the Christmas season, we need to discuss some changes. I won't make any waves until then. We all need to figure something out. I don't want to become a husk."

Krampus felt something powerful pounding on the barrier around his house. A gingerbread man burst into the room. "Master, there is an army of shadow sticks outside. They are bombarding the house with cannonball Christmas ornaments."

The Ghost of Christmas Past looked at him. "This is because of me. Scrooge wants me back. Let me talk to him."

He shook his head. "No. This is about them getting back at me for escaping. They want you as a prize for stealing you away from the others. Don't give them the satisfaction. Believe me, I have enough backup to take them."

"Is there anything we can do to help?" Yeti asked as he slipped his hood over his face. Once he did, the dark touch of his power came back. Krampus ignored it this time.

"You three go upstairs and man one of the turrets. Berman here will show you the way up there. If you got any attack magic up your sleeve, then it would be a good thing to have," Krampus told them. The gingerbread man waved his arm for the others to follow him.

Once they left the room, Emerald came in with a panicked look in her eye. "What's going on? All these things are outside with cannons and riding skeleton reindeer."

Krampus touched her face. "The Scrooges kidnapped me and convinced Persimmon to help them. They want her back, and they figure they can take my seat of power. That's not going to happen. I want you to go upstairs into the closet, press the rock that looks like Santa's jolly ass, and wait in the room for me there."

"I can help you."

"Please, Em. Don't fight me on this. I know you can take care of yourself, but if they get in here, I don't want them taking you away while I'm fighting them off. I don't know what would happen if I lost you."

She kissed him as another explosion rocked the castle. "Okay." She left the room and went upstairs.

Without her being a distraction, Krampus went into the foyer and looked out of the window. It was true. Cannons were firing at the castle. They had an army of Scrooges riding reindeer skeleton. He couldn't count how many there were, but he figured at least a thousand out there. "They want a fight. They're going to get it."

Already his tin soldiers and gingerbread men were mustering as they waited for his orders. He walked back into the armory where the tin soldiers made their home. They all stopped and saluted. "What are your orders, Master?" A faded paint job on the soldier and his lack of one eye showed he was the general in the bunch. Krampus couldn't recall his name. Behind them were the nutcrackers. In the back pantry, lines of gingerbread men were ready to do battle.

"I want ten of your best soldiers upstairs guarding the door to my bedroom. My wife is isolated up there. I don't want anyone or anything coming in to get her. The rest of you, they can only come at us from the front gate and the southwest. Unless they can fly or climb, they can't get to any other parts of the castle. It's time we take them down. How many of you are hungry?"

A unanimous yell came from all his creatures.

"Then take no prisoners and feast well."

Chapter Six

Krampus stood outside the house in front of the lines of tin toy soldiers, carnivorous nutcrackers, and the gingers who all feasted on one another when they got a little bored. He held out his hand and summoned the magic that came with his office and a sharp blade of ice grew in his hands. Stuffed into the waist pouch at his side was an arsenal of bells he had turned into bombs. He glanced up at the sky and saw the darkening of the night. He pulled out one of the bells, held it in his hand, and thought about Nyx. Krampus needed some help and he was going to use all his friends to get it too. The army of Scrooges grew larger by the minute. He needed reinforcements. A cold breeze stirred his pelt as he summoned the snow to blind his enemies. The cannons continued to lob ornament balls. The bell in his hand grew colder and lighter.

He brought the bell to his lips that had turned mostly to ice and whispered against it. "Call the others, I need assistance. Bring the night and the frost." He threw the bell up into the air and watched as it was carried upward by the wind. All he had to do was wait for the others to arrive. The redheaded Scrooge who was after Persimmon raised his hand and the cannon fire ceased. He walked up to the line of no-man's-land between them and cupped his hands together to yell across.

"Give up now, Krampus. Give us the girl. If you do that, then all of this goes away," he shouted.

"Not going to happen. You can't have me or her. Don't think that you're going to take my place here or use my power. This is my realm. You have no foothold here." Krampus gathered the cold around him. He stomped his foot and a wave of frigidness swelled out. It rolled the ground as the frost heave picked up speed. When it reached the frontlines of the army, it was four feet tall and it knocked out the first two lines of the soldiers and downed the cavalry. He raised his sword and sliced the air with it -- the sign for his men to charge. The gingerbread went forward. After them were the nutcrackers and then the tin toy soldiers. They raced toward the Scrooges as he sent another wave of cold. Krampus charged with the tin soldiers. He was able to break into the upheaval and take advantage of the Scrooges. He sliced a few of them down before they reoriented, and he found himself in the thick of things.

They swarmed him from all sides. The tin soldiers and the nutcrackers circled around him in a protective barrier to keep him safe. Krampus collected more magic and brought the blinding snow. He could see through it and he made sure to put the cold behind it. He couldn't feel it, but the Scrooges were shivering. A great explosion sounded. The next thing he knew, he was flying backward through the air and sliding across the frozen ground. It took him a moment to get his bearings. He stood up and looked down where he saw colored glass in his pelt. He moved his arms and felt the pain. A large piece of purple glass stuck out of his shoulder. He gritted his teeth and pulled it out. The tin soldiers were scattered in pieces around him. He heard a yell and saw Scrooge twirling something in his hand above his head. A leather sling with something loaded in the pocket aimed at Krampus. The ornament bomb landed a few feet from him. Another slice of agony hit him across his mid-section. He touched his belt and came away with blood. This time he had been seriously hurt. He grunted and tried to pull his magic to him to heal. The whiteout lessened, and he could feel the stitching of his wound as the cold flashed through his body.

The assault upon the castle continued, but he was losing ground. His soldiers were falling to the ornament bombs and their whips of Christmas lights. He continued to swipe with his sword and take out the other Scrooges coming at him. His meager army was depleting faster than he liked. He reached into his bag and pulled out a couple of bells. He threw them into the advancing enemy. They exploded, sending metal shrapnel. The sound when it hit forced everyone to their knees. He took the moment to regroup, but his troops were scattered around the battlefield.

The Scrooges advanced. His remaining troops surrounded him to keep him safe. But the enemy kept coming. The wind kicked up and the white-out grew darker. The flakes from the storm grew crisper with the hardness of metal.

"Heard you needed some help." A husky voice next to him said.

When he looked over, Nyx stood dressed in a silver-and-gold battle dress of armor with her black skin a stark contract against the silver. Next to her was a shorter man with pale white skin. His blue Mohawk was braided down his back. He wore a chain mail shirt made of hardened frost and had a short sword in hand.

"Am I glad to see you two!" Krampus smiled.

"Emerald gave us the quick rundown of what's going on and then Nyx told me about the Christmas Spirits. I've come across these Scrooges before. They are a pain in the ass," Jack Frost replied. He ran his blue nails over his shirt and the design changed.

"I appreciate you coming." Krampus winced as another ornament bomb exploded next to them.

Nyx sighed. "This has gone on long enough. Krampus, would you pull back your storm a bit, please?"

Krampus reined in his magic. Nyx touched her shoulder and pulled out a comet shooting across her flesh. It glowed orange and yellow in her hand and was the size of an orange. She threw it in the direction of the Scrooge army.

"Shield your eyes," she instructed them.

Krampus turned around and shut his eyes. Even with them closed, he could see the glow of the comet and feel the blazing heat it released when it hit the ground. The force of the explosion rocked him, but Nyx and Jack remained at his side. When the heat subsided, he turned to examine the destruction. Those Scrooges who hadn't been injured or killed were slowly retreating from the devastation.

"Don't think this means we are done with you, Krampus," Scrooge, who had originally shown up, shouted to him.

"Oh, it means you $are@ done with him and Persimmon," Nyx said to him. "Come after them again, and I'll make sure your entire Scrooge Incarnation is wiped out ,and there won't be any more Scrooges."

He balked. "Y-you can't do that."

Nyx grinned. "Try me. You piss me off enough, I can make your existences a living hell. You forget who you are talking to. I control the night and the vast expanse of the universe you exist in. I'm not just the Incarnation of Night. Planets, stars, and galaxies make up my entire being. Don't tell me I can't do it."

"Yeah, and I'll make sure to freeze all your dicks so they shrivel up and you can't use them anymore," Jack Frost added.

The leader limped over to the other Scrooge and

put a hand on his shoulder. He quickly shook his head and raised his hand. "Peace. We don't wish any harm to come to our brethren. We will never darken Krampus's doorstep or pursue the Ghost of Christmas Past again." He tugged on Scrooge's arm until they faded away.

"Thanks for that," Krampus said to the both of them.

Jack kissed him with a little tongue. His fingers slid over Krampus's pelt and cupped his cock through his pants. "Anytime. I've missed you."

"Jack. Leave Krampus be. I'm sure he wants to go check on Emerald." Nyx brushed her lips across his cheek. "Once this is settled we both want to have a night with both of you. Sound good?" She nibbled on his ear.

"Works for me. I'll give you a shout. Thanks again." Krampus headed back to the house, hoping Emerald was okay.

Chapter Seven

Krampus rushed into the house to find Emerald in the kitchen trying to help mend some of the shattered gingerbread men. Many of them were in pieces and beyond repair. The nutcrackers and the tin soldiers who had survived were bringing in the pieces of the other soldiers to either be melted down or repaired. He slipped his arms around Emerald and nuzzled her neck, relieved she was okay.

"You're safe." Emerald turned around in his arms and pressed herself against him. She sobbed into his pelt.

He ran his hands down her back to comfort her, then pulled way. "It's okay. I'm okay. Why did you come out of the safe room? You could've been hurt."

"Nyx and Jack told me it was okay to come out. They said they were going to help."

He nodded and wiped the tears away from her eyes only to see the love she had for him. "It's all taken care of. Don't worry about it. Where are Yeti and the others?"

"In your study, I think."

"I'll be back." Krampus left the kitchen and went into the study to find the others snuggling together on the couch. Persimmon sat in the middle. He watched them for a moment, and when they started kissing one another, he coughed. Persimmon jumped, and he caught the blush on her cheeks. "Sorry to interrupt, but I wanted to check on you now that the Scrooges have gone. It seems like you're working things out."

"Yes, we've been talking." Permission got up and walked over to him. Yeti and Cornelius stood behind her. "I wanted to thank you for everything that you did. We still have some things to sort out, but I think it'll be fine."

Cornelius grabbed Krampus's hand. "Thank you so much. We're indebted to you."

"I'm glad it's all good. Let me know how it goes," Krampus told them.

Persimmon took the other spirits' hands and together they faded away in a glow of red and green, leaving behind a smell of evergreen and vanilla. Once they had left, Krampus let out a sigh of relief now he had his house back. He headed back into the kitchen as his stomach growled. Using so much of his magic left him famished. He went into the pantry and pulled down one of his human sausages from his stores he made when he had the chance. He tore a hunk out of it and found Emerald sitting at the table with a line of tin soldiers waiting for her to try and patch them up. He felt somewhat bad for them, but they had done everything they were created for. Watching how Emerald cared for the soldiers made him have a pang of loneliness. She was great with all of them.

He set the sausage down and slid his hands over her shoulders and massaged them. She moaned as he found the normal spots on her that knotted. "All right, boys. Take those who can be fixed back to the barracks. Those of you who are able, put all the pieces of those too badly damaged in the forge so I can start rebuilding your numbers. Tell the same to the nutcrackers and the gingers."

"Yes, Master." The tin soldier saluted and shuffled off as the others followed.

"Why did you do that?" Emerald asked.

"Because I wanted to spend some time alone with my lovely wife." He snuggled her neck and flicked his tongue over her flesh, tasting the sweetness of it. "The battle has me hungry for everything, especially you, knowing you're okay. And some sweet, pudgy children. I think some of the human stock have some out back."

"Can we not talk about you eating people right now?" Emerald moved away from him.

Krampus looked at her with a confused look. She understood he had a craving for human flesh and mostly he got it from the human stock he raised on the land. They weren't like the regular humans he kidnapped from Earth. Those were special. The ones on the farm were nothing more than overfed cows with hardly any intelligence. He wanted -- no, $needed@ -- to give in to the hungers raging inside him. His wife was not making it easy for him. He closed his eyes and wrangled his emotions so he could talk to his wife and figure out what was going on with her.

"Em, is there something you're not telling me? You know I eat human meat. We came to an agreement about it. You've been with me long enough to know that this time of year makes me hungrier for long pig and hornier than the Easter bunny on Easter."

"I know. It's… forget about it." She rushed behind the counter again and began cleaning up the damage from the barrage. He took her hands while she picked up pieces of broken pottery and set the pieces back on the counter.

"I'm not going to forget it. Something is bothering you and I don't understand why you don't want to tell me. You've always been frank with me. Sometimes too much so. I love that fire in you."

"You always go on about eating children and people. Sometimes it gets to me and it makes me wonder if you would eat $any@ children."

He eyed her, trying to figure out what she meant. "You're talking in circles. I only eat the naughty ones I catch in the human world who are irredeemable or from the human stock that I farm." He ran his fingers down her cheek. She turned her face into his palm and kissed the inside of it. Something in her seemed to relax when he said that. "Love, please tell me what's the matter. What are you afraid of?"

She took his hand and guided it down to her stomach. She held it there and he still didn't understand what she was trying to get at. Her eyes widened and crested with tears. Her lip quivered. Then it dawned on Krampus. A swell of joy went through him. "You're pregnant?"

Emerald nodded. "Are you happy?"

"Happy?" He picked her up and spun her around. "Of course I'm happy."

His wife squealed, and he put her down. He captured her lips in a hungry kiss and pressed against her. His teeth scraped her bottom lip until Emerald pulled away.

"Are you okay?" he asked.

"I'm fine. I just need you." Her fingers walked down his pants and cupped his cock.

"Won't that hurt the baby? I mean… we can get a bit rough."

She shook her head and squeezed his dick. "Not at all."

"How could you think I would want to eat our baby?"

Emerald shrugged. "I don't know. I should've known the answer, but my sight has been obscured since I've gotten pregnant. I've been a little out of my head with worry, and you've been so focused on getting ready for the holidays. All the talk about human meat… it just… I don't know. It's a bit irrational."

He wiped the tears from her eyes. "It's not irrational. I understand. I would never hurt you or any of our children."

"I know you wouldn't. Which is why I know it's crazy."

Krampus scooped her up and carried her back up to their bedroom. The joy in his heart knowing he was going to be a father overwhelmed him. He needed to show his wife how much he needed her in his life and how happy the news made him.

Krampus set her down before the bed. She reached for him, but he stepped away and walked behind her. She struggled to turn, but he tugged on the zipper and undid the intricate ties that held her garment on. Krampus pushed the shoulder down and kissed the bend in her neck as his hands roamed under the cloth and over her breasts. The nipples hardened against his palms. He nibbled her flesh, biting her harder until she moaned just the way he liked it. Emerald slipped her arm around his neck holding him to her. She arched her back when he nipped a tender spot on her throat. Her encouragement and his need for her made him drag his canines over the skin until he tasted her blood. His hunger overwhelmed him when he tasted her blood. Her nails dug through his pelt and into his flesh. Her breathing increased.

Krampus could feel the beast rising in him. He didn't think he could contain it. He spun her around, twined his hands through her hair, and mashed his lips against hers. Emerald tried to keep up with him. He sucked on her bottom lip until he tasted more blood. Krampus couldn't hold back anymore. He raked his fingers down her back. She shivered in his arms. He shredded the rest of her dress and her undergarments until she was naked.

Emerald breathed hard with blood on her lips. He could smell her desire. Her pale skin was flushed. He pushed her down onto the bed and knelt before her as he opened her legs. Her soft red patch of curls glistened with her desire. He slid his palms over her thighs. Krampus glanced up and saw the hunger shining in her eyes. He flicked out his forked tongue and laved her clit. Emerald pushed against him as he sucked on her hard bump. Her breathing intensified. He looked up and saw her bouncing breasts, which stirred his craving even more. Krampus drew Emerald to the brink, stopping only when she uttered her little pleasure sounds that drove him wild, letting him know she was about to come.

"Please, Clo," she murmured.

Krampus took one of her firm nipples into his mouth, sucking on it. She reached for him, but he batted her hands away. He needed her. He slipped his thumb along her inner thigh, dragging the talon along her sweet flesh. Krampus entered her with his finger, careful to only bring her pleasure and not harm her with his sharp claws. The rhythm increased as she tried to use his fingers to bring her to fulfillment. But Krampus pulled out of her pussy, leaving her whimpering. He sucked on his finger, enjoying the spice.

"Why are you torturing me?"

"Who said anything about torture? I'm just getting ready to fuck you. I'm having a hard time controlling my hunger. I don't mean to be so rough." He sucked in her other breast and teased the nipple with his tongue. He dragged his teeth over it and that made her jump when his teeth caught the firm bud.

"Harder. Please. I need you."

Krampus couldn't deny her. He stripped and

stroked his erect cock, hardening it even more. Emerald licked her lips and opened her legs wider, only egging him on. He couldn't wait any longer and grabbed her around the waist. He lifted her up and drove into her wet pussy. Emerald wrapped her legs around his waist as he impaled her. She grabbed his horns and ran her hands over them as if working his cock. The light touch sent chills through him. Krampus lost it and backed her into a wall. He increased their rhythm with her weight bouncing against him. He felt the warmth of her tongue run along one of his horns. Krampus stumbled and brought her back over to the bed. He lost his balance as they still continued to make love.

Emerald moved with him until Krampus felt himself giving in to the ecstasy. He clenched his teeth as his wife climaxed. Her scream drove him over the edge. He kept pumping into her until he collapsed on top of her. His wife snuggled up next to him and ran her fingers through his pelt. "That was wonderful."

"You say that all the time."

"But I mean it all the time. I love how you make me feel." She pinched his nipple, catching him off guard.

Krampus jumped as she laughed. He leaned on his elbow and looked at the shape of her. As he examined her closer, he could see the slight roundness to her belly he hadn't noticed before. He cupped the little bump as Emerald put her hand over his. "I didn't notice before."

"I wasn't starting to show until the other day. I'm a little scared."

"You'll be a great mother. I'll have to suppress the urge to not want to eat the pudgy thing."

Emerald poked his chest. "That's not funny."

He smiled. "I thought it was." He pressed his lips to her stomach.

"I told you we'd come too late."

Krampus looked up and saw Jack and Nyx standing at the foot of the bed, each wearing robes. "I thought we were going to give this a little time before you showed up."

Nyx shrugged. "Couldn't wait. We can leave if you want."

Emerald sat up and trailed her fingers over Krampus's thigh, stirring his cock once more. "You don't have to go. I think we can accommodate you." Emerald got up and kissed Nyx. Seeing the two of them making out made him want more.

Jack Frost knelt before Krampus and cupped his cock. The touch made him shiver as Jack put some power behind the caress. "I did miss this."

"Me too." Krampus claimed his lips as the frost power flashed through him. He threw his head back and watched as his beautiful wife made out with Nyx. Emerald caught him staring and winked at him. Seeing her do that and knowing he would soon be a father made him proud and even hornier.

Y'all Tied Up

Crymsyn Hart

Aniston awakens to find an intruder in his house kneeling in front of his Christmas tree. Expecting a white beard and a jolly laugh, Aniston is shocked to find this is not Santa. Aniston is kidnapped and whisked away into a world of giants where Krampus is the master of the house.

Clive rescues Aniston and together they survive among cannibal gingerbread men, oversized nutcrackers, and tin soldiers roaming the house and guarding over Krampus' sack. Aniston can't help but be drawn to Clive and finds comfort in his arms. They only know of one way to get home. They must escape or spend Christmas a long way from home.

Chapter One

Two weeks until Christmas. Aniston glanced outside. Frost designs had formed on the window. A light snowfall added to the foot of snow already in his yard. The forecasters were predicting snow for the rest of the week. Carols played in the background. It would be a perfect night for Santa to come down the chimney laden with his bag of gifts. Glowing coals burned in the fireplace. The warmth of the fire made him sleepy.

Aniston inhaled the scents of pine and peppermint as he examined the bell in his hand. He had found it in the attic, in a box of ornaments. The bell appeared to be a hundred years old, but the ringer inside was frozen so it didn't make any noise. Aniston looped the ribbon on the bell around a branch of his tree. He checked the dying embers and switched off the lights as he went to bed. As he lay his head down to sleep, he heard the faint jingle of a bell.

Something jostled Aniston from his sleep. He glanced at the clock. Two-thirty in the morning. A sudden bang from the roof jerked him awake. *Probably just snow sliding off the roof.* He waited a moment, then heard another thump. It sounded distinctly like a footstep. All went silent. The thud happened again. This time it didn't come from the roof but from downstairs in the living room. His heart skipped a beat. *What the fuck is that?*

He got up. Grabbing the baseball bat kept by the door, he slowly crept down the stairs. The heady scent of gingerbread, and the heavy musk of some animal stung his nose. He blanched at the aroma. Aniston caught a glimpse of someone dressed in a red suit kneeling by the tree. Next to the person was a large red sack. When his foot hit the last step, it creaked. He winced.

The creature looked over its shoulder. Aniston wasn't sure what he was seeing. He blinked several times. By the time it registered, the being roared and rushed him. He dropped the bat. The thing's putrid breath enveloped him. The world no longer smelled like gingerbread, but the rancid odor of bad breath mixed with sulfur. The reek overwhelmed him and he passed out.

* * *

Taking in a long breath, he caught the fragrance of pine and nutmeg. *It was all a dream.* Relief flowed through him.

Then he opened his eyes. Aniston discovered himself curled up with large green spikes suspended over his head. Panic gripped him. His hands were bound behind him. He moved his feet and saw he was tied with some silver rope. The ground shook beneath him so violently the green spikes above him came down in a flurry. Each one was six or seven feet long. They fell all around and over him, until they covered him completely. Aniston struggled against his silver bindings and the light green spikes burying him. The intense smell of pine assailed his nostrils.

"Hush." A firm hand pressed against the middle of his back.

Aniston tried to see who was talking to him.

"Stop moving. Don't make a sound," the man said in a hurried whisper. "He'll hear us."

Dread filled Aniston at those words. He had no idea where he was. The last thing he remembered was being rushed by a creature who had invaded his house. His heart slamming in his chest, he tried to stay calm. The ground quaked. More weight fell on top of him. It felt like he was suffocating. Aniston tried not to panic. The presence of another man behind him kept him grounded. He bounced off the ground several inches from the tremors as they got closer. The same grotesque odor from earlier infused the air. He tried to hold his breath, but a gag had been stuffed in his mouth. A loud crash exploded a few feet from him. The impact made him wince. The following roar chilled him to the bone.

He whimpered.

"Shhh." The man behind him jabbed him in the ribs.

Aniston squeezed his eyes shut, trying to quiet himself. His pulse echoed in his ears. He tried to take in slow breaths as his body shook. Another growl sounded above him. It might have been words, but he couldn't make them out. The ground shook more as the large footsteps moved away as if going out of a room. Once they were gone, something cold slipped against his fingers.

"I'm going to cut this tinsel and free you. Then I'm going to ungag you. You have to be silent. Do as I say until I can get you out of here. Understand?"

Aniston nodded. What the hell had happened to him? After a moment, his hands were cut free. The man behind him released the gag and pressed something into his hand.

"Cut your feet free."

He did what he was told and saw he had a shard of something wrapped in cloth. Aniston sawed through the silver rope. He touched the bindings and felt its waxy surface. Tinsel. *What the fuck is going on here? Where am I?* Once free, he turned around to the man behind him. He had on a black hat with a chin strap and a red uniform with silver buttons and black boots.

"What the hell are you?"

"Shh." He grabbed Aniston's hand and yanked him backward.

He followed him through the green spikes toward towering square structures. All the structures were in different colors. Gold and green. Red with white stripes. As he was yanked backward, he realized the green spikes were pine needles. The man tugged on his arm and dragged him toward a crack in the wall. He wanted to stay and examine his environment. The toy soldier shoved him into the crack in the wall out of sight.

Inside, he slid down the wall. Aniston looked around. A gathering of threads and cotton were fashioned into a couch. Scraps of cloth were blankets. Wooden thread spools acted as tables. Someone had been living here and it wasn't a mouse. He glanced back at the man who had rescued him.

"Where I am? Who are you?"

"You're welcome," the other man spat. He set the sharp blade down next to him and took off his hat. He ran his hand through his blond hair. Sharp blue eyes stared at him until Aniston glanced down at the floor.

He realized then he was still in his red boxers and nothing else. Aniston drew his knees up against his chest. "Sorry. Thank you for untying me. I don't mean to sound ungrateful."

"Don't worry about it. I didn't mean to snap. It's been a while since I've had someone to talk to. He doesn't often bring live presents back."

"Presents? Is that what I was? Who was that?"

"Hold up. Before we get into this, you need to get some clothes on in case you go back out there." His rescuer went to a trunk and pulled out another outfit like his. He laid it at Aniston's feet. "It's my spare. It'll help you blend in. I think it'll be big on you. If you have to venture out, it won't give him an excuse to stop you."

Aniston glanced at the outfit. "Thanks. But who is him?"

"Krampus."

"Who the fuck is Krampus?"

"He's like the anti-Santa Claus. He punishes people for being naughty during the year. And I'm not talking about slipping a lump of coal into your stocking. We're talking about stringing you up by your intestines and hanging them on the tree for decorations. Sometimes, if you catch him in the act of leaving something, he'll bring you back to give to his children for Christmas."

Am I hearing him right? The creature, the thing, he had seen by the Christmas tree was some anti-Claus. He had somehow gotten kidnapped and brought back to its house for a present for its children. "Shit."

"Yeah. It's a lot to take in. I'm Clive, by the way." He stuck out his hand.

Aniston shook it. "Aniston. Nice to meet you."

"I know it's a big adjustment. Did you hang an old fashioned bell on your tree?"

"Yeah. It was in a box I found in the house I moved into. Most of the decorations were falling apart. The bell was neat, so I stuck it on the tree. Then it happened like you said. I found him by my tree with a sack next to him. I surprised him. He came at me and his breath knocked me out."

"That's what happened to me, too."

"How long have you been here?" Aniston asked, tugging on the pants Clive had given him. They were both too snug and too long, but they were warm.

"This is my third Christmas here."

"Three years?"

"Yeah. I was like you. There was another guy here with me that Krampus gave to his daughter. I saw what she did to him. I ran away to this place. I figured I wasn't the only one since there was stuff here already."

"He was normal size by my tree. Why is everything here so... big?"

Clive shrugged. "The best I can figure is that in our world he's normal sized. This is his realm so he's a giant. Everything is giant. I like to think we've gone to the top of the beanstalk with Jack and we found giants. It helps me cope. It's good to have someone to talk to. I was under the tree when I saw him bring you in."

"I owe you for saving me. I don't want to be treated like some Ken doll for the anti-Claus. How the hell do we get out of here?"

* * *

"Whoa! Slow down. You can't click your heels together three times and assume you're going home. There's only one way I know of to get out of here. Somehow, you have to get into his sack. He takes it with him whenever he leaves. The only time he leaves is when one of the bells ring. That's when he knows it's someone who has been naughty."

"But I wasn't naughty. I didn't ring the bell. The ringer inside of it wasn't moving. I just thought the bell was neat so I hung it up. That doesn't make me a bad person."

Clive eyed him and shrugged. "I'm not passing judgment. All I know is what I've observed hiding in this damn hole. Believe me. I've tried to get into his bag. It's guarded by these tin soldiers. I've taken a couple of them out, which is how I got the uniforms. Then there are the nutcrackers." He shook when he talked.

Aniston rubbed his balls just thinking about what these evil nut cracking beings might do. All of this was turning into some kind of bad Christmas nightmare he couldn't wake up from. "The next thing you're going to tell me is there are gingerbread men running around here too."

His companion kept a dead stare and his rigid expression didn't change. "They're cannibals." Clive lifted his pant leg and pointed to angry scars on his calf muscle. "One of them got me when I ripped off a piece of their gumdrop buttons. I was lucky to get away with only a little bite taken out of me."

"Shit. Man. I guess you *have* seen a lot."

"You don't know the half of it."

Aniston laid his head back trying to rationalize what he'd heard. This was no dream, but a Christmas nightmare. He didn't think he would ever think of Christmas again in the same vein. First, he had to get out of here alive. "Okay so we have to get past the tin soldiers, the nutcrackers, and the cannibalistic gingerbread to get into the bag. Anything else?"

"No. Obviously, if it was easy I wouldn't be here."

"Dude, I'm not saying it is or that you haven't tried. I'm just trying to get this all right in my head to formulate a plan. This is a whole bunch of fucked-up."

Clive chuckled. "Yeah, it is. Look, we aren't going anywhere tonight. I've never heard two bells ring in the same day. Let's just relax. You're going to need your head about you before we try any of this."

Aniston pulled on the shirt Clive had given to him. As he did, he looked over at Clive and saw him

studying him. The other man looked away and his
cheeks turned red. Aniston smiled to himself. Clive
was well built. The uniform stretched over his frame.
His blond hair was nearly white. His intense blue eyes
were nothing like Aniston had seen before. Was the
other man a supernatural being like an elf? He didn't
want to think about that right now. They had to worry
about getting the fuck away from Krampus.

"Right. Okay. What do we do now?"

"You hungry?"

Aniston's stomach rumbled. "Yeah. I guess. I
didn't eat dinner last night. Too busy decorating. I
don't even know what time it is here. Do you?"

"Dinner time. I can tell by the smells. Mrs.
Krampus started cooking an hour ago. The children
will come clattering in sometime soon from lobbing
snowballs at the feral reindeer that pull his sleigh.
Think zombie Moose. It's the best way to describe
them. Dinner will be meat pies, man stuffing, with
horseradish sauce, and peppermint pies for dessert."

"Man stuffing?"

"Oh yeah. They breed humans here like
livestock. The same way we do with sheep. She puts
them in the stuffing."

"Why don't they eat the ones he kidnaps from
our world?"

Clive walked to the corner of the room. He lifted
a small cup, removed the lid from a wooden barrel,
and dipped the cup inside. He took a long drink of
water then handed Aniston a cup. "Because the
humans here are dumb. Can't speak. Can't do anything
really except mill around in their pens. They are taller
than us, but not giants like him. They average about
nine feet. Hell."

"What?" Aniston asked, noting the water had a

peppermint flavor to it.

"I'm rambling. It's been a long time since I've had anyone to talk to. I've nearly gone crazy being alone. With the everyday fighting for my life, I think I've forgotten what it is to be nice to someone." Clive sniffled and turned away from him.

Aniston felt his pain. "Look, it's okay." He touched Clive's shoulder. It hit him how his savior had had to endure horrific things. The man had been here for three years with not a soul to carry on a conversation. His heart ached for the man.

Clive turned around and drew Aniston into a quick hug. It took him by surprise, but he didn't care. He patted his back. Clive hugged him harder. "I've been so alone."

"I know. It's going to be okay. We are going to get out of this."

Clive withdrew and met his eyes. Aniston wiped the tears from his cheeks and touched his chest. The other man put a hand on his cheek. He leaned in and then pulled back a moment. Aniston felt the heat ignite between them. The man was attractive. He wasn't going to deny him touch or personal comfort.

Aniston tugged on his shirt and drew him in. He put his hands on the sides of Clive's face and kissed him slowly. Clive melted against him. His hands trailed down Aniston's sides and tugged at his shirt. Then he thought against it and moved to his ass instead. He clutched Aniston's butt and squeezed it hard. A moment later Clive pulled away and seemed a little bit out of breath.

"I'm sorry. I shouldn't have done that. It's just…"

Aniston put a finger on his lips. "It's okay. I get it. No human contact for three years. Fighting off cannibal cookies. Stupid humans used for food. It's enough to drive anyone batshit crazy. You didn't feel me push you away did you?"

"No. And you're right, but I didn't know if you were into guys. And you're gorgeous, by the way. I could totally…" He stepped away and put his hands up.

"What's the matter?"

"I was about ready to tell you I could give you a blow job."

A small smile turned up Aniston's lips. "If you think I kissed you out of pity, you have another think coming. You are one sexy soldier. Your ass in those pants is something else. The thought crossed my mind, but I didn't want to be too forward, you know. This is the craziest situation I've ever been in. I don't think this is a dream. I know you're real. You saved my bacon. I should be getting down on my knees and sucking you off as my way of saying thanks for saving my life."

Clive blushed at his words. "I wouldn't expect you to do something like that."

"Really?" Aniston jerked on Clive's shirt until it came loose from his pants. The other man didn't stop him. He pulled it up and trailed his fingers over the other man's hard abs. "Because I *can* go over in the corner and leave you alone. I am a little tired, but… it's been a long time since I've been with anyone. I know it's been longer for you. I ditched my last boyfriend when I found him cheating on me."

He'd turned to walk away when Clive grabbed his hand and pulled him into a hug. He hit the other man hard. Clive slipped his fingers through Aniston's brown hair, growling and panting as he pushed his lips against Aniston's. Clive's tongue darted between Aniston's lips and met his in a hungry kiss.

He pulled Aniston against him as if he needed to mold their two bodies together. His fingers raked down Aniston's back. Aniston gripped Clive's waist, trailing his hand around the waistband of Clive's pants.

Clive groaned as Aniston slid his hand lower and cupped Clive's hardened cock. Aniston's nerves flared with anticipation. The surprise of what they had been through so far had already worn off.

"Do you want me to stop? If this makes you feel uncomfortable, us being virtual strangers and all."

"Has that stopped you in the past?" Clive asked.

"No. But… I don't want you to think I'm easy."

"Shut up and fuck me. We can worry about labels later."

Chapter Two

"Ram my ass. Suck my cock. I don't care. Just don't stop," Clive commanded.

Aniston quickly unbuttoned Clive's slacks and went to his knees before the other man. Clive's engorged prick pointed at him once it was free of its bindings. He licked his lips at the thought of what it would taste like. He tugged the trousers down until they were around Clive's knees. He glanced up and saw the other man's eyes glistening with desire. He trailed his fingers down the center of Clive's stomach to a thick patch of blond hair.

Clive whimpered when he touched the shaft of his dick. The man was halfway there. His breathing had increased. Just a few touches could get him off. But it was understandable because he hadn't had anyone there in so very long. The yearning for human contact, not just fantasies or his hand getting him off, had to be strong.

Aniston didn't wonder any longer. He didn't want to leave Clive wanting. It would be interesting to hear Clive calling out his name when he was on the bed with Aniston on top of him. He could imagine Clive tied up with tinsel while being tortured for the pleasure of it. He used to play similar games, but his ex-boyfriend was always rougher with him than he enjoyed. Maybe Clive would enjoy being tied up. He could see him wrapped in the tinsel with Aniston taking advantage of him.

He flicked his tongue around the rim of Clive's prick. Clive's hips thrust forward. Aniston chuckled. He slid his tongue over the smooth shaft. The salty taste of his lover's flesh on his tongue combined with the taste of cloves which made his own passion rise.

He shifted his knees as his prick firmed. He needed release. But he could wait.

Clive's length slid between his lips. His fingers wrapped around Aniston's hair and jerked his head back. "Stop playing," he seethed between clenched teeth.

Aniston cupped Clive's balls and squeezed. "You have to release my head if you want me to please you. You're the master here."

Clive shut his eyes and his pained expression made Aniston drool. Clive let his head go. Aniston sucked in his lover's prick until it hit the back of his throat. He moved his lips over Clive's length slowly, swirling his tongue. He smoothed his hands over Clive's thighs and cupped his ass. Clive's hips thrust forward. His breathing intensified.

Aniston focused on the soft flesh of his lover's ass. He clutched it and spread his legs a little further apart. He tasted the saltiness of the pre-cum as it slid down over his tongue. He could see himself bending Clive over this cotton ball sofa back in the real world. Fucking him from behind, getting off when Clive cried out. It would be great to take him that way, pumping together until they came.

"Oh, yeah. Just like that."

Clive held onto Aniston's head with both hands and kept him steady. Aniston dragged his teeth along the tender flesh. His lover hissed in a breath of pain. Clive's fingers raked over his scalp. His body trembled against Aniston's. Clive rocked forward on his heels. It was all Aniston could do not to stop sucking on his cock and claim his mouth once more. Clive moaned as he pumped himself into Aniston's throat. Aniston took all of him, and as he twisted his tongue around the shaft one last time a burst of warmth came into his mouth. He swallowed everything while holding fast to Clive. Clive pulled away as Aniston sat back to catch his breath. His eyes glowed with the pleasure of the aftermath.

"You know that wasn't necessary. You didn't have to feel obligated."

"Shut up and just enjoy it. I already told you, I find you attractive."

He stood up, staring at Clive, who was putting himself back into his pants. He stifled a yawn and adjusted his cock. It ached with the need for release, but he wasn't about to say anything to the other man.

"Sorry. I'm not used to company. And yes, I find you attractive as well." Clive buttoned his trousers back up and walked over to Aniston. He touched his prick and smiled. "I can't leave you hanging with blue balls." Clive massaged him through the material.

Aniston's eyes fluttered. "Shit. You don't have to do…"

Clive captured his mouth and thrust his tongue between Aniston's lips in a rough kiss. He shoved his hand down Aniston's pants and captured his cock. He backed him up against the wall as he rubbed his prick. Aniston broke the kiss and gulped in some air. The other man flashed him a devilish grin.

"God, I love how you feel." Clive pressed his nose to Aniston's neck and inhaled. "And how you smell. I've missed the rich smell of another human. The gamey, rancid stink of our host gets to you."

Aniston heard him, but Clive's words came to him on an echo. All he could feel was Clive's hand on his prick. The rhythm alternated between fast and slow. Clive knew how to work him, bringing him to the brink then letting him ease down until it was sheer agony. Maybe he was already an expert at torture and wouldn't mind being tied up.

Aniston arched his back against the wall and a cry slipped from his lips. Clive covered his mouth with his free hand. "Shh. Not so loud. Don't want anyone to hear us. Understand?"

Aniston bit his lip to keep from screaming. Sucking in a quick breath. He was panting now. "Please."

Clive nipped his throat and plunged his tongue into his ear. "I like to see you suffering like this. I have to admit when I saw Krampus put you underneath the tree, all tied up in tinsel, it made me hot. Seeing you squirm like this. I'd rather have you tied up and see what you are going to do then."

"Funny, I was thinking the same th-thing… ahhh." Warmth exploded through him. Aniston swallowed his moan so he could be quiet. "Fuck."

"Oh. I like how you moan." His lover pulled his pants down the rest of the way until his prick was completely free. "I could do this for hours with you."

"I can't…"

"I know. Maybe some other time." Clive increased his rhythm until Aniston thrust his hips upward and came.

Aniston slid down the wall and let the pleasure wash over him. Clive sat down next to him. "I wonder what else we have in common besides trying to get out of this place."

Before Clive could answer, the boards began to shake. Aniston heard some chittering coming from outside of the hole. Clive shot up. "Fuck. He let them loose. Quick, help me slide this across the hole."

Aniston raced over to the other side of the mouse hole. Clive had dragged something he had a hold of. He groaned and lifted the other end. A large piece of wood covered the hole, but the skittering came closer. Before they got the wood across the hole, Aniston saw what was coming toward them. They resembled the gingerbread men he had seen on Earth, but these were as tall as he was. All of them had gumdrop buttons down their middles and frosting around their outlines, but their mouths were full of sharp teeth. Some of them had large chunks taken out of them. Their eyes blazed red, and they were coming at them. Clive slammed down the board that held it in place.

"Damn that was close," Clive said.

"Cannibal gingerbread?"

"Yeah. He lets them out at night to patrol in case some of his prizes get away. He must have noticed you weren't underneath the tree."

"Right. How do the cookies know not to go under the tree and snack on his prizes?"

"Beats me. They just don't."

"Great." Aniston shivered as he thought of the scar Clive had shown him on his calf. He didn't want to come up against one of those creatures. If he was going to make it back home, he was willing to face anything because he didn't want to spend the rest of his life cooped up in a mouse hole, dressed as a tin soldier, fighting off crazed gingerbread men and who knew what else.

"Don't look so glum. I'll make sure you get home. You just have to believe."

"What about you?"

"I don't plan on staying here. I'm going with you. With two of us, it can be possible. We have to wait for another bell to ring. I have a feeling it'll be soon. Everyone is decorating their tree. He has his bells on the trees and when someone puts one on their tree in our world, then his rings. Just be patient."

* * *

Being patient was easier said than done. They had been cooped up in the hole for three days. The only way Aniston knew when it was day or night was from Clive telling him. Soon, Aniston began to learn the rhythm of the house. In the morning the floorboards shook from the household being awake. They had moved back the board for fresh air. The smells coming from the kitchen enticed Aniston, but he knew better than to dash out into the room in case something tried to eat him. The gingerbread guard hadn't banged on the door. Maybe they had given up looking for him and decided he was a lost cause. Whatever the reason, he was grateful.

On the fourth day, Clive poked his head out of the hole and looked around. "We're going to get the lay of the land this morning. Follow me. Do as I do. We need to pinch more food from the kitchen so we have a store. You can only live off of so much gingerbread."

Aniston's stomach growled. They had finished the last of the food the night before. At this point he didn't care if he ate gingerbread as long as they didn't eat him. "Great." He adjusted the chinstrap on his hat. Then he straightened his jacket so he could look more like the tin soldier he imitated.

Clive beckoned him forward as they slipped out of the mouse hole. They moved slowly around the molding and underneath the massive Christmas tree. Aniston looked up and couldn't see the top of it. All he saw were the large ornaments. Blue and silver colored globes the size of hot air balloons hung from the branches. Long, thin twisted silver strands he knew were tinsel. Golden spheres he recognized because of the one hanging on his own tree were the bells Clive had talked about.

They moved slowly around the perimeter of the tree until they arrived at an open space. All the floors in the house were wood. At his tiny size, it seemed the expanse of the hallway into the kitchen was seven football fields long with only minimal furniture along the way in case they needed to hide behind something.

They got to the corner of the room. Clive put his finger to his lips to quiet him. He stood up straight. Aniston did the same. He righted his uniform and moved his arms robotically swinging slightly at his side. As Aniston walked he felt like Frankenstein's monster wobbling back and forth on his stiff legs. He just knew they would be caught as soon as they were out in the open. Minutes ticked by as they walked along the hallway. The aroma of food made him hungrier and his stomach grumbled.

They made it to the center of the hallway when a line of soldiers walked past them. Clive stopped, drew himself up, and saluted. It took Aniston a moment before he followed. He kept his eyes straight as the lines of ten tin soldiers went past them. Some carried bayonets and others had nothing in their hands. They saluted Clive and Aniston as they passed. They joined in at the end of the parade, pretending to be one of them.

Aniston couldn't believe this had happened. They hadn't gotten caught. Following the tin soldiers through the house into the kitchen gave Aniston a lay of the land. If they were to dash right back over to the mouse hole under the tree they would be screwed. He didn't think he could sprint that far. Although he didn't think he had to worry about the tin soldiers running after them. They didn't seem to have any knee joints, which was why they walked so stiffly. Another line going the other direction passed them. All of them wore the exact same uniform, though the color of their hair differed. Their painted skin had an orange hue. Small red circles formed their cheeks. Their mouths and eyebrows were black lines. They had no noses on their round faces. The only sign of life they had were their eyes. Aniston saw a spark in them, but he had no idea if it was real intelligence or a soul. If it was a soul, maybe a person, he pitied the poor individuals who had gotten locked away in there.

The line wound through the kitchen. As they passed the counter, Clive darted to the side and hid behind one of the legs of the long table. Aniston pressed himself against the wood.

"What now?" he whispered. "We can't climb up onto the table." He looked up at the hundreds of feet above him to the tabletop. Luckily, they hadn't encountered Mrs. Krampus or the children yet.

Clive put his finger to his lips and pointed to the wall closest to where they were hiding. Another mouse hole hidden behind a large crate. Clive indicated they had to run fast to get to it. He checked to see if they were clear, counted down to three with his fingers, and then ran. Aniston bolted after him until they were behind the crate. He could barely fit behind it. They slipped into the crack and emerged into the pantry. The array of shelves and food made his mouth water.

Clive slid down behind a sack of flour and took a swig from a flask he pulled from the belt around his waist. Aniston saw it had several black pouches on it he hadn't noticed before. Clive handed it to him. He took a swig and found out it was water.

"Did you think it was hooch?"

"I didn't know what it was. Thank you. It's a bitch to get over here."

"No shit. That's the reason I don't do it often. I take what I can fit into my sack. Then I take a rest. Sometimes I spend the night in here. Although that can be risky with the rats. Big fuckers the size of bulls." He pulled a bag out of a different pouch and threw Aniston another.

"Where do we get all the food?"

Clive gestured to the shelves. "We climb and pick off what we can. I hope you're not afraid of heights." He pulled out a pair of gloves and slipped them on. Aniston followed behind him. On one side, handholds had been carved or chipped out of the wood deeply enough that it resembled a ladder. Clive gripped them and began to climb. Aniston looked up at how high the ceiling was. He could have been looking at a hundred foot skyscraper, himself the size of an ant at the bottom of it. It went on forever.

Clive had already gone up. Aniston put his feet and hands into the grooves and climbed. It was obvious these had been carved into the wood over time. There must have been other humans who had done it in the past. The same with the things in the mouse hole. *How many humans had Krampus kidnapped and brought back to his realm for his children to play with? How am I ever going to get home*?

Aniston shook off the thoughts before they bloomed into depression. He had to be positive. *Clive has survived for three years. I can, too*. As he climbed, he couldn't help but notice how fine Clive's ass looked and how the muscles bunched. Aniston focused on those sexy mounds instead of the tireless ascending. His palms started sweating. When he looked down, he must have been thirty feet off the ground. Clive wasn't above him. He wobbled and nearly lost his footing. Clive grabbed his arm and hauled him onto the platform.

"Whoa. You're okay. Just don't look down. I learned that a long time ago."

Aniston tried to catch his breath. "Fine. I'm fine."

"Good. It's time to go shopping. She keeps all the cheese and hard sausage here. Sometimes I get lucky and get bread, too. Let's see what we can get." Clive wove between the jars. "Jackpot."

Aniston followed him to a very large wheel of cheese. Clive had taken out another knife and sliced a piece off the rind and threw a couple of slices to him. He sniffed it. The stench reminded him of old gym socks.

"Eat it. Trust me."

He tested it with the tip of his tongue. It actually tasted better than what it smelled like. More like a cheddar mixed with blue cheese. He munched on it while placing the other slices Clive carved off into his sack. From there they went further down the shelf and found some sort of dried sausage. Clive passed him a piece. Before he ate it he remembered what Clive had said about raising men for stuffing.

"What now?"

"There's no human in this, is there?"

Clive stared at him long and hard. "I told you they raised them as livestock. I can't tell you what's in them. I used to think the same way you did after I saw them. Then my stomach got the better of me. You've been eating it since you got here. Why do you object now? This is a whole other world here and we're on the bottom of the food chain. Eat it or not, but -- Run. Hide!"

The shelf shook. A sausage rolled. Clive grabbed the slices and raced to the back behind some large Mason jars. The jars clicked together and the shelves bounced. Aniston pressed himself against the wall and the glass hoping he wouldn't be seen. He had a good view of the pantry. In walked a large creature wearing a purple dress. It had three fingers and a thumb with long sharp claws on them, and brown hairy arms. It spoke in a language he couldn't understand.

Horror filled him when a large blue eye came into view. The hand reached back, patting around for whatever it was on the shelf she wanted. He could make out a snout and a pointed ear. Aniston held his breath. Short horns curled out of the mass of hair on the top of its head. Claw points raked his arm. They curled around the Mason jar and pulled it out. Aniston waited for a yelp. When he looked out, the beast had its head turned. He raced and hid behind another jar. The woman walked out of the pantry and closed the door. Aniston slid down the wall and saw his life flash before his eyes. Clive dashed over to him and took his hands.

"Are you okay?"

Aniston wasn't sure he could answer.

Clive touched his cheek. The sudden gesture made him glance up. He kissed the other man quickly before hugging him.

"Hey. It's going to be okay. I should've warned you about coming face to face with them for the first time. It's a bit overwhelming, but you did it. You made it."

"Right. We should get the stuff and get back to where we are not out in the open."

"Sure. Come on."

Clive led the way as they climbed up to another shelf. They gathered more dried meat and some bits of bread. They packed what they could carry, including some chunks off the potatoes and carrots stored on the bottom shelf. Laden down with goods, they made their way back down the ladder. They snuck out of the crack and hid again behind the table leg. The kitchen had quieted down. The halls were poorly lit. They had a long trek back. He would feel safe again when they were back inside the mouse hole. No patrols of tin soldiers came around. Aniston waited for the gingerbread, but he didn't see them. Instead, a pair of shadowed forms approached them. Their heavy feet echoed in the house. What came into view were the nutcrackers Clive had spoken about. They were ten feet tall. They looked like the nutcrackers he was used to, all dressed up with black hats, white tufts of hair sticking out from underneath their hats. Their huge mouths hung open, ready to crack something more than walnuts. The nutcrackers clacked their mouths together as they patrolled. Clive put a finger to his mouth. Aniston didn't need to be told they had to be quiet. He didn't want to have his head squished between their wooden jaws.

Once they were out of sight, Clive motioned for him to run. Aniston moved as fast as he could with his load. They made it to the other side of the hallway. But they still had a ways to go before they were safe and hidden by the massive tree. They walked as fast as they could until they returned to the living room.

As they rounded the corner, Clive stopped him.

"What is it?"

"Krampus."

* * *

Aniston looked over at the tree. The sack lay open. The giant creature stood by the tree. The red suit he wore was dirty and in tatters. He didn't wear any boots. Instead, he had cloven hooves for feet. A short bushy tail hung down from the back of his pants. Large round horns curled over the back of his head. The awful smell in this house surrounded him. Aniston blanched, but didn't pass out. He had to make sure he wasn't seen.

He couldn't see what the beast was doing. After a moment, a bell rang on the tree. He glanced back at Clive.

"The bag. Get into the bag. Go. Quickly. You never know when you'll have another chance at being this close. Come on." Clive pushed him toward the sack.

"I can't leave you."

"Who says you're leaving me? Run!"

Aniston and Clive dropped their bags and darted toward the large sack. Aniston reached it first. He grabbed onto the cloth and climbed up. His hands and muscles ached. They screamed for him to stop, but he kept on going until he reached the furry rim of the bag. A trumpet blared. Tin soldiers had surrounded Clive and held him at the points of their bayonets. Clive looked up and smiled before giving a slight nod. He mouthed one word.

"Go."

Aniston couldn't leave the man who had helped him survive in the giants' house. He wasn't about to leave him. He began to climb back down, thinking of how he was going to save Clive. Krampus grabbed the sack. Aniston lost his balance and fell backward into the dark abyss. He landed on something hard. When he knocked his head, he couldn't fight the blackness that overcame him.

Chapter Three

Aniston opened his eyes when he felt a thud. Light shone above him. It beckoned him along with the fresh air. He climbed the stacks of boxes in the satchel and leapt toward his salvation.

As he climbed out of the bag, his arm suddenly got longer. His palm rubbed against the carpet. He swung his leg over and pulled himself the rest of the way out. Aniston crawled away, knowing he was free. Everything around him was normal size. Once he was outside Krampus' bag, he returned to his normal size. He found himself in someone else's living room. A fake white Christmas tree with neon pink lights lit up the room.

"It's about time you got out of there," a gravelly voice called from across the room.

Aniston peered into the darkness as his eyes adjusted to being out of the satchel. Krampus sat on the couch with another captive tied up and gagged next to him. Aniston glanced around searching for a weapon but found none. The anti-Claus was uglier than he had imagined. He had the head of a billy goat with long shaggy black hair. Horns on the top of his head curled over until the ends turned in on themselves. His snout was short and filled with tiny sharp points. His teeth ground together around whatever he was eating. Something was struggling to get out of his hand. As he took another bite, a shrill scream filled the room. Aniston cringed. He went closer and saw a two-foot-long gingerbread man with several bites taken out of it in the beast's hand.

"Would you like some? Wife made them fresh this morning." Krampus offered the cookie to him.

"No thanks."

"Suit yourself. They're best when they still have some punch in them. Fresh nutmeg is the secret." The cookie took a swing at Krampus.

"I'll keep that in mind the next time I make them."

"Take a seat, Aniston. I won't bite."

Aniston didn't trust him, but he wasn't about to go against the anti-Claus. He took a seat across from him, taking the time to glance around the living room. Whoever lived here was into horses, judging by the figurines and paintings on the wall. His gaze returned to the person on the couch. It was a handcuffed man with red hair and a ball gag in his mouth. Krampus put a hand on the man's head and patted him. The man opened his eyes. Once those eyes met Aniston's, recognition washed through him. He opened his mouth to say something, but Krampus beat him to it.

"One word about him and I'll make sure your former lover boy gets real friendly with the gingerbread. They love man-flesh."

Something hissed from the shadows. Shapes moved and gingerbread cookies emerged from the darkness. Aniston didn't want his ex to get hurt even if he had cheated on him in the past. But then again, he could have been talking about Clive. Aniston couldn't see Clive hurt. He held up his hand in defeat.

"Good boy. You're wondering why I'm letting you go?"

"I am."

"Seems I made a mistake about you. The ringer on that particular bell was no longer in service. It never should have rung. Left over magic, I guess. Fortunate for you, that you fell into my bag when you did."

"You're just going to let me go?"

"No harm done. I'll even get you back home."

"Why are you being so nice?"

Krampus grinned showing off his long pointed teeth. "Call it the Christmas Spirit. I do have a little of it."

His mind turned back to Clive. He hated leaving the other man behind. If Krampus knew about him being in his bag, then he had to know about Clive. If he didn't, Aniston didn't want to give the other man away and jeopardize his life. His gaze darted to Barry. One of the gingerbread men licked his calf. He struggled in his bonds.

"What happens to him?"

"He's been a bad boy. All those years you were together he spent screwing old men out of their life savings. He even killed one. He'll get what's coming to him. Ready to go?"

Aniston found it hard to believe, but he wasn't going to question Krampus. "Sure."

"Ho. Ho. Ho."

On the third Ho, the world dropped out from beneath him. Cold surrounded Aniston until he thought he would freeze to death. Then his ass settled upon something solid. Aniston found himself back in his apartment. Everything looked the same, but when he checked his digital clock it showed how many days he had been gone. It hadn't been a dream. It had all happened.

Aniston wanted nothing more than to scream at the top of his lungs because he had made it out alive. But even as he rejoiced, his thoughts turned to Clive. He already missed the other man's voice and the softness of his touch. His heart ached not knowing if he would see him again. *There has to be a way for him to be free.* An idea popped in his head, but he nearly dismissed it because it was crazy. Then again so was everything about where he had been.

Fuck it. It can't hurt.

Aniston raced to his kitchen and grabbed a pen and paper. He sat down and shook his head. *If this doesn't work, I don't know what will.* He cleared his head and wrote his one request.

When he was done, he sealed it in an envelope and wrote *To Santa* on the front. He set the letter on the mantle above the fireplace.

* * *

Aniston got his life back on track. His sister had left him a message about the family gathering at her house. That meant her four children, his two brothers and their children and spouses. It would be over twenty-five people if everyone showed up. He always enjoyed his nieces and nephews and being with the family, but he could only take them for so long. As the days ticked down to Christmas and his five hour drive to his sister's house, his gaze strayed to the letter on the mantle. It hadn't moved. He thought about Clive as the minutes and hours ticked away. He replayed the moments they'd spent together before they went to sleep. His cock was throbbing for the man, and his heart was ready to burst. In the short time he had been with the man, he had fallen in love with Clive. He didn't know much about him, but he wanted to know more.

And now they were worlds apart.

On Christmas Eve day, Aniston grabbed the letter, packed his bags and drove the five hours to his sister's. When he got there, he spent time playing with the children. After everyone went to bed, he sat in front of the fire, sipping his beer.

"Are you okay?" Angie asked.

He looked up from the dancing flames. "Yeah. I'm fine."

"I know that look. You have a man on your mind."

"You know me too well."

"I took care of you all. Momma was too busy working after Daddy had left us."

"I know. Momma tried her hardest."

"She did. Who is the boy?"

"Someone I met. He helped me out during a bind."

"He's not a criminal?"

"No. He's not."

"What happened?"

"Long story. We were separated by circumstances beyond our control. And I don't know if he's alive or dead. He sacrificed himself so I could escape."

"What the fuck happened?"

"Don't worry, Angie. I'll be fine. Someday when it's less painful I'll tell you all about it. Right now you should go on up to bed. Don't want to be awake when Santa comes."

His sister kissed his cheek. "Don't stay up too long, because the same goes for you."

Aniston nodded. His sister left the room, and all grew quiet in the house. While staring at the coals, he took the letter he'd written from his pocket, thinking about Clive one last time. He kissed the letter and threw it into the flames. "I hope you're well. I'm so sorry I had to leave you behind. I miss you."

He sighed as the letter caught on fire. A blast of heat came out of the hearth. A gust of peppermint reached his nose. Aniston chuckled and slipped into the guest room. As he fell asleep the events he had endured played through his mind. His last image was of Clive, his amazing smile, and intense blue eyes.

Aniston opened his eyes and heard something loud on the roof. *More snow falling from the eaves*. His sister had more of it than he had. He settled his head back into the pillow. Another large thud sounding on the roof. He rolled his eyes. *Not again*. Aniston got out of bed and went downstairs. The rest of the house remained silent. It seemed he was the only one affected by it. When he got downstairs, a figure leaned over the table by the tree. It was dressed in a red suit.

"There is no bell on that tree. What the hell are you doing here?"

The figure turned around. Instead of the goat, Aniston found a jolly older man with red cheeks and a snow -white beard. His blue eyes sparkled. A red hat adorned his head.

"Oh shit." Aniston's mouth fell open.

"Language, Mr. Wade."

"S-sorry. S-santa."

"I'll let it go this one time."

"Thanks. Why are you here?"

Santa reached into his red jacket and pulled out a charred letter. "I got this."

"Fu-Fudgesicles."

"That's more like it. I don't make it a habit of going to see my nemesis."

There was no hope for Clive. "I see."

"I said I don't make a habit of it, but I made an exception. I saw your ordeal with Krampus when I touched your letter. He let you go, which is something he never does. We traded a few things. Sometimes we have to. You might find your present outside."

Aniston looked at him and then at the door. "Seriously?"

Santa's large stomach shook as he laughed. "I can't tell a lie. Oh, and always remember the spirit of Christmas isn't just this time of year. It's all year round. We always like to hear it more than just this time of year."

"I'll remember that. Thank you."

Santa put his finger to his nose and crouched down. With a tinkle of bells, he disappeared in a shower of golden glitter up the chimney. Aniston couldn't contain his glee. He raced to the door and opened it. Standing on the stoop in a long red cape with a hood was a man.

"Clive?"

The man turned around. His intense blue eyes told Aniston all he needed to know. He pushed his hood back from his head. Aniston drew him into his arms and kissed him. Clive returned the kiss with hunger. Warmth rushed over him. The soft material of the cloak rubbed across his cheek. Clive pulled away from him and touched his cheek.

"I don't know what the hell you did. It must have been incredible. You rescued me from the impossible. Krampus nearly shit when he saw Santa in his living room. The gingerbread men ran away screaming from the big man. I didn't hear what they said, but it did the trick. They made some deal, and I got to leave with him."

"I wrote Santa a letter and prayed he would get it. Shit, I didn't think it would work. I never wanted to leave you behind. I didn't know if you were going to be eaten by the gingerbread men."

"Almost. But I had a few tricks up my sleeve."

"You know. I never asked where you were from. Your family, I'm sure they want to know where you are and how you've been."

Clive trailed his fingers down his chest. "My family never wanted me in the first place. I went into the army when I turned eighteen. I was a soldier for a long time and got lost in my job."

* * *

"Come in out of the cold. You can meet my family. I want you to stay with me."

Clive's eyes brightened. "I'd like that. I know a good way to get warm." He walked his fingers down Aniston's chest and stopped at his waistband.

"I think we can accommodate that. But we'll have to be quiet."

The other man pulled out something from the pouches at his waist. A ball gag and some silver rope. "Santa also gave me a couple of presents. Unless you aren't into…"

Shock hit Aniston first, which blossomed into expectation of what was to come. "Oh no. I'm good with it."

Clive cupped his cock. "Good. Because I have a couple other things too."

Aniston took his hand, led him inside and closed the door. He went upstairs with his Christmas present. Clive dropped his cloak. He ran the rope through his hands.

"Will you trust me with this?"

"You saved my life. I trust you."

"Then drop your pants and get on your knees," Clive commanded.

A thrill went through him as he thought back to his fantasy. Of course, he had been the one giving orders, but he didn't care. The man he loved was before him once more. He knew he could give himself up to whatever Clive had in mind. After what they had already shared, it would be a spectacular experience. Aniston slipped off his pants and went to his knees. Clive went behind him and placed the ball gag in his mouth. He bit down on the rubber ball as Clive cinched the leather strap.

"Is that too tight?"

Aniston shook his head no.

"Good. If this gets uncomfortable or you want me to stop, hold up two fingers. Nod if you understand."

Aniston nodded.

"Put your hands in front of you." Clive came around front and tied his hands together and then bound the rope around his chest with his hands pressed against his torso. "Now sit on the bed for a moment."

Aniston perched on the edge of the bed. Clive stripped giving Aniston a feast for his eyes. As each article of clothing came off, Aniston trembled with anticipation. He squirmed against the coils of rope. His hands ached to touch the solid form of the man before him. All the fantasies he had dreamed about the man were nothing compared to this. He had thought he would be the one tying Clive up, but this worked for him too. His ex and he had each played the dominant role. He didn't know what Clive enjoyed, yet. He was happy to have the man back with him. All he wanted was to experience the exquisite torture this man had planned for him. His entire body yearned for the pleasure of Clive's touch.

Clive put something in his mouth. As Clive's head went down, Aniston felt his lover's lips enclose his prick. At the first touch of his lips, he felt his cock firm. As it did, Aniston felt something tighten around his flesh. When Clive's head came back up, he had a devilish smile on his face. He caressed the base of Aniston's shaft.

"Ever used a cock ring before?"

He shook his head.

"Oh good. You'll enjoy this."

Clive spread Aniston's legs a bit more before sliding his tongue along his length. He didn't move his gaze from him as he shivered. Aniston thrust his hips up, but he wasn't able to move since he was bound. The sensation in his length as the desire built in him made him squeeze his eyes shut. His lover took him into his mouth so he sucked on the ring as well, circling his tongue around and slowly coming back up with a strong suction. Clive scraped his fingers over Aniston's thighs.

He tried to moan his pleasure, but he was effectively silenced.

"Yes. I know. But it feels wonderful, doesn't it?"

He took the soft head and sucked on it, nibbling the smooth skin with his teeth. A tear slid down Aniston's cheek. He couldn't hold on much longer. He tried thrusting his hips upward again as Clive increased his tempo just taking part of his length in. The cock ring made his dick thrum with pleasure. He needed to let go, but he couldn't. It kept him hard and filled. His nerves burned. He pressed his fingernails into the meat of his palms. The pain helped him to focus. Clive dragged his teeth along his prick one last time. Aniston nearly screamed.

His lover kissed his stomach between the bindings and took a nipple into his mouth. He bit down on the pert nub. Clive twisted the other one between his fingers. "Yes. You're all mine. And I'm all yours. Turn around and bend over on the bed."

Aniston climbed on the bed and knelt down,

resting on his knees and elbows. Clive smacked his ass. The crack made him jump. The pain made him want more. His lover swatted him again. Aniston wiggled his butt, asking for more. Clive chuckled and hit him one more time. He spread Aniston's ass as he got up behind him. Something cold and wet rimmed his ass. Clive's hands gripped his hips as he inserted his cock into Aniston. He grabbed a hold of Aniston's cock and worked it slowly.

"God, you feel so good."

Aniston pushed backward as Clive thrust into him. They created a pace that increased as Clive got closer to coming. Aniston's jaw hurt from biting down so hard on the ball gag. All he wanted was to cry out and call Clive's name. Being bound was intolerable because he couldn't hold onto his lover. Aniston's prick hurt. Clive drove into him. His lover moaned and worked him harder. Even with the cock ring, Aniston couldn't hold back any longer. He needed to come. Clive pounded into him one more time and buried his head into his shoulder. Aniston hung his head and tried to catch his breath. His lover's weight added to the satisfaction humming through his body. Clive kissed his shoulders and slowly brought him back up.

He undid the gag and pulled it out of Aniston's mouth. Once he was free of it, he claimed Clive's lips. Clive kissed him and pulled away. "I missed you."

"I missed you, too. Did you enjoy that?"

"Yes. But can you untie me?"

Clive undid the ropes so he was free. He took Clive in his arms. It felt good to hold him and know he was there and all of this hadn't been a dream. "Did I tell you that I love you?"

"I love you, too."

"Next time, I'd like to see you all tied up."

"We can certainly do that, but maybe another night."

"Right. A lot has happened. There's a bathroom off the guest room if you want to take a shower."

Clive smiled. "A shower would be wonderful. You want to join me? I promise no monkey business."

Aniston stood up. "I'd like that."

* * *

The next morning, Aniston brought Clive downstairs to meet his sister. Carols were already playing on the radio. Angie was humming along as she prepared Christmas breakfast. The children didn't make any comments about her singing. They kept looking at one another and giggling.

"Are you going to introduce me to your friend?"

Aniston blushed. "This is Clive."

"Nice to meet you," Clive said. "Forgive me for showing up in the middle of the night. I was able to get a ride at the last minute."

"It's fine. I can see you mean something to Aniston. You're welcome to stay. Just don't break his heart. If you do, I might have to tie you up and leave you for the kids to tickle."

Aniston nearly choked on his coffee. "You might find he enjoys being tied up."

Clive ran his hand over his thigh. "I'm not sure she wants to hear about our personal lives."

Angie set her cup down and stared at him. "You'd be surprised what I hear. Now why don't you two stay in here and help me with the cookies? I have a bunch of gingerbread I have to make."

Clive blanched. Aniston's stomach turned at the thought of it. "I don't think gingerbread is my favorite anymore. Long story."

"Okay. Well then, you two will just have to help out later. Go on and enjoy Christmas. The rest of the family will be here soon." Angie shook her head on her way back to getting ready for the rest of the family to arrive.

Aniston took Clive into the living room and looked at the tree. His heart swelled knowing Clive was back with him. They would be together through all kinds of things that might come up. He imagined what Christmas could be in their future. Santa's words echoed in his mind. Clive was living proof the Christmas spirit was alive and well. And if they were tied up, they would share the ropes together.

"Merry Christmas, Clive."

"Merry Christmas, Aniston."

Crymsyn Hart

Crymsyn Hart is a National Bestselling author of over eighty paranormal romance and horror novels. Her experiences as a psychic and ghostly encounters have given her a lot of material to use in her books. Vampires, grim reapers, shifters, and other paranormal creatures tend to end up in her books no matter how hard she tries to keep them away.

She currently resides in Charlotte, NC with her hubby and her three dogs. If she's not writing, she's curled up with the dogs watching a good horror movie or off with friends.

Crymsyn at Changeling: changelingpress.com/crymsyn-hart-a-188

Changeling Press E-Books

More Sci-Fi, Fantasy, Paranormal, and BDSM adventures available in e-book format for immediate download at ChangelingPress.com -- Werewolves, Vampires, Dragons, Shapeshifters and more -- Erotic Tales from the edge of your imagination.

What are E-Books?

E-books, or electronic books, are books designed to be read in digital format -- on your desktop or laptop computer, notebook, tablet, Smart Phone, or any electronic e-book reader.

Where can I get Changeling Press E-Books?

Changeling Press e-books are available at ChangelingPress.com, Amazon, Apple Books, Barnes & Noble, and Kobo/Walmart.

ChangelingPress.com